CREED

Look for other books by Chuck Black

The Kingdom Series
Kingdom's Dawn
Kingdom's Hope
Kingdom's Edge
Kingdom's Call
Kingdom's Quest
Kingdom's Reign

The Knights of Arrethtrae
Sir Kendrick and the Castle of Bel Lione
Sir Bentley and Holbrook Court
Sir Dalton and the Shadow Heart
Lady Carliss and the Waters of Moorue
Sir Quinlan and the Swords of Valor
Sir Rowan and the Camerian Conquest

The Wars of the Realm
Cloak of the Light
Rise of the Fallen
Light of the Last

The Starlore Legacy
Nova
Flight
Lore
Oath
Merchant
Reclamation
Creed
Journey
Crucible
Covenant
Revolution
Maelstrom

www.ChuckBlack.com

Author's Commentary

It is with much prayer and extreme carefulness that I present this story to you. Today, our lives are immersed in worldly entertainment, from the innocent to the blasphemous. But rarely, if ever, does the secular entertainment industry point us to Jesus Christ as the exclusive author of our salvation. Therefore, it is my heart that the Starlore Legacy books might entertain while heralding the inerrant Word of God as true and acknowledging that there is no name given among men whereby we can be saved other than that of Jesus. As Jesus taught through parables, allegory, and metaphor, this is my attempt to likewise inspire people of all ages to search out the Holy Scriptures and follow our Lord and Savior.

These books are not intended to replace, distort, or confuse God's Word. These books are also not intended to teach theology or doctrine. Therefore, please do not make the mistake of rigidly applying this loose allegory to such and thus misunderstanding its intent. I am grateful and humbled to be able to share my passion for serving God through literature with you. Thank you.   ~Chuck Black

As a **BONUS FEATURE** for Episode Seven, there are full color images of significant characters, scenes, and technology to help illustrate the story. It is recommended that the entire chapter is read first and then view the corresponding images for that chapter. Don't look ahead or you'll find spoilers. You'll find the images by chapter at **www.chuckblack.com/creed** or you can also scan the QR code below. Enjoy!

THE STARLORE LEGACY

CREED

EPISODE SEVEN

CHUCK BLACK

PERFECT PRAISE PUBLISHING

Creed

Published by Perfect Praise Publishing
Williston, North Dakota

ISBN 978-1-959574-20-0

Printed in the United States of America

Library of Congress Control Number: 2025903388

Contents

CHAPTER

1

Whispers from Beyond

Transference –The process of capturing the essence of a human being by utilizing Immortal quantum technology which maps every memory, synaptic pathway, and molecular biological construct of the human body in exquisite detail. The device used to capture the essence of the human is a nephesh matrix, often carried in a small transportation chamber or reliquary. Although the process of transference can occur up to two days prior to and two hours after death, the quantum law of anti-duality denies the possibility of the living one in the realm of humanity being regenerated into the realm of the Ruah without death first occurring.

Regeneration – The process of infusing the transferred essence of a human from his or her nephesh matrix into a mapped Ruah bio-equivalent body, initiating a final domain of immortal existence. Transference and regeneration are singular irreversible events for each human.

Fifty-three years earlier...

Lord C'fir Dracus sat in the captain's chair on the bridge of the *Diabolus*, his new star cruiser class flagship for the Torian galactic fleet. The *Diabolus* was one of Admiral Kyrsa's elite designs. Sleek, powerful, and deadly, the *Diabolus* was equipped with the most advanced weaponry, sensors, and propulsion systems that existed in the Ruah. Four squadrons of Torian fighters were hangared in 12 launch bays to provide escort and quick response when necessary. An accompanying array of support vessels, including battleships, destroyers, and frigates, were always part of the space force strike group.

The dark and devious mind of Dracus was focused on the hovering display before him, where the words of the ancient Raylean oracles scrolled upward...Eziam, Darnullay, Iyhaz, Micaba, Sabella and secondary oracles. He scowled as he considered the perfect fulfillment of their words—words that had been given to them from Ell Yon. If he could thwart even one of these prophecies, then all would be negated, and the flaws of Ell Yon would be exposed to humanity.

"Why do you study the words of these obsolete and subjacent oracles?" Admiral Kyrsa asked as she approached from the turbo lift. "Whether Ell Yon forces these petty prophecies to come true or not, we still rule the galaxy."

Dracus rotated the captain's seat to face Kyrsa. "How do you think I've come to rule the galaxy with such dominance?" Dracus lifted his hand to the display. "This is a roadmap for us to decipher and subvert the plans of Ell Yon. Do you really think Ell Yon intended to govern merely one small obscure planet in the Kahn system while I rule over thousands of planets and trillions of subjacent humans?"

Admiral Kyrsa's brow lifted as she considered Dracus's analysis. "And what do the words of these oracles tell you now?"

Dracus rotated back to face the display. "The Merchant's arrival is close, but Ell Yon has a trick up his sleeve...of that I'm sure." Dracus leaned forward. "According to the oracle Micaba, '*He shall free prisoners from Gehenna and lead them through the stars.*'"

"Well, that seems obvious enough," Kyrsa replied.

Dracus shook his head. "No...there's more. Somewhere there's—." Dracus let his incomplete thought hang.

Kyrsa waited. When Dracus was satisfied, he turned to look at her. "We will kill the child when it arrives or make his mission so painful that he will submit to me. The one thing Ell Yon's Merchant will not understand is the power of human pain—something I've perfected."

Kyrsa offered a crooked grin.

"I assume you are here to deliver good news in person," Dracus tilted his head forward to indicate he would accept nothing else.

"Yes, my lord." Kyrsa straightened. "Per your directive, our resource division has discovered one of the richest deposits of andelucite we've ever found. It is located just inside Malakian-controlled space near the uninhabitable Thenus System."

Dracus lifted his head and smiled. The mineral andelucite possessed extremely useful properties for building the hulls of ships. Its yield strength, ductility, and resistance to slipstream travel stresses made it the premier and nearly exclusive choice as a composite additive for ship hull construction, both for the Torians and the Malakians.

"The research was conducted without the Malakians' knowledge, so they're unaware of this rich deposit," Kyrsa continued. "All we need to do is expand our space boundary in the Bravo quadrant by four parsecs and it's ours. Shall I give the order?"

Dracus aligned the tips of his fingers together then brought them to his lips, his devious mind formulating the perfect plan.

"No."

"But, Lord Dracus, this deposit of andelucite would advance our ship-building capacity years ahead of the Malakians," Kyrsa protested.

Dracus's eyes narrowed. "Hail our phystech director." He then turned to look directly at Krysa. "In one week, I want you to leak our discovery of the andelucite deposit to the Malakian intelligence and reconnaissance organization."

Kyrsa's eyes opened wide. She opened her mouth to protest, but Dracus would have none of it.

"Do it, Admiral."

Present day...

Daeson Starlore looked out the canopy of his Starstreak down onto the grand city of Jalem, the capital of Rayl. Time was running out—it was time to return to a planet in a treacherous region of space.

Deep in the central region of the Aurora Galaxy, there exists a cluster of systems that orbit a massive black hole. It is a frightful region of space. The brightness of a thousand suns in this tightly packed region of space refuses to let even dusk appear on any of the hundreds of planets unfortunate enough to have formed here. From a distant perch in space, this region appears on fire and is appropriately called the Gehenna Cluster.

There are no slipstream gateways that lead there—at least none that humanity has been able to find. It is a place unreachable and therefore unknowable. But this does not stop the telling of ancient mythical tales by spacefarers with vivid imaginations and an affinity for fanciful orations. It was well believed by all of humanity that life in such a dreadful place could not exist. They could not possibly be wrong, for how could such a fiery domain harbor life? But in the realm of the Ruah, Gehenna hosts billions of people who have undergone transference and regeneration, a process of bringing a human life into existence in the dimension of the Malakians and the Torians.

Unfortunately, because of the diabolical impact of Deitum Prime on all life in both realms, the regeneration process is not fully realized, and continual energy must be absorbed to sustain life. Only in this region of space is the concentration of cosmological particle energy great enough to allow regeneration of human bio-scans into a replicated form of the original being. And once recreated, this energy force is what sustains the lifeforce within them. However, Gehenna is a place of separation—a place of waiting and a place of torment necessitated by the reality of Deitum Prime. Whether respite or agony, the cluster is a prison for all transferred and regenerated humans.

In this unreachable region of space, Ell Yon's Malakian tech force gathered those that remained loyal to the Sovereign onto a protected planet of waiting— Brahm's Cradle. Although this planet offered respite from the perils of Gehenna, there was the continual knowledge that they were prisoners to the cluster until the Solution was implemented by Sovereign Ell Yon...the Solution that would free them from this interim respite, giving them the lifeforce that was being temporarily maintained by the high concentration of cosmological particle energy.

However, the Gehenna Cluster was also the place where C'fer Dracus and his Torians revived their human pawns into beings of servitude in the Ruah, having conducted their own acts of transference in the realm of humanity before death. Dozens of planets were home to the vast mines of beryl and kyawthuite. For the unfortunate souls that awakened under the iron fist of the Torians, the most despairing knowledge was that of absolute hopelessness—a horrific state of existence where not even death was a release from the toil of their every waking moment.

Daeson Starlore's awakening from his transference had been joyful, for he was greeted by Raviel and his dear friends, Tig and Kyrah. He had been regenerated into a younger version of his body, one in peak condition, yet something was drastically missing. All of them were bound to this dreadful Gehenna Cluster. Brahm's Cradle was protected by a network of equatorial geosynchronous stasis generation satellites. This global stasis field provided protection from deadly radiation while still allowing the life-sustaining cosmological energy particles entrance. This region of space was heavily occupied by their enemies, the Torians, but without the highly encrypted frequency access codes, none could reach low orbit or enter the atmosphere of Brahm's Cradle.

Daeson conducted a quick check on his sensors before his thoughts began to stray. Earlier that morning, Admiral Lucien had arrived with a squadron of ships to deliver a mission to Daeson.

"Navi Daeson Starlore, the Commander has issued a critical mission for you and Navi Raviel Starlore that will take you off world and back to Rayl." Admiral Lucien's stern countenance was difficult to read.

Daeson glanced over at Raviel then back to the admiral.

"How is this possible, Admiral?" Daeson asked. "We can't survive outside of the Gehenna Cluster?"

The admiral looked concerned. "Both of you will be given an injection that will sustain you outside of the Gehenna Cluster for sixteen hours. You must return before this allotted time expires, or you will die. Additional injections will not be effective, so there is no way to extend your out-time. Do you understand?"

Daeson and Raviel both nodded. "What is the mission?" Daeson asked.

"You will utilize the training you have received in the Starstreak to rendezvous with the Commander over the city of Jalem on Rayl. There you will assist him in whatever capacity he needs."

Daeson was confused.

"Forgive me, Admiral, but how can we accomplish what you or any Malakian warrior or pilot could not?"

The corners of Admiral Lucien's mouth turned slightly downward. He hesitated. "Sometimes the ways of Ell Yon are as much a mystery to us as they are to you."

That subtle confession by one of Sovereign Ell Yon's highest-ranking admirals was startling. Daeson dared not ask anything else.

"I understand, Admiral Lucien. When do we launch?"

"Immediately," the admiral replied. "We will escort you to the boundary of the Kayn System, but you must manage your return flight. Your window of survival is narrow."

That final conversation with Admiral Lucien was ten hours and eighteen minutes ago. Daeson Starlore tapped on his center display to activate his Starstreak cloak. Since that conversation, he and Raviel had completed their mission to fly in support of the Commander of the Malakians, Jeshu Starlore, in his battle with Dracus over the skies of Jalem.

The brief encounter with their daughter, Brae, was having a profound impact on Daeson's emotions. He could only imagine what Raviel was dealing with. At least Daeson had memories with Brae. Raviel only had stories that Daeson had shared with her. With every story he told, he could feel the ache in Raviel's heart deepen. It was the ache of a mother lamenting for the time she had not lived with their only child. Daeson struggled to know if the stories he spoke of Brae would diminish or increase her sense of loss. At times she seemed eager and delighted to hear them. At other times, Daeson sensed her heart was too broken to hear what she had missed.

Seeing Brae in a Starstreak battling with the foes of Ell Yon was both joyous and frightening at the same time. Then, to be so close, separated only by their canopies and a few feet of space, was nearly more than he could bear. He had wanted to embrace Brae and tell her that eventually all would be well. Though Daeson didn't know the future, he sensed that Ell Yon and Jeshu's battle with Dracus was far from over, and Brae was irrevocably connected to the plan for the restoration of humanity.

Daeson looked off his right wing. Though invisible to the world, Raviel's Starstreak displayed as a simulated image on his visor.

"You okay, Rav?"

There was a ten-second pause before the mic clicked.

"No...not really. I don't want to go back to Gehenna."

Daeson didn't know how to respond. The truth was that he didn't want to go back either. It took everything in him not to follow Brae back to the surface and run to her. He waited, thinking about what might help Raviel.

"I understand. I don't either." Daeson let his words of confession linger for a few seconds. He knew she needed to hear him speak the words they both knew to be true...words that might give them the strength to push on to the end. "We'll be with her again. Our time in Gehenna is almost at its end, but only if we return quickly. We must survive to see her."

Daeson continued to circle the city of Jalem in a broad arcing flight path. He couldn't leave Rayl until he knew Raviel was ready. He looked down at his console to see their survivability time clock steadily decreasing. Seven hours and forty-three minutes remained, but the slipstream jumps back to Gehenna would take over seven hours. Death awaited them both when it reached zero. Daeson gripped the engine throttles a little tighter, waiting. He knew that Raviel would find the emotional strength to do what was needed if he just gave her enough time—but time was their enemy outside the Gehenna Cluster.

Daeson's finger hovered over the mic button, ready to press and push Raviel on.

"I'm ready. Let's launch," Raviel's voice boomed over the headset.

Daeson took a breath. "Copy, Saga Two. Prepare for trans-atmospheric flight." Daeson tapped in the coordinates for a position that would place them in high orbit above Rayl and transferred the codes to Raviel.

"Coordinates received," Raviel replied.

"Engage now."

Daeson pushed his throttles forward, feeling the powerful engines of the Starstreak accelerate and push him into his seat. He gently pulled back on the stick until he was in a 70-degree climb. He glanced over to see Raviel just a mile off his right wing, matching his flight parameters. Ten minutes later they arrived at a position 250 miles above the blue and white orb of Rayl. Since their Starstreaks were equipped with the non-gateway slipstream jump-drive engines, they only needed to be free from the effects of Rayl's gravity field for longer jumps. Even still, the distance to the center of the galaxy where Gehenna was located was too far to safely make in one jump. They had taken three jumps to get to Rayl and would follow the same profile back.

Daeson looked over his left shoulder at Rayl. This single planet was the cradle from which the rescue of the galaxy would come. He thought of Brae and her journey there as one of Jeshu's Navi. *How would this next chapter in the episode of humanity turn out?* he wondered. *What part would his daughter play?*

Daeson communicated with his Starstreak's Artificial Intelligence Flight Assistant, AIFA, to calculate the arrival coordinates for their first jump and transmitted them to Raviel. This would be a two-hour and twelve-minute jump spanning more than 8000 light years.

"Saga Two, de-cloak and prepare to engage jump drive engine on my mark," Daeson radioed. So far, the Malakians had not figured out how to remain cloaked while performing a slipstream jump drive. Something about the two technologies were incompatible. Typically, this was not a problem, but on long range jumps like this, it meant being exposed to enemy radar for a few brief seconds until they could re-cloak.

"Copy, Saga One," Raviel replied.

Daeson waited until her ship appeared visually a hundred feet off his right wing.

"Engage."

Their first two jumps were successful. Daeson commanded AIFA to calculate their third and final jump back to Brahm's Cradle. He transferred the coordinates to Raviel and was about to make the call when Raviel hailed him over their com channel.

"Saga One, I'm getting faint and unusual hits on my long-range scanner, 119.3 by 286.4."

Daeson directed his Starstreak's long range scanner to look there.

"Copy, Saga Two. I'm seeing the same hits but have no I.D. yet."

"Same, Saga One," Raviel replied.

Daeson looked at their survivability time clock—four hours, sixteen minutes. Investigating this anomaly was certainly not within the scope of their assigned mission, and diverting would make their narrow survivability window even smaller. He thought of Raviel and realized the risk was too great.

"Saga One, I think we need to investigate," Raviel interrupted his thoughts. "Jeshu's mission on Rayl is at a critical juncture, and this could mean something."

Daeson took a deep breath. His gutsy Raviel would never be okay with complacency.

"Saga Two, we have four hours, and this will add another jump. We'd be cutting it close...real close."

"I understand," Raviel replied, not offering any safe way out.

Daeson calculated a new jump destination and transmitted the coordinates to Raviel.

"New coordinates received," Raviel radioed.

"We get there, take new scans, and get out. Copy?"

"Copy," Raviel replied.

"Initiate jump drive on my mark." Daeson's finger hovered over the jump drive engine's engage button. One tap of his finger could mean the final death of both of them. As he was about to pull back, the image of their daughter's face looking at him across the small gap between their Starstreaks filled his mind. *Could their investigation alter her success as one of Jeshu's Navi?* he wondered.

"Engage!"

When Daeson and Raviel exited their slipstream jump, his radar lit up like the stars of the Aurora galaxy, and so did the visual through his canopy. They had exited the slipstream jump and arrived right in the middle of a massive Torian armada. At a quick glance, Daeson estimated at least two full Torian fleets complete with star cruisers, battleships, destroyers, frigates, and hundreds of fighters. Daeson felt the immediate rush within his muscles.

"Initiate cloak!" he radioed but Raviel was one step ahead of him, disappearing just a fraction of a second before he had completed his command.

"AIFA, full stealth mode!" Daeson commanded, knowing Raviel would initiate the same.

AIFA shut down every energy producing and consuming process on the Starstreak, leaving only his visual and radar cloak tech and minimal life support online.

"Stealth mode initiated," AIFA responded.

Daeson's heart was racing. Here in the middle of a massive Torian armada, they were sitting ducks, floating helplessly and hoping against hope that in the 2.5 seconds they had been visible, the enemy hadn't noticed them. Daeson held his breath as he visually scanned three hundred sixty degrees around himself for some sign of detection.

What could this mean? Daeson wondered. *And why such a massive armada this far out in space away from anything significant?*

Although Daeson had only heard speculations as to the size of the Torian galactic space force, he imagined that the ships he was seeing had to constitute a significant portion. *Why wouldn't Dracus have these ships marshaled and engaged in the battle for Rayl?* None of it made sense.

Daeson took his first breath a full minute after their arrival when he had so far not seen any response. The armada didn't seem to have any particular purpose in their movements, except perhaps to be gathering for some future mission. Daeson and Raviel found themselves in a serious dilemma. They couldn't power up and jump without being detected, but the armada wasn't moving away from them, so the clock on their survivability was ticking. They had two hours and thirty-four minutes left with a two hour and twelve-minute final jump to make. As Daeson considered their limited options, a Torian battleship with thirty Torian escort fighters and three accompanying frigates began to close in on them from behind. In stealth mode, he couldn't even get a simulated visual on Raviel.

As the Torian ships came closer, Daeson's legs began to ache with unutilized adrenaline. *Did they know?*

Everything inside Daeson wanted to power up and either fight or flee, but logic dictated a wait-and-see tactic. He could hardly bear it as the battleship loomed large off his right wing. With Raviel positioned between him and the battleship, she was even closer to the Torian vessels. Fighters zipped past them, one just a few feet from colliding. *Would Raviel and her Starstreak be obliterated by a collision with the massive battleship?* he wondered. He found himself holding his breath once again, relieved only slightly by the fact that this Torian vessel group didn't appear to be sweeping the space they occupied, and thus apparently knew nothing of their presence.

Once the battleship had passed, Daeson glanced at the survivability time clock—two hours, sixteen minutes. They now had four minutes to spare. He risked transmitting an encrypted message via their quantum entanglement communicator. Although the QEC transmission itself was not detectable because of the quantum entanglement principle, the power to generate the communication was.

Jump coordinates, 299.3 by 106.4. De-cloak and launch in 60 seconds.

Daeson waited for a reply, but none came. *Had Raviel been struck and become incapacitated?*

Thirty seconds.

Daeson entered the jump coordinates.

Twenty seconds.

"AIFA, on my mark, power up, decloak, and initiate the slipstream jump drive."

"I have no confirmation with Saga Two," AIFA replied.

"I'm not giving the order until I see her Starstreak," Daeson replied.

Just then two Torian fighters broke from the battleship group and circled back on an intercept heading. Daeson was now certain they had detected his transmission!

Fifteen seconds.

"AIFA, de-cloak and bring weapons online!" Daeson ordered, hoping he could draw the fighters to his location and give Raviel a chance to escape.

As soon as his Starstreak decloaked, the Torian fighters opened fire.

"Saga Two, ready to jump!" he heard Raviel radio.

Daeson glanced over to see Raviel's Starstreak appear.

"Engage!" Daeson said just as two massive plasma bursts filled his canopy.

WHAM!

Daeson felt the first plasma round impact his left engine nacelle just as his jump drive engine engaged. His stomach flipped as he entered slipstream. At first the visual was unusual and severely distorted. His mind instantly flashed to years earlier when Raviel had experienced her slipstream anomaly…an event that eventually killed her. Would he suffer the same fate in the Ruah? Ten long seconds ticked by as he experienced the wild contortions of the spacetime jump. He felt nauseous. Then in the blink of an eye the distortion cleared. He waited…hoping. Two hours passed. Daeson wondered if he would reemerge inside the galaxy's black hole and be snuffed into oblivion.

The survivability clock passed zero and was now counting negative. The jump drive disengaged, and Daeson appeared only a few miles outside of the Brahm's Cradle global stasis field.

"Daeson—do you copy?" Raviel's urgent voice blared over the radio.

"I copy. Are you okay?" Daeson responded.

"Thank Ell Yon! You're an hour later than you should be. I thought—" Raviel's voice was trembling.

"I'm okay. Let's get inside the global grid. You should be there already!" Daeson chastised.

Daeson quickly set their course, and they successfully entered Brahm's Cradle atmosphere. A few minutes later they had landed at the central space port. Raviel ran to Daeson, wrapping her arms around his neck.

"I thought I'd lost you," she said, holding tight to him.

"I'm okay. I'm not sure what happened up there, but I'm okay." Daeson held her then released her so he could see her face. "We need to report this ASAP."

Raviel looked shaken, knowing that if Daeson had been lost, he would have been lost forever. With eyes red, she nodded. As they made their way to headquarters, Raviel refused to let loose of Daeson's hand. Whatever they had discovered was now up to Admiral Lucien to figure out.

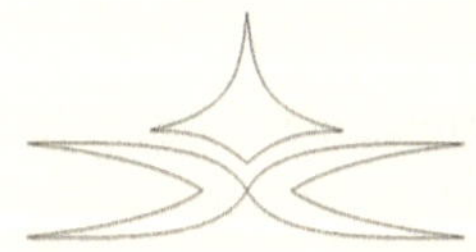

CHAPTER

2

Transference

He came into the galaxy, but humanity did not receive him. He came to reclaim that which Deitum Prime had destroyed. He was light in the darkness, but the darkness rebelled against his light. Yet those who follow him are initiated into his reclamation by the creed of his words.
– Iyhaz, Oracle of Ell Yon

The Merchant's Day of Execution...

In the realm of the Ruah, First Admiral Kalem and Admiral Galec and their warriors looked on in horror. The smoke of battle lifted upward from their fierce encounters with the Torians. They had won this precious space above the Ring through sheer might and epic battle, but now an eerie silence ensued as the execution of the Son of Ell Yon commenced. Reinforcements from a dozen fleets had arrived, giving them the capability to end this frightful execution by these miserable humans, but the order to engage was never given. Jeshu hung silently in the power of his love for humanity, and Kalem could hardly bear it.

"One word, my lord...just one," Kalem whispered, eager to unleash the might of Ell Yon's galactic fleet on the Torians and their human pawns of evil.

As Jeshu hung in tortuous agony, slowly being stretched by the powerful unrelenting force of the magnetic collars around his wrists and ankles, the pain of each grissler lash magnified as his skin was drawn taut by the electromagnetic engine powering the force of distention. In the hallowed halls of sacrificial deeds, this moment in time by this perfect man was the crown of them all. The galaxy held its breath as Jeshu folded his life into a gift of perfect Solution to rescue the souls of humanity. Galec was tasked with conducting Jeshu's transference into the nephesh matrix. Normally this was done at or moments before the point of death, but for Jeshu, not so. Although the risk of a degraded transference increases with each minute waited after death, Jeshu gave explicit direction as to the timing of his transference. There would be no transference until the unforgettable sting of death had been fully realized. Jeshu wanted to remember every microsecond of this great and painful sacrifice.

"Of all the elements that makes me most human, death is the binding agony that must never be forgotten. Death by Deitum Prime is a bitter wine that must be tasted in full measure," Jeshu had said to Kalem and Galec.

In the invisible realm of the Ruah, the two admirals stood upon an anti-grav platform positioned next to their beloved Commander as he hung within the Ring, death eager to finish its grisly task. The anti-grav platform was tethered to an advanced command transport just above them as two hundred accompanying warriors stood guard, encircling the Ring with weapons ready. To Jeshu's last breath, Kalem waited for the command to stop this horrid execution, but no such command escaped the lips of the Sovereign's son. Death lashed out upon the perfect man, and Jeshu did not retreat from its vicious sting.

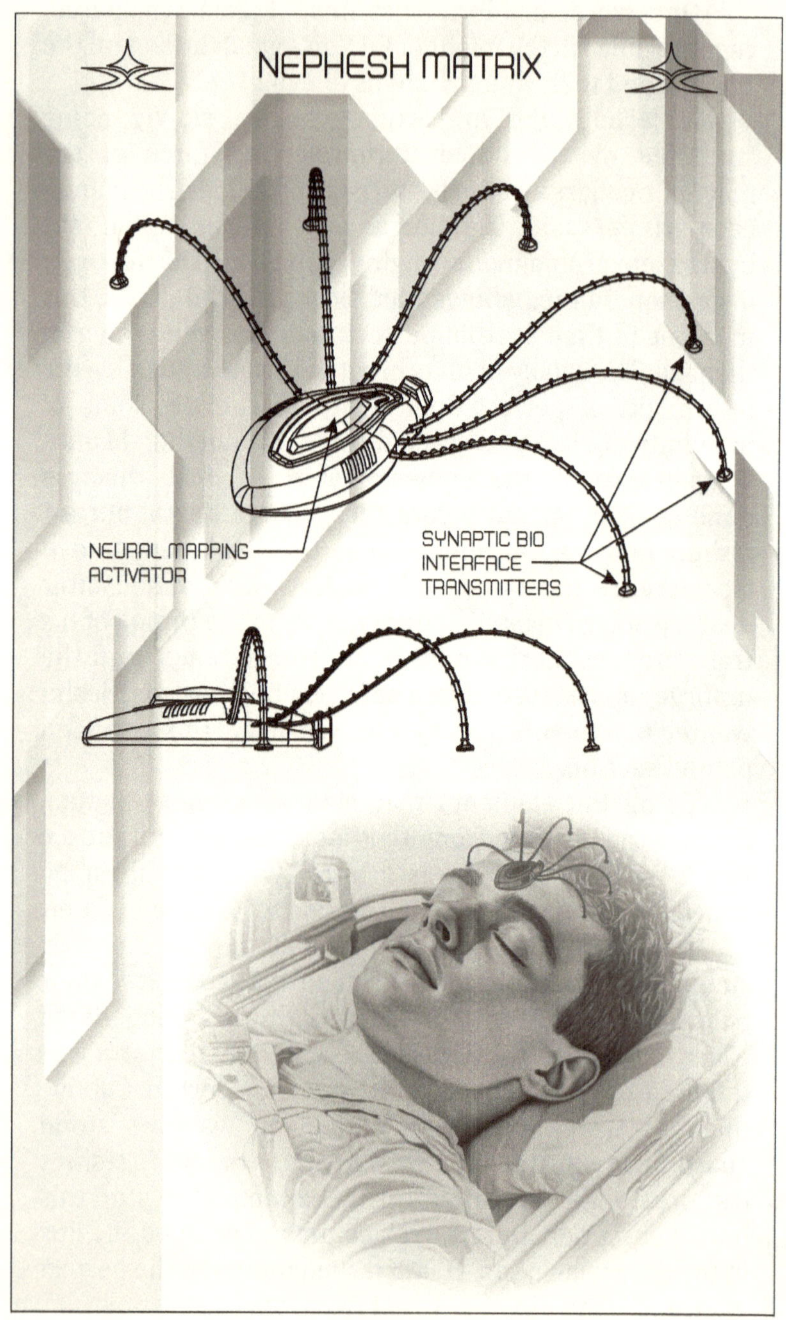

NEPHESH MATRIX
NEURAL MAPPING ACTIVATOR
SYNAPTIC BIO INTERFACE TRANSMITTERS

Seconds after Jeshu's death, Galec placed the nephesh matrix on the noble brow of the Son of Ell Yon under the watchful guard of Kalem and his warriors. Galec pressed the jewel in the center of the nephesh matrix device, initiating the transfer of the essence of their mighty Commander, capturing every memory, synaptic pathway, and biological network scan in perfect detail. Time was of the essence, for the Protectors would not wait to execute their final proclamation to the galaxy—power already surging.

The amber jewel in the center of the matrix crescendoed to a brilliant glow then diminished. The six tentacles of the device quickly retreated from their perches on Jeshu's head. Galec lifted the device, placing it carefully within an ornate armored reliquary about the size of his hand. He looked over at Kalem, offering a subtle nod. Kalem nearly trembled at the thought of their next mission. From this moment on, Kalem and Galec would never be out of arm's reach of Jeshu's nephesh matrix.

"We leave now!" Kalem ordered.

At that moment, the fury of Dracus and all his grisly minions erupted in a ferocious attempt to destroy Jeshu's nephesh matrix. The region surrounding Rayl was ablaze with space battles on an unprecedented scale as the Torians tried to penetrate the defenses of Kalem's fleet forces. This would be their only hope of victory against Sovereign Ell Yon and the Commander, for if the death of Jeshu could purge the people of Dracus's Deitum Prime, his return to life would seal the future of trillions and shatter all plans to usurp the reign of Ell Yon.

Kalem and Galec retreated on the platform into the underbelly of the command transport. A squadron of Starstreaks materialized from cloak to escort the command transport and its precious cargo back to Kalem's flag ship, the *Advent*. Inside the command transport, Galec looked down at Jeshu's reliquary, then set his eyes on Kalem.

"Never before, nor ever shall be again, has the Commander allowed such vulnerability. It is a frightful thing."

Kalem felt the full weight of Galec's words. He locked eyes with his fellow admiral.

"To die for those who reject him. To offer a thing so precious to a people so undeserving." Kalem dared to shake his head once. "A frightful thing indeed, Galec. The love of Ell Yon and his son is beyond my understanding."

Galec lowered his gaze back to the reliquary. "There is none in all the universe, save him, that could accomplish such a profound thing. It makes me feel…small."

Galec's words pierced the heart of Kalem with crushing truth. He swallowed hard, trying to steel himself for what was to come, but for a few brief seconds, Kalem could not escape the powerful emotions shattering his fortress of duty. He turned away, looking toward the cockpit as they launched upward and away from Jeshu's place of execution. *How could C'fir Dracus have rebelled eons ago against the flawless command of Ell Yon's son— one so absolutely perfect in purpose, deed, and heart?* he wondered.

A Torian destroyer's salvo of weaponry ratcheted the command transport before a battleship from *Advent Fleet* unleashed its full battery of 32 arc cannons and 12 high-yield class four plasma cannons.

Kalem glanced back at Galec. "That's too close," he said as he and Galec made their way to the command cockpit.

It took fifteen minutes to recover back to the *Advent.* Then, for the next thirty minutes, the two admirals coordinated a well-planned tactical extraction in response to Dracus's attack. Fleets across the entire Kayn system were engaged in battle more fierce than anything the warriors of Ell Yon had seen before, including Kalem himself. Then, as quickly as it began, it ended.

Kalem and Galec stood in the *Advent's* command center evaluating the actions of the Torians.

"We're getting reports from every fleet across the Kayn system that the Torians are pulling back," Kalem's first officer announced.

"This is unexpected," Galec said. "Do you suppose he knows our destination?"

Kalem kept his eyes on the tactical displays, making sure he wasn't misreading the actions of their enemy.

"We both know how intelligent Dracus is. I'm sure he knows the writings of the oracles better than anyone. Though the message is cryptic, I'm certain he's figured it out." Kalem turned to look at Galec. "Daeson Starlore's unexpected encounter on his return flight to Gehenna gives us a pretty clear picture of Dracus's intentions."

The reclamation energy wave initiated by the death of Jeshu raged outward to the four corners of the galaxy, initiating the purge of Deitum Prime. Every living organic lifeform on every planet, moon, and habitable body trembled in silent contemplation, looking upward toward the realm from which the taste of eternity had come. The reach of promised reclamation held all life in its tender, righteous grip, exposing darkness in hearts, heralding hope for many, and calling all to the arms of Sovereign Ell Yon. But as is the natural corrupted state of the human heart, many cried out against this Immortal sacrificial act in rebellion, raising fists against the one who had died for them. Jeshu's death was an unrepeatable gift of unconscionable price, yet trampled underfoot by most, for the love of Deitum Prime was a willful prison for their minds. How then shall such a purchase of the souls of humanity be offered? Why then should such a thing so despised be given so cheaply to those so undeserving?

Each of the Navi of Jeshu contemplated such great ponderings in utter distress. Was it all for naught? Had they ruined their lives for the fleeting bliss of a fading visionary? The mysteries of Ell Yon were hard to bear in the aftermath of the Master's execution.

Although the morning after Jeshu's death stood saturated in bleak despair, none anticipated nor could comprehend the surging power of Ell Yon through the lifeless body of his son. The birth of new hope awaited.

Brae Thornton and Rhett Stryker held each other, clinging to a shred of comfort in the wake of such tragedy.

"Will they come?" Brae whispered, her head pressed against Rhett's chest.

They had arrived at a secret rendezvous in the north region of the eastern continent. The trees and ground were already dusted with snow as the warm season ended. Fifty-two acres of rolling hills moderately forested in patches of evergreens, this was Rhett's emergency retreat, a place he called *Arcton Hold*. A modest home with a suitable workshop and a few other outbuildings comprised the structures on the property. Brae had learned that Rhett had lofty plans for *Arcton Hold*, but those plans were cut short by Jeshu's invasion into his life. As it was, Rhett had equipped the getaway with ample provisions to support a dozen people for six months. *Arcton Hold* was intended to provide a temporary haven of safety from the enemies of Rayl should the nearby hostile planets ever align in a concerted effort to attack. Rhett had confided to Brae that he'd never imagined *Arcton Hold* would one day harbor the followers of the Merchant.

"I don't know," Rhett returned. "Fear has the ability to bring out the best and the worst in people."

Brae could feel the floor beneath them begin to vibrate, the only indication that something of significant mass was setting down. She jumped up to peer out the large front room portal to see the swirl of snow dust just a few hundred feet away.

"Someone's come, and since it's still cloaked, I'm guessing it's one of ours!"

A few seconds later, a Spacehawk resolved in the flurry of settling snow. Bridger and Kase exited the cockpit. Brae closed her eyes.

"Thank Ell Yon...it's your brothers."

On the porch, Brae and Rhett greeted them with enthusiasm, and each embrace was held tighter and longer than typical. Kase's usual smile was noticeably absent.

"Any news of the others?" Rhett asked.

Bridger shook his head. "There was such chaos with everyone scrambling to get away. I saw at least two other Spacehawks escape and the *Aviel*, but I don't know who was flying them or where they were going. I just hope—"

Bridger was cut short by the distant rumble of two more Spacehawks setting down. The mere sound settled Brae's heart in a way she couldn't describe.

"More inbound!" she exclaimed.

Within the next three hours, eight Spacehawks, the *Aviel*, and all eleven loyal sectators had gathered at *Arcton Hold*. The reunion was an odd mix of joy, sadness, and apprehension. Brae separated herself from the group to get something to drink. When she returned, she stood and listened to the rumble of conversations about what had happened and what might happen to them now that Kylos had succeeded in killing Jeshu.

"Surely they will hunt us down."

"Where can we go that they won't find us?"

"We are enemies of both Rayl and Moria—there's no place to hide."

"Was this really Ell Yon's plan?"

"Why didn't the warriors of the Ruah help him?"

"Do we hide forever? What are we supposed to do now?"

With each question and comment, Brae's heart fractured a little more. Of the eleven remaining sectators, she was the one who had been given a front row seat to this epic event. She heard and felt their apprehension, but deep down, something was missing—something none of them yet understood.

"We have to go back," she blurted out.

All ten sectators turned to look at her, bewildered by her comment.

"Surely you don't mean back to Jalem," Shayde said.

"I do."

"They'll kill us, Brae," Cilla exclaimed. "What good would that do?"

Brae shook her head. "I don't know, but I just— Look...we all saw his power. What just happened," Brae said pointing south to Jalem, "can't be the end. Jeshu defeated by Kylos? You all know he could have stopped it at any time. This isn't over, and I want to see what's next."

Brae's decisive trust in Jeshu and in Ell Yon silenced the room with conviction for more than a few seconds.

"Before leaving Jalem, one of the Raylean Guard pilots told me that the Keepers had taken Jeshu's body and locked him away in one of their crypts," Quill said.

"That doesn't make sense," Mazon commented. "I would have thought they had incinerated him instead."

Quill shook his head. "No, the pilot was certain. Almost as if they were treating Jeshu's death with honor."

"But the Keepers are the ones that hated him! They orchestrated his execution," Kase added.

"Not all Keepers," Bridger said. "There are a handful who secretly believed in Jeshu."

Brae remembered the evening Jeshu spent with one such Keeper...Codemus. The conversation she had overheard was profound, and she remembered wondering how the Keeper was going to reconcile his novel understanding about who Jeshu truly was with his own role in the order that was opposing the Son of Ell Yon at every turn.

"Brae is right," Rhett interjected. "Though I was slow to believe, I've seen too much to think this is the end. Nothing about this ending makes sense. At least not yet. I'll go with you."

"Do you think Major Kamp could put us in contact with Keeper Codemus?" Brae asked. "Perhaps he would be a good place to start."

"I'll reach out," Rhett replied.

"I need to see this too," Bridger added as he stood.

Kase looked like he was going to volunteer, but Bridger cut him short. "I don't think Mother and Father could stand all three of their sons being captured and executed in the same week." Kase frowned but stayed silent.

"Then count me in," Shayde piped up.

No one else volunteered or protested, so the investigation team was set.

"At least disguise yourselves a bit," Jaym said. "There's no need to make it easy for them."

Rhett smiled. "Fair enough. Let's get some sleep, and we'll leave at first light. Does that work?" he asked Brae and the others.

They all nodded.

Preeminent Keeper Fasa Kylos approached Morian Subchancellor Pylok in his great hall of Judgment, his footsteps echoing throughout the large chamber. Ribbons of amber and green lights accentuated various features in the room, but they could not overcome the gloomy gray sky that darkened the massive circular window just behind Pylok's command chair.

"Subchancellor Pylok, with all due respect, did you authorize two men by the names of Codemus and Sephner to take possession of the body of the anarchist?"

Pylok glared back at Kylos, seeming to understand that there was an accusation in the question.

"Tread carefully, Kylos. You are here only at my pleasure, and I'm not feeling very pleased at the moment."

Kylos apologetically bowed his head ever so slightly.

"Forgive me, Subchancellor. I only ask because I am concerned for the preservation of peace on Rayl, a testimony to your benevolent rule."

The exchange between Kylos and Pylok was always an elegant dance of nuanced meanings and subtleties of words, as well as the silence between them. Pylok's eyes narrowed, fully grasping the intent behind Kylos's tactful words.

"I was told that Codemus and Sephner belonged to your Keeper and Builder orders. Is this not true?"

Kylos proceeded carefully. "They were, your grace, but they have just recently renounced their vows."

Pylok became annoyed. "It is not the obligation of my commandos to keep track of such petty things. I granted those men possession of the body, and that is that."

Lines formed above the brows of Kylos. "That is most unfortunate, Your Excellency, because—"

"He's dead, man! What more do you want? I am weary of mediating your ridiculous grievances." Pylok leaned forward from his governing chair. "And I will not be persuaded to utilize the power of the Morian Empire to execute your nefarious schemes again...is that clear?"

Kylos paused, offering an appropriate amount of time for Pylok's rebuke to settle.

"Perfectly, Subchancellor. It's just that there were preposterous claims made by this Jeshu character that he would be revived and live again." Kylos offered a squeamish smile. "As absurd as this sounds, can you imagine the chaos that would occur throughout Rayl if his followers were to orchestrate some charade of such a claim?"

Pylok's frown eased as he processed Kylos's words. It was just enough of a fissure in Pylok's forceful rebuttal that Kylos dared continue.

"With all due respect and for the sake of your continued established peace, I would propose that guards be posted at Codemus's crypt to preclude such a conspiracy. Morian guards at that," Kylos added.

Pylok looked hard at Kylos for a long while. "This insignificant planet will be my undoing. Tribune Daros," Pylok shouted across the hall. "Give Kylos six commandos to guard the crypt of his dead nemesis."

Pylok then glared at Kylos. "Away with you, Kylos, and don't set foot in my hall again."

CHAPTER

3

The Prisons of Gehenna

Ell Yon is ever before me, and I rejoice that I will not remain in Gehenna. Neither will the body of the Merchant decay in the grave. He will show me life, and I will stand at the right hand of my Sovereign. In His presence is everlasting joy. – Darnullay, Oracle of Ell Yon

Admirals Kalem and Galec were preparing to lead an armada of over three hundred ships into the heart of the Aurora Galaxy—destination...Brahm's Cradle in the Gehenna Cluster. There, at the planetary regeneration complex, Galec would deliver Jeshu's nephesh matrix and oversee his regeneration. For the billions of regenerated humans on Brahm's Cradle, there was one and only one way they could be set free from this prison of protection, and it was Galec that would deliver the one who could free them.

Galec felt the burden of billions of souls on his shoulders. But even more than that was the weighty knowledge that the essence of the Commander was in his hands...literally. He looked down at the precious reliquary holding Jeshu's nephesh matrix and trembled. No mission in the history of the Malakians was as important as this.

Aboard the *Advent*, First Admiral Kalem led the armada with unmitigated resolve, and Galec was thankful for it. Being uniquely responsible for personally transporting Jeshu's reliquary disallowed Galec from fully engaging as a strategic and tactical admiral. His first officer was given command of his own fleet while Galec was tasked with this unique and supremely important mission. Until the reliquary was delivered, Galec could think of little else.

After the armada had completed their second slipstream jump, Kalem sent 22 vessels to various jump coordinates near the Gehenna Cluster to try to locate the assault force that Daeson Starlore had reported was waiting for them.

"Where are you, Dracus?" Kalem murmured. "Sensors...what does our long-range fleet network detect?"

The officer at the sensors station was assimilating the combined data of over one hundred ships and their long-range scans. His fingers flew across the glass panel with the speed of a Surian cat. He stopped, turning to face Admirals Kalem and Galec and the first officer.

"Assimilated scans from our fleet and all 22 of the advance vessels are all clear, admiral."

"Is it possible that Dracus believes the Commander's nephesh matrix might be taken directly to the Omega Nebula?" Kalem's first officer asked.

"Highly unlikely. Dracus is too shrewd to miss the Sovereign's promise to the regenerated prisoners in Gehenna, even though it's subtle," Kalem responded as he continued to absorb the endless data being presented on a dozen displays.

Kalem frowned. "This is where we part, my friend. I must rendezvous with Admiral Rafel and receive the Commander's Protectors from Sovereign Ell Yon before engaging with Dracus's armada...wherever they may be. Is your crew ready?"

Galec nodded.

Kalem held out his arm. "Ell Yon be with you. I'll hold nothing back to win the day."

Galec grasped Kalem's arm. "Nor will I. See you on Brahm's Cradle," he said then entered the turbo lift with two massive Malakian warriors on his left and right, plasma rifles drawn and ready.

In the lift, Galec opened the reliquary to convince himself that Jeshu's nephesh matrix was still there. The central amber jewel glowed softly within the reliquary chamber, signaling that Jeshu's transference was intact and stable. Galec took a deep breath, closing and sealing the chamber once more. He placed the reliquary inside his tunic chest pocket. Galec was certain that Dracus would deploy every available vessel in his fleet to stop him from delivering the Commander's reliquary. During the brief hours of transportation of the Commander's nephesh matrix, Dracus would only have to contend with the Malakian fleets and their warriors. It was the one time in the history of the Malakian-Torian war that the Commander would not be present to stand against his nemesis in the flesh.

Galec and his armed escort arrived at *Advent's* launch bay one. The bay door's six panels rotated away like an opening iris as Galec approached. Inside the bay was a recently-commissioned small Malakian warship that was stealthy, powerful, and deadly—the *Firestorm*. This ten-crew-member vessel was fully armed yet as agile as a two-seat fighter craft. The purpose of this design was singular—deliver the Commander's nephesh matrix to Brahm's Cradle and then lead the billions of regenerated prisoners home to the Omega Nebula.

As Galec approached, the crew of the *Firestorm* snapped to attention, all waiting in perfect formation. Each crew member had been hand-picked by Galec himself, most of them from his own fleet.

"Captain Vin, is she ready?"

"Aye, admiral—as are we."

Galec handed his first officer an encrypted micro-drive. "Here's our slipstream jump profile. With the *Firestorm's* reduced slipstream jump signature, the Torians will have no way of tracking us, but as a precaution we'll be making a few extra jumps before arriving at our final destination."

Only Galec and Kalem knew the *Firestorm's* seven-jump slipstream profile. They were taking every precaution to ensure absolute security.

"Aye, sir." Captain Vin turned to his crew. "Man your stations and prepare to launch."

The next 24 hours would determine the fate of the galaxy.

The *Firestorm* launched from the *Advent's* largest bay. Within a few minutes, they were approaching the entrance coordinates for their first slipstream jump. Galec wondered just how many enemy ships awaited them. Would their devised tactic of a backdoor entry to Brahm's Cradle actually work? Galec knew the capabilities of his crew and of this advanced warship, yet he cautioned himself against underestimating C'fir Dracus. The Torian commander had proven his shrewd tactical genius time and time again. Galec sat in the captain's seat in the center of the *Firestorm's* command center cockpit.

"Ready to jump, Admiral," Captain Vin announced.

One of the advanced technologies built into the *Firestorm* was its ability to calculate and slipstream jump in just a few seconds. Typically, this could take up to two minutes, but the *Firestorm* was designed to be a nimble slipstream ship. This would allow Galec and his crew to skip-jump across the galaxy quickly and with little possibility of the enemy's following or intercepting them.

"Hold this position," Galec ordered. He tapped a sequence on his command console. "Nav, I want our time between the next three jumps to be less than ten seconds."

Captain Vin's eyebrows raised, but he nodded. "Aye, sir. Ensign Prager, enter the coordinates. Lieutenant Kash, I want a full sensor scan during each ten-second span. Major Zensi, bring arc cannons and shields online as soon as we're through. Is that clear?"

"Aye, sir!" came the unified response.

"Engage!"

Dracus leaned forward in the captain's chair aboard his star cruiser *Diabolus*. He had assembled the largest force of warships the galaxy had ever seen. Although he hadn't prevented the Merchant from fulfilling his mission on Rayl, he still had a perfect opportunity to thwart Ell Yon's plans. The oracles had foretold of the Merchant's mission to Brahm's Cradle in the Gehenna Cluster after his death, and now with the Son of Ell Yon's essence captured in a nephesh matrix, there would be no other time in history when he would be so vulnerable and powerless.

Dracus smiled as he thought of destroying the Commander of the Malakians before the Son of Ell Yon could be regenerated. However, the lord of the Torians couldn't subdue an annoying and rising anxiety about certain oracle references to an event that was not specified clearly enough for him to ascertain. *Ell Yon's arrogance in foretelling his plans through the oracles will be his undoing*, Dracus thought. And yet, a few secrets existed which Ell Yon had hidden from everyone since the beginning. Dracus wondered if the planned regeneration of the Merchant would hold just such a secret.

"Get Admirals Kyrsa and Yelrod on com," Dracus ordered.

A few seconds later, the two admirals appeared on the forward display of the *Diabolus's* bridge.

"Are your fleets prepared?" Dracus asked.

"Yes, Lord Dracus," Yelrod replied. "Obviously the destination is Brahm's Cradle. So why do you have us positioned and ready over 130 light years away? They could slipstream jump from an infinite number of approach coordinates."

An evil smile ebbed across the dark lord's face. He tapped on his control console.

"Phystech Director Devex, transmit the quantum tag array display to Admiral Kyrsa on the *Nightshade* and Admiral Yelrod on the *Wraith.*"

The sensor display showed a map of the entire galaxy and then began to populate with hundreds of indicators, most of them in concentrations around the planet Rayl, the Omega Nebula, and the Gehenna Cluster.

Kyrsa and Yelrod began to assimilate the information as the display zoomed in to the outer limits of the tagged indicators.

"What are we seeing, Lord Dracus?" Kyrsa asked.

"Fifty-three years ago, we handed one of the richest deposits of andelucite over to the Malakians," Dracus explained.

"Yes...I remember," Kyrsa said with a scowl.

"Before we leaked the location information to the Malakians, I ordered Director Devex and his phystech team to taint the entire deposit with thousands of molecular andelucite quantum tags."

"What is a quantum tag?" Yelrod asked.

A visual of Director Devex appeared.

"A molecular quantum tag uses the principle of quantum entanglement, except that we have developed the technology such that we can now positionally identify the remote entangled particle by monitoring its associated home particle's synchronized acceleration information," Devex explained. "Knowing the Malakians would use the andelucite as a composite material for the fabrication of their ship's hulls, we identified and logged each quantum tag and have been tracking their newest ships for the last two decades.

The realization of what this meant shattered Kyrsa's and Yelrod's composure.

"Why haven't we been told that we had this capability?" Yelrod demanded, his face red with anger.

Dracus slowly stood, his countenance dark with indignation toward Yelrod's obvious breach of respect. He glared at the admiral. Yelrod swallowed hard.

"Forgive me, Lord Dracus," Yelrod recanted. "It's just that we could have used this technology hundreds of times in the past two decades to gain the advantage on the Malakian fleet forces."

Dracus held his silence a bit longer. "Don't you think I know that, Admiral Yelrod? I've patiently laid a trap to deal a final and fatal blow to Ell Yon and his miserable son once and for all. We could not give any indication whatsoever that we could detect the positions of their ships until this very day...the day of vengeance! Don't ever question me again!"

Yelrod lowered his head in subjugation. "Of course, my lord. It will never happen again."

Dracus allowed the humility of his admiral to linger for a few seconds. "Observe...it's clear that Admiral Kalem is positioning most of his fleet forces to make a run to the Gehenna Cluster to deliver the nephesh matrix of the Merchant."

"One fleet is detouring to the Omega Nebula," Kyrsa added.

"Yes," Dracus agreed. "No doubt to acquire the Protectors the Merchant wants once he is regenerated.

We need not be concerned with that. If we can destroy the nephesh matrix, there'll be no need for the Protectors."

"Based on the size and position of their main fleet, we should be able to predict their final slipstream jump coordinates and attack before they ever reach Brahm's Cradle," Yelrod declared enthusiastically.

"One would think." Dracus directed the quantum tag array display to zoom into one particular area of the map. "But Kalem is too clever to make such a direct run to their world in the Gehenna Cluster. He knows he would face the power of my fleets and considers such an engagement too risky for the Merchant's nephesh matrix." Dracus zoomed in even further until one lone quantum tag was isolated and separated from the thousands of others. The identifier displayed, "*Firestorm.*"

"There you are, Galec," Dracus said with a dark gleam in his eye. "The messenger of the Merchant would certainly be his courier as well. The *Firestorm* is their newest warship. Our quantum tag has indicated the ship was commissioned just two months ago. The main Malakian fleet force is a diversion so Galec and the *Firestorm* can backdoor their approach to Brahm's Cradle."

Dracus looked at Kyrsa and Yelrod, a dark and fierce resolve in his eyes. "That's our target, admirals." Dracus pointed to the highlighted target on the display. "We intercept when the *Firestorm* is one jump from Brahm's Cradle."

"But Lord Dracus, we can track them, but we can't predict how far they will jump," Kyrsa said as she scrutinized the data.

"True." Dracus's face contorted with a wry grin. "On their last jump, we will know their exact heading, so we will set up a wall of ships in their path as a barrier. The *Firestorm's* ship collision safety protocol will automatically bring them out of the slipstream jump right into firing range of our entire fleet."

Kyrsa offered a crooked grin. "It's genius."

"We'll track Galec's ship until his final jump heading is directly toward Brahm's Cradle. We must be close enough to intercept them before they arrive. Dedicate everything we have to the destruction of the *Firestorm*. Am I clear?"

The two admirals snapped to attention.

"Yes, Lord Dracus. We'll prepare at once," Yelrod replied.

Galec had faced the fiery edge of vicious Torian warriors' stasis blades and fought in a hundred dire battles against the forces of Dracus near planets and moons across the galaxy, but bearing the responsibility of couriering the priceless nephesh matrix of the Son of Ell Yon brought greater angst to his soul than all the previous threats combined. Galec placed his right hand on the Merchant's reliquary resting in his breast pocket just next to his heart as he intently watched the bridge displays. Their exit out of the first jump was upon them. A few seconds later, streaks of vibrant slipstream aura dissolved as the fabric of normal space rematerialized. Trillions of stars of the Aurora Galaxy sparkled in jeweled brilliance before them.

"Sensors clear," Lieutenant Kash announced.

Galec waited as new slipstream parameters were calculated.

"Set heading 19.55 by 273.14," Captain Vin ordered.

The nav officer quickly aligned the *Firestorm* to the new heading.

"New heading set and slipstream jump calculations complete," came the response.

"Engage," Captain Vin ordered.

Normal space melted away into the shining slipstream aura so familiar to veteran spacefarers.

"We clocked 11.3 seconds," Captain Vin said with a frown. "Let's tighten that up on the next jump."

"Aye, sir," came the unified response.

Galec relaxed ever so slightly and took a breath. He figured the first jump and the last jump were the most dangerous since those would be the only ones the Torians could possibly even speculate as to what their entry and exit coordinates might be. One jump down and six to go.

The next five jumps were flawless and without cause for concern of any kind. But as they neared the end of their slipstream jump profile, Galec became uneasy once again. The *Firestorm* crew had perfected the ten-second interval and were ready to initiate their seventh and final jump.

"Engage," ordered Captain Vin.

This was one of the longer jumps—53 minutes. Galec drummed the console with his fingers, waiting. As the seconds clicked by, something deep in Galec's soul seemed off, but there was little that could be done now.

With 12 minutes remaining in the slipstream jump, the *Firestorm*'s anti-collision alarms began to blare. The *Firestorm*'s AI computer voice announced the problem. "Slipstream collision imminent. Exiting jump profile in three...two...one..."

Before Galec or Captain Vin could issue commands, the slipstream kaleidoscopic visual dissolved away to reveal a terrifying nightmare of battle. The space around them filled with an unending torrent of arc and plasma cannons, phaser fire, and trans-light missiles on every side. Hundreds upon hundreds of Torian and Malakian battleships, destroyers, frigates, and fighters were engaged in the fiercest space battle the Aurora Galaxy had ever witnessed, and Galec instantly knew it was all because of the small reliquary he carried near his chest. Right in front of them loomed one of Dracus's largest star cruisers, Admiral Yelrod's flagship, *Wraith*. It unleashed its massive class-four cannons as a squadron of twenty

Torian fighters swooped in from a flanking position, adding to the crippling blows of the star cruiser.

"Evasive maneuver bravo two!" Captain Vin shouted. "All reserve power to the shields!"

Galec grasped the arms of his seat as the *Firestorm* ratcheted from a cacophony of energy weapon hits. Even their best ship couldn't take this abuse long.

"Reengage our jump drive engine and get us out of here," Galec ordered.

"There are too many ships in line with our next heading, sir," the nav officer reported. "We must reposition."

Galec considered authorizing any jump that would take them out of this deadly furball but then realized they had somehow been compromised. If Dracus could predict this carefully planned jump, there was no telling what their next jump would bring. Somehow they at least had Malakian support here. Their next jump had to be directly to Brahm's Cradle.

"Shields at 42 percent," Major Zensi called out from his weapons console.

Just as it seemed they would not survive the next few seconds, 28 Malakian fighters intercepted the attacking Torian fighters as the *Advent,* Admiral Kalem's star cruiser, positioned itself between the *Firestorm* and the attacking *Wraith* star cruiser.

"*Firestorm*, this is Admiral Kalem of the *Advent*. Make your heading 335.2 by 163.8. We'll clear an opening for your next jump."

"Make it so and quickly," Captain Vin ordered.

Galec watched as the two massive star cruisers exchanged crippling blows of fierce fire power. Massive explosions began to occur on both star cruisers as the *Advent* depleted her energy weapons in a sacrificial attempt to save the *Firestorm*. The *Advent* unleashed a final salvo of six trans-light missiles into the belly of the *Wraith,* ending the fight. The midsection of the *Wraith* exploded in a fiery storm, splitting the massive vessel in half. But the resulting damage to the *Advent* was complete...itself a crippled floating mass of explosions and debris.

"Kalem!" Galec exclaimed.

"We have a solution!" the nav officer reported.

Galec took one last look at the disintegrating flagship of his commanding officer and his friend.

"Engage," Galec ordered.

Their last jump was 12.3 minutes and brought them to the very edge of the Brahm's Cradle global stasis field boundary. Within seconds of exiting the slipstream jump, they were safely tucked inside the protective dome of the global stasis field. Galec's heart lay heavy, wondering if his friend had survived. He was already mourning the loss of thousands of gallant Malakian warriors who had sacrificed themselves to allow Galec to bring their Commander's nephesh matrix to this obscure planet in the heart of the Gehenna Cluster.

The *Firestorm* set down on the designated space port landing pad next to the regeneration complex. Billions of people filled the streets, terraces, and walkways of the largest city on Brahm's Cradle, all waiting for the arrival of the Merchant's reliquary.

As the engines shut down, Galec found it impossible to move.

"Give me any information we have on the status of the battle," Galec ordered.

"Yes, sir," Captain Vin replied. "Evidently, as soon as we jumped, the Torians disengaged. I'm getting battle reports now."

Galec remained as he scanned the reports...hoping.

Kalem stayed aboard the *Advent* until the last possible minute, overseeing the evacuation of his crew. Many had lost their lives in this battle of the ages, but the *Firestorm* had survived. Too many Torian outposts were positioned throughout the Gehenna Cluster, so he authorized the self-destruct sequence of the *Advent*. For centuries he had commanded Sovereign Ell Yon's Aurora Galactic Fleet from the bridge of the *Advent*. Part of his heart tore as the vessel exploded into a million pieces.

By the time Kalem's transport landed on Brahm's Cradle, the *Firestorm* had already landed at the designated space port landing pad and was surrounded by thousands of heavily armed Malakian warriors.

As Kalem approached the ship, Admiral Galec disembarked and met him on the pad. Galec saluted Kalem, and then the two men locked arms.

"It's very good to see you, Admiral Galec," Kalem said with a subtle grin.

"How, Kalem? How did you know?" Galec asked.

"Based on Daeson Starlore's recon report a couple of days ago, an MRT7 reconnaissance team was able to get a fix on one of Dracus's fleet positions. They observed that each time the *Firestorm* made a slipstream jump, the entire fleet changed headings, almost as if they knew the direction of your jump. Since I knew your jump profile to Brahm's Cradle, it became clear to me that the Torians had devised some way of tracking your position, even hundreds of light years away."

Galec's eyes opened wide.

"I know," Kalem added. "Our scitech teams are already working on it."

"At those distances, they must have made some advancement in quantumtech. I'd get those teams involved as well," Galec offered. Quantumtech had been Galec's field of expertise as a young officer in Sovereign Ell Yon's fleet before Dracus rebelled.

"Agreed," Kalem said. "By your fifth jump, I abandoned our diversion plan and directed our fleets to rendezvous near Brahm's Cradle. The MRT7 recon team then relayed the final heading of the Torian fleet, and I knew they were on an intercept course with the *Firestorm*. We triangulated your seventh jump heading with theirs and were able to predict where they were planning on hitting you. We arrived just a few minutes before you and engaged."

Galec was usually difficult to read, but not here—not now. The stoic general's eyes softened as he gazed at Kalem. Galec removed the reliquary from his chest pocket, briefly glancing down at the priceless treasure, then back to Kalem.

"The galaxy owes you and your fleet a great debt of gratitude. Thank you, my friend."

Kalem lifted a hand toward the regeneration complex entrance. "The galaxy awaits...shall we?"

Galec nodded. Amidst the protection of their mighty Malakian warriors and the billions of human onlookers, the two admirals made their way to the antigrav lift within the complex that would take them to the place of hallowed importance.

This was the moment billions of regenerated souls had waited for—some for thousands of years. The population of the entire planet of Brahm's Cradle had assembled to witness the event of eternity—the regeneration of the Commander of the Malakians back into the glory of his former being. The anticipation of the singular event held every person spellbound in solemn wonder. There was risk, but the promise of Ell Yon held them.

The pinnacle of the regeneration complex was designed and reserved for this day. One thousand feet in the air, the marbled terrace had been carefully constructed to host the event of the ages. Kalem and Galec stood side by side—an armed escort of fifty elite warriors stood guard just a few paces away. One hundred Malakian warships hovered in perfect formation, the gleam of the sun dancing off thousands of brilliant surfaces.

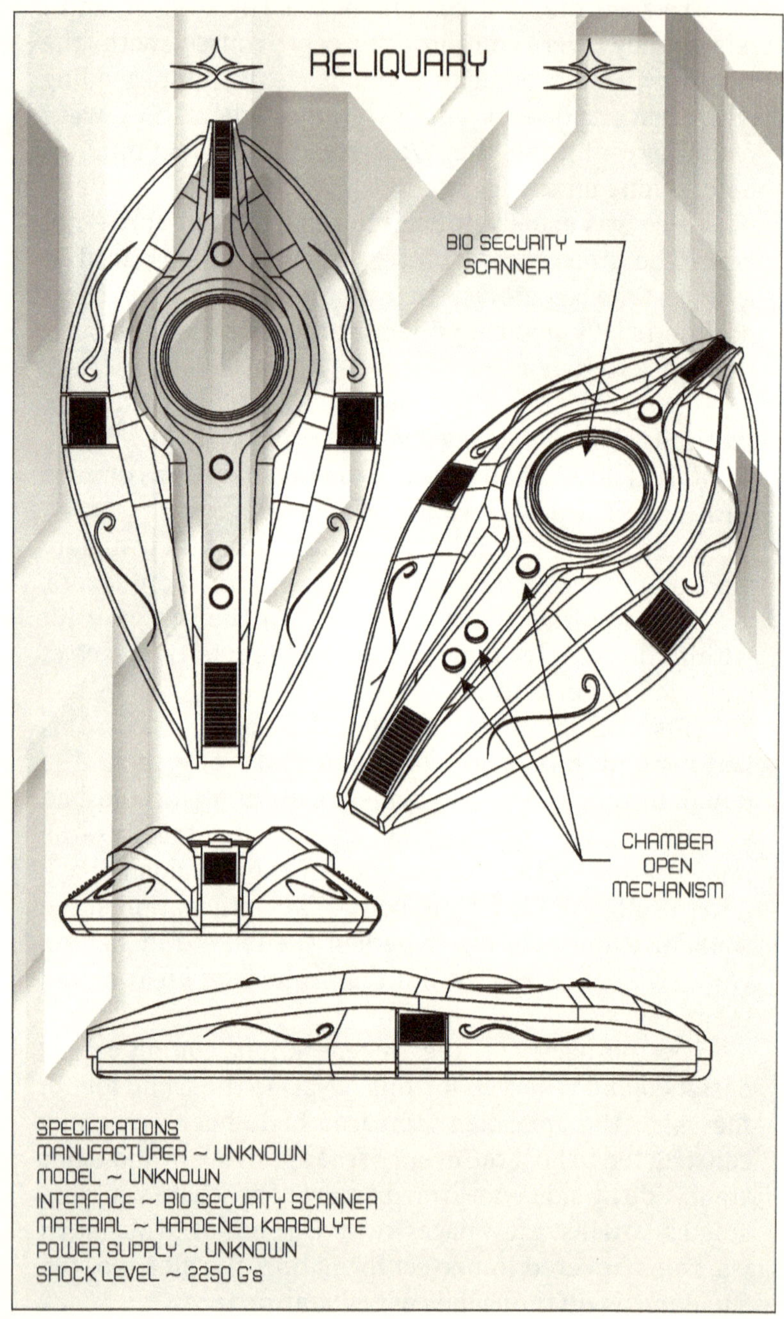

RELIQUARY
BIO SECURITY SCANNER
CHAMBER OPEN MECHANISM
SPECIFICATIONS
MANUFACTURER ~ UNKNOWN
MODEL ~ UNKNOWN
INTERFACE ~ BIO SECURITY SCANNER
MATERIAL ~ HARDENED KARBOLYTE
POWER SUPPLY ~ UNKNOWN
SHOCK LEVEL ~ 2250 G's

Kalem gave the signal to the chief of his marshal warriors. The chief turned to face the warriors of Sovereign Ell Yon and the sea of endless souls behind them, stretching farther than the eye could see. Hundreds of floating holographic displays peppered the sky, stretching to the farthest watchful soul, each one displaying the events that were occurring on the terrace at the pinnacle of the regeneration complex.

"Ten-hut!" the Chief commanded. Ten thousand warriors instantly snapped to attention.

Kalem first approached the hallowed place of regeneration, a broad, raised marble platform called the chancel. In the center of the chancel was a sleek elevated circular platform, the focal point of Ell Yon's power to regenerate Jeshu from his nephesh matrix. In the middle of the platform stood a fifty-foot tall elaborate and highly technologically advanced pedestal. In receivers on each side of the pedestal, Kalem placed the two Protectors that Sovereign Ell Yon had charged him to carry and deliver for this day.

Kalem retreated, then nodded to Galec. The second admiral stepped forward into the chancel, reverently placing Jeshu's reliquary in a specifically designed receiver at the base of the pedestal.

Galec opened the reliquary and lifted the nephesh matrix out of the chamber. The memory of a hundred fierce battles flashed across the mind of Kalem as he considered this epic moment in time. He watched Galec carefully place the Commander's nephesh matrix into a depression in the raised pedestal. He then pressed the glowing amber jewel in the center and six tentacles extended outward then down into ports designed to receive them. Galec took three steps back, then bent to one knee. Kalem and the rest of the planet followed suit.

For ten long seconds, Kalem, along with billions of watchful souls, held their breath...waiting...hoping. Finally, the jewel on the nephesh matrix began to glow with a brilliant white light. Within seconds the expanding light was too bright to gaze upon, for it superseded even the sun of Brahm's Cradle. As the people shielded their eyes from the power of Ell Yon, the Protectors energized and began moving up the sides of the pedestal, adding a fierce blue intensity to the concussion of holy light. The entire region began to tremble as the power of Ell Yon held the galaxy's gaze. The Protectors ascended to a hovering position just above the top of the pedestal. At the command of the Protectors, fragments of molecular substance ascended from the orifices around the perimeter of the regeneration platform and began to assemble at the top of the pedestal, aligning in perfect fashion according to the nephesh matrix. The stars roared and the seas billowed as the Commander regenerated into the form of his previous glory. After two minutes, the explosion of power subsided, and the creative supremacy of Ell Yon was complete.

Jeshu...Commander...Merchant...Son of Ell Yon stood in brilliant power with two Protectors forever fastened to his arms, a royal robe flowing about his regenerated body. Before Kalem could react, Jeshu raised his arms, and the power of the Protectors crescendoed with Sovereign Ell Yon's ultimate Solution for the prisoners of Brahm's Cradle. Jeshu opened his hands, and a wave of purifying power exploded outward, healing and fulfilling the missing life force to free the people. Every single soul on Brahm's Cradle felt the fulfillment of Ell Yon's promise as the spilled blood of Jeshu won them the cure from Deitum Prime forever and completed their own regeneration, freeing them once and for all from the Gehenna Cluster.

Silence settled onto the world and its inhabitants once the purifying power of the Protectors was complete. Jeshu turned his radiant face upward, his arms still lifted high.

"By the word of Sovereign Ell Yon, it is complete, and I will accomplish his plan for humanity!"

All at once the world lifted their voices in deafening shouts of adoration and cheer. And how could they not shout with total abandon, for they had been saved, restored, and set free. Deitum Prime no longer enticed them away from Ell Yon by their own affections, nor could it ever again. The inner struggle they had all felt in the realm of humanity was fully purged from every fiber of their being, and they were jubilant.

For the next three days, Jeshu, fully restored, spoke to the inhabitants of Brahm's Cradle, teaching them about the things Ell Yon had done on Rayl and giving promises for centuries to come...promises to defeat Lord Dracus and to one day restore the entire galaxy with immortality. It was a time of great celebration for the people of Brahm's Cradle, but for Rayl, a time of great peril was quickly approaching.

At the end of his time on Brahm's Cradle, Jeshu called for Admiral Kalem. The First Admiral met his Commander at the pinnacle of the regeneration complex. Now every time Kalem saw the Commander in the flesh, he breathed a great sigh of relief, especially since Jeshu had now fully returned to the Ruah.

Jeshu gazed out over the vast cityscape of Brahm's Cradle as thousands of transports were lifting and marshaling in the airspace before them.

Kalem softly approached to stand beside the Son of Ell Yon. He remained quiet, waiting for Jeshu to complete his reflection on the planet that had been home to billions of regenerated humans.

"The time has come to free these people from the prison of Gehenna and bring them home," Jeshu said, not shifting his gaze from the expanse of the city.

"Will Dracus try to stop us?" Kalem asked. Most of the Gehenna Cluster was dominated by Torian warships.

Jeshu turned his eyes toward Kalem. When Jeshu was fully human and ministering to humanity on Rayl, there was a gentleness in the Commander's countenance that had surprised Kalem. But now, the fierce look of command returned, and fire flashed in his eyes…the eyes of a zefflyn.

"It has been communicated to Dracus that unless he wants the oracles of his demise to be accelerated, he will stand down and allow passage of every ship out of the Gehenna Cluster."

Kalem could imagine C'fir Dracus scowling at such a command but also submitting to the power of a restored Jeshu.

"The last of the transports are being marshaled into the restoration armada as we speak," Kalem offered.

Jeshu offered one subtle nod.

"What will become of Brahm's Cradle?" Kalem asked.

"It will remain forever empty, an eternal monument to remind all of the devastation Deitum Prime wrought on humanity." Jeshu turned to fully face Kalem. "I will lead these people to Tsiyyon, but we will first journey to Rayl. My regeneration isn't yet complete."

Kalem looked at Jeshu—concerned. "Not complete, my lord?"

Jeshu turned his resolute gaze on his First Admiral. "Select your two finest first marshals. When we arrive at Rayl, you and your men will accompany me to Jalem."

Kalem saluted and left to prepare his men and his ship. Perhaps Jeshu would offer some measure of explanation on the journey back to Rayl.

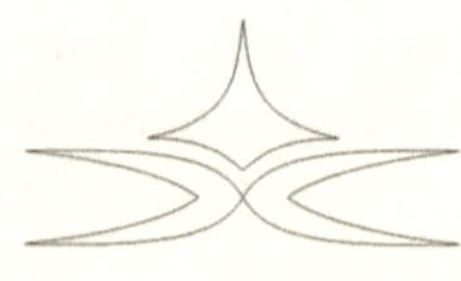

CHAPTER

4

Immortality Revived

Stabil Retention Field (SRF) – a semi-transparent energy field that can be varied in its intensity to offer a variety of application effects. At its lowest setting, the SRF can allow passage of dense solid objects and biological life forms while preventing passage of gases. The SRF is useful for doorless space bays which can retain an atmosphere within a spacecraft's launching bay while allowing smaller vessels to enter and exit the bay. At its strongest setting, the SRF will prohibit passage of any object regardless of its density.

Brae, Rhett, Bridger, and Shayde launched in the *Aviel* shuttle and set course for Jalem before the sun had risen. Brae had to admit that this trip into Rayl's capital city so soon after Jeshu's execution would be risky, but she felt inexplicably compelled to find out what had happened to Jeshu's body. If what they had heard of Keeper Codemus was true, perhaps they would find at least one friend there.

"If they recognize the *Aviel*, they'll know we're sectators of Jeshu," Bridger said.

"We'll set down at a small port just east of Jalem, then take a speeder the rest of the way," Rhett offered.

Bridger nodded. Brae liked the idea too.

Before long, the four sectators were strapped into a six-seat speeder and departing the space port where they had left the *Aviel*.

"Kamp gave us a rendezvous location," Rhett said as he navigated the traffic routes of outer Jalem. It was still very early in the morning so there was very little traffic to contend with. "Hopefully Keeper Codemus will meet us there and not a squad of Raylean Guard."

Brae didn't find Rhett's quip funny, but then again, maybe he wasn't trying to be.

When Rhett brought the speeder to a halt, Brae didn't recognize this part of the city. It was near a newly constructed trade mall in the southern district of Jalem, an area that was rapidly expanding. Rhett motioned for Brae, Bridger and Shayde to follow him. He led them through the entrance of the mall and then to a sleek eatery where a young woman greeted them. Without Rhett saying a word, the woman seemed to recognize them, which made Brae nervous.

"Follow me," she said, leading them through a closed-off section of the eatery toward the back of the facility. Brae scanned for any signs of skullduggery, but there was little to go on other than the growing knot in her stomach. The young woman brought them to a door, stopped, and lifted her hand as if to say, "You go first...I'm leaving."

Rhett paused, glancing toward Brae and the others. He tilted his head. "Well, this is what we came for, isn't it?"

The young woman then promptly exited as Rhett took a step toward the door. It immediately swished away into the wall, revealing a quaint dining room large enough to seat 15 people. Brae followed Rhett through the door to see two men and a woman standing at the far end of the room having a quiet conversation. As soon as the four sectators entered, all three members of the group engaged in conversation turned to face the incoming group. Brae recognized Keeper Codemus, which brought no small relief, but she was surprised and a bit alarmed that there were two additional people. Codemus and his companions came to greet them. He held out his hand.

"Welcome. I am Codemus. This is Sephner and Tazra," he said, motioning to the man and the woman respectively.

Each of the sectators accepted their greeting in turn.

"It's good to see you again, Keeper Codemus." Brae gave him a careful smile.

"We're not Keepers or Builders anymore," Codemus replied.

"We have renounced our vows," Sephner said. "Your teacher has changed everything."

"He's much more than a teacher," Shayde replied.

"Yes," Tazra returned. "Of that we're convinced. But with his execution, we're not sure what that means."

Tazra's comment resonated with Brae and her companions.

"To be honest, we're not sure either, other than the fact that Jeshu said this was all going to happen just as it did." Brae already felt something kindred about these three former sanctum officials. "This isn't the end...it's the beginning."

"We believe that coming here may give us some answers as to what comes next," Rhett added.

Codemus, Sephner, and Tazra all seemed relieved to hear that.

"Come, let's sit, eat, and talk. We have many questions," Codemus said as he motioned toward a table with fruit, drinks, and brioche bread.

Once they were all seated and had given thanks to Ell Yon, Rhett asked the first question.

"We understand that you arranged to secure Jeshu's body. Is that true?"

Codemus nodded. "I petitioned Pylok for the body." His gaze lowered to the bowl of fruit before him. "I wish now I had done more to stop his execution. I thought I should at least honor him by offering my crypt."

"We'd like to honor him as well," Brae said. "Can you get us access to the crypt?"

"Yes, of course," Codemus replied. "But I would recommend against it, at least until the six Morian commandos have been released from the duty to guard it."

Brae glanced toward Rhett. He frowned at hearing the comment. "Regardless, if we could have the access code to enter, we would be most grateful."

For the next thirty minutes, Codemus, Sephner, and Tazra asked intriguing and meaningful questions about Jeshu's missions and his future promises. The four sectators did their best to satisfy them, but there were many areas of conversation and interest for which they had no answers...at least not yet.

When they parted ways, Brae felt as though they had true allies in the three former sanctum officials. *Who knows how Sovereign Ell Yon might use these new friendships in our missions as Navis?* she wondered.

When they exited the trade mall, the sun was just breaking the horizon. Their next stop would be the crypt in which Jeshu's body lay.

Admiral Kalem and his two first marshal warriors followed behind the Commander as they approached the crypt where Jeshu's temporal body lay. This moment in time would anchor the reclamation of humanity forever.

Kalem had seen a thousand battles and experienced the victory and horror of war for thousands of years. Rarely did any new threat or thrill quicken the beat of his heart, but here in the quiet of a dead man's crypt, the First Admiral of the Aurora Galactic Fleet felt his heart pounding. The entire journey of the Commander into the domain of humanity had been saturated with extreme struggle and tenuous missions for every one of the warriors of his fleets. The Commander had and still was exposing himself to very real and imminent danger by taking on the fully human form of a man. What his Commander was about to do had never been attempted—revive and rejoin a transferred and regenerated Ruah being with its physical human bio structure. If Kalem was completely honest, he didn't fully understand how Ell Yon was going to accomplish it through the Protectors, nor did he grasp what it would mean. *What would be the final state of his Commander's existence? Would he still exist in the Ruah...would he exist in the domain of humanity...perhaps both?* Kalem's ponderings were upsetting. He didn't like the unknown. Unknowns meant risk, and often risk meant loss.

Just outside the crypt entrance, six Morian commandos stood guard. Kalem's two first marshal warriors briefly translated into the realm of humanity and rendered them unconscious with a broad burst of their dual plasma-phaser rifles. Jeshu pointed to the Stabil retention field transmitters on each side of the entrance, and Kalem destroyed them both.

They entered the crypt, and Kalem watched as the Commander stood over the dead form of his human body. He placed his hands on the curved transparent glass of the interment capsule, and both Protectors instantly began to pulsate with energy. A minimal discharge deactivated the capsule's protection protocols. A few seconds later, the transparent glass slid away to reveal the still form of Jeshu. Kalem and the two first marshal warriors knelt in solemn reverence. Although billions of souls waited aboard the restoration armada, nothing would rush this moment of extreme significance. While still abiding in the realm of the Ruah, the Commander laid himself down into the capsule, super-imposing his living being onto the dead form of his human body. Kalem looked on in wonder and great apprehension. In the fragile silence of this crypt, Kalem heard the Commander proclaim his purpose.

"I am the first and will restore immortality to humanity. By the hand of Ell Yon and the power of his Protectors, I yield myself to this cause."

Both Protectors began to arc with brilliant flames of energy, filling the crypt with the presence of Sovereign Ell Yon. Kalem and his first marshal warriors shielded their eyes, but it wasn't enough. Within seconds, the crypt was filled with the brilliance of the sun. They could not bear it even with their faces covered and heads turned away. Just as Kalem was about to order their retreat from such holy power, it stopped, and they breathed once more. Seconds passed before they dared to glimpse their Commander again.

"Rise up, Admiral Kalem," the Commander's strong voice ordered.

Kalem and his warriors lifted themselves to their feet, gazing at the glowing figure of the Commander. His human body was no longer in the capsule. Kalem and his warriors had witnessed life from death—a thing so profound Kalem could scarce believe his eyes. With great wonder on his face, he looked upon the majestic form of the captain of Ell Yon's forces.

"What does this mean, my lord?" Kalem asked. "Are you of the Ruah or of humanity?"

Oddly, Kalem couldn't tell.

"I am both, Admiral," the Commander replied.

Kalem tilted his head. Clearly the Commander's presence was manifest in the realm of the Ruah...but—

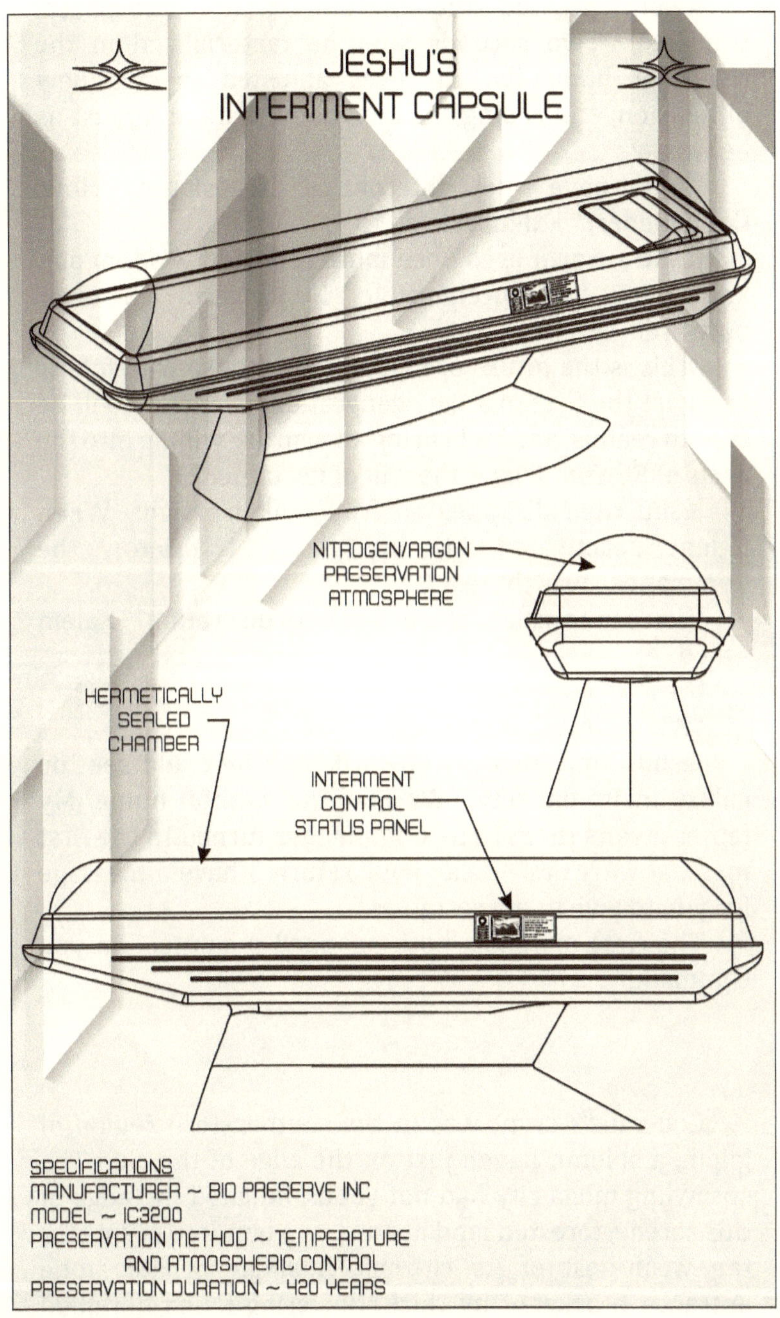
JESHU'S
INTERMENT CAPSULE
NITROGEN/ARGON
PRESERVATION
ATMOSPHERE
HERMETICALLY
SEALED
CHAMBER
INTERMENT
CONTROL
STATUS PANEL
SPECIFICATIONS
MANUFACTURER ~ BIO PRESERVE INC
MODEL ~ IC3200
PRESERVATION METHOD ~ TEMPERATURE
AND ATMOSPHERIC CONTROL
PRESERVATION DURATION ~ 420 YEARS

Kalem pressed the button on his interphasal translator. Two seconds later he materialized in the realm of humanity. His eyes adjusted to this new dimension, still seeing the Commander standing just as he was.

"You have no interphasal translator. How, Commander?" Kalem asked.

Jeshu's warm eyes once more reflected wisdom and knowledge incomprehensible. He spread his arms outward.

"This is the future of humanity for those who follow me. I am the first of a new generation. My abode will be in both realms, and I will bring all who are willing into the arms of Ell Yon. This is the will of my father."

Jeshu then disappeared from Kalem's sight. When Kalem deactivated his interphasal translator, the Commander was there.

"You can translate at will and with discretion?" Kalem asked.

"Yes."

"What now, Commander?"

Jeshu lifted his eyes upward, as if he could see the galaxy in its entirety. "We take our faithful home. My father awaits them." The Commander turned to the first marshal warriors. "Delay your return. I have a message for you to give to my sectators."

The first marshals both snapped a salute. "As you command."

Codemus's crypt was in the southeastern region of Jalem, a solemn haven just on the edge of the city. The sprawling mega city had not yet assimilated the edge of this serene, forested land hosting two hundred crypts for the wealthiest of its citizens. A single ornate stone entrance bracketed by thick, flowering fauna heralded their arrival to hundreds of crypts. A Stabil retention field was active and glowing.

"Codemus gave me his access code for entrance into the crypt plaza," Brae said. "But only two are allowed to enter."

"You two go," Bridger said. "Shayde and I will wait here and let you know if anyone of concern is coming."

"I'm afraid our concern is already waiting for us in there," Rhett said with a glance toward the entrance. "Codemus said that Pylok had assigned six commandos to stand guard. That changes everything." He fixed a hard glare on Brae. "This is going to end badly."

Brae inwardly admitted that pressing on seemed foolish, but the compulsion to see inside the crypt was unassailable.

"I know it doesn't make sense, Rhett, but I have to go. I'll do this alone," Brae said as she tapped in the access code. The Stabil retention field diminished to half of its former strength but did not disappear.

Rhett shook his head. "In what world could I ever let that happen?"

Brae and Rhett stepped through, and instantly the Stabil retention field re-illumined to full power. They looked back at the slightly hazy images of Bridger and Shayde.

"Com check," Rhett radioed.

"Check," Bridger's voice came through loud and clear. "Be careful."

Brae's heart quickened as they walked the marbled path leading to the specified area. It was early morning, the ground and greenery still wet with dew. A low-lying mist swirled around their feet as they proceeded. It didn't take Brae and Rhett long to find the two crypts owned by and reserved for Codemus. When they arrived at the entrance, Brae's blood turned as cold as the icy waters of the Northern Sea. Six Morian commandos lay prone on the ground as if someone had shot them in cold blood. But even more frightful was what she instantly attributed this unrecoverable crime to—an android was kneeling over the body of one of the commandos, his hand around the man's throat. The android turned its head to cast its steely-eyed gaze in their direction.

"Rivet!" Brae whispered. Chills flitted up and down her spine as she considered what had happened and what this would mean. She didn't know what to do.

"Are you sure it's him?" Rhett asked.

Brae nodded as Rhett's hand moved to his blaster.

Rivet slowly stood to face them. In the silent face-off, Brae's mind ran wild with speculation. *How had he come to life? Who was responsible, and what altered programming would have allowed such an atrocity?*

"Lady Brae, it is good to see that you are well."

Hearing his voice amplified the chills she was experiencing. "Rivet...is it really you?"

Rivet began walking in their direction but stopped once Rhett lifted his blaster toward the bot.

He glared at Rhett, tilting his head slightly, then looked back at Brae. "It is me, Lady Brae. You need not be afraid."

Brae's eyes darted to the prone Morian commandos. "Did you do this, Rivet?"

Rivet followed her gaze then looked back at her. "No. These commandos were unconscious when I arrived."

Brae let out the breath she'd been holding in a deep sigh. She went to Rivet, eyeing every detail of his form. He was exactly as she had rebuilt him, or so she thought. One slight alteration in his forearms caught her attention.

"Halt!" shouted one of two approaching commandos from behind them. When Brae and Rhett turned about, the commandos spotted the blaster in Rhett's hand and immediately opened fire.

In the flash of a moment, Rivet leapt in front of Rhett and Brae. He held up his left hand, which instantly projected some type of protective energy shield. The commandos' blaster fire impacted the shield but dissipated without effect. Rivet held up his right hand, and a fraction of a second later a broad-span phaser burst exploded from his palm, hitting the commandos with such force that they flew backward. Both landed unconscious on their backs, sending swirling waves of mist outward from their bodies. Rivet turned back to look at Brae and Rhett.

"That, I did."

Brae looked at the android in stunned silence. "I didn't build that into your new body, Rivet."

Rivet looked down at his forearms, rotating them about as if inspecting them for the first time. He lifted his gaze back to Brae. "I can't explain it, my lady, but I am Rivet."

Brae went to him, lifting one of his arms to inspect it more closely for herself. Whatever modification had been made was technologically beautiful and sleek. She then lifted her gaze to Rivet's eyes. Rhett approached to stand protectively beside her, apparently still nervous about the bot.

Brae looked deep into Rivet's eyes...questioning... hoping.

"When I was eleven years old, Dad insisted that I take you with me on a picnic I wanted to have in the woods. What did we see there?"

Rivet hesitated. "You called me Clunk, because I was instructed by Daeson Starlore to hide my identity from you. In the woods we encountered a namorian panther. What you do not know is that it had been stalking you for over a mile. I transmitted a high frequency sonic pitch to make it go away."

"Even then, you were protecting me," Brae said, her heart warming to the hope that Rivet had returned to her.

She wrapped her arms around the android. "I'm so glad you're alive, Rivet."

Rivet gently returned the embrace until Brae released him.

"Why are you here?" Rhett asked.

Rivet turned his head toward the entrance of the crypt. "I'm not entirely sure. For some inexplicable reason I was drawn to this place at this time." He looked back at Rhett and Brae. "Is this the grave of Jeshu?"

"Yes. Former Keeper Codemus offered his crypt to preserve the body of Jeshu," Brae answered.

All three of them set their eyes on the entrance of the crypt. The powerful Stabil retention field present at all the other crypt entrances was noticeably absent here. The field transmitters on each side of the entrance were charred and smoking from some apparent sabotage.

"This is all wrong, Brae. We need to leave before more commandos come," Rhett muttered as they approached the entrance.

"I must agree, Lady Brae. You are in danger," Rivet added.

Brae shook her head. "I have to see."

She stepped through the entrance and into the eerie silence of the crypt, the forest mist slowly ebbing across the cold marble floor before them. Soft-glowing amber lights gently pulsated, indicating the crypt's integrity had been compromised by some unknown force. The chamber to the right would hold the interment capsule. As they turned the corner and peered in, Brae's heart nearly stopped. Standing on each side of the open capsule were two massive warriors with drawn Talon-style weapons glowing hot white. Brae had seen their semblance before...warriors of the Ruah, but to which faction she did not know. *Had Dracus been victorious in his battle against Jeshu's admirals and stolen Jeshu's body as some victory prize?* she wondered.

The warriors seemed as stone, standing guard to an empty crypt...why?

"Where have they taken Jeshu?" Brae dared ask.

Both warriors fixed their eyes on her, and she nearly fled from the terror of their gaze.

"Why do you look for the Commander among the dead?" one of them asked. "He is not here. He is alive, never to die again."

As soon as the words were spoken, both warriors touched a small device on their belts and dissolved away in fading wisps of their former visage.

Brae, Rhett, and Rivet stood paralyzed by the message from beyond for a few seconds. Rhett grabbed Brae's arm.

"Come on, Brae...we need to leave now!"

CHAPTER

5

The Creed of Jeshu

I will free them from the perils of Deitum Prime and will give them a new heart. I will protect them and give a new promise that will never be taken away. – Eziam, Oracle of Ell Yon

Back at *Arcton Hold*, Brae scanned the solemn faces of her fellow sectators as Rivet stood quietly against an adjacent wall just a few feet away...motionless. The story she and Rhett had relayed garnered a plethora of responses from their fellow sectators. Some looked hopeful while others were dubious. Lubin and Salara looked utterly distraught. Perhaps the most common expression she could discern was apprehension. Each sectator had become a public figure, standing beside and helping Jeshu on his short mission to Rayl. Now their futures were not only uncertain but also threatened. How could they move on from here? Should they attempt to return to some semblance of a normal life? But how would that be possible after witnessing the profound and supernatural events that Jeshu had shown them? Brae became lost in her silent contemplation amidst the quiet mingle of three different conversations in the room.

"His body has been taken. The Malakians could easily do that," Brae heard Salara say. "But how does that help us? We're left here dealing with the aftermath."

Brae couldn't deny the rising apprehension within her own heart. Things were so strange and uncertain. She glanced over at Rhett to find that he was staring at her. He offered a wisp of a smile, but it did little to hide those same feelings reflected in his eyes.

"What do you think, Brae?" Cilla asked.

"I'm sorry...think about what?"

"After everything we saw and were a part of, none of us imagined it would end like it has. What would Jeshu want us to do now?" Cilla explained.

The room fell quiet to hear how Brae might respond, but she had no answer. After a few seconds of awkward silence, Kase interjected.

"I don't get it...Jeshu seemed powerless at the end. Did Ell Yon and the Protectors truly abandon him? How are we supposed to respond to that?"

Lubin wrung his hands together, lifting his bowed head. "Let's be honest...we're all ruined. We publicly stood beside Jeshu and are known by everyone. The Keepers and the Builders are against us, Prefect Terrok is against us, and the Morian Empire executed Jeshu. In what bizarre existence does this end well for any of us?"

Lubin's dramatic but truthful words fell on the other ten sectators like a wall of granite. The solemn silence was suffocating.

As Brae searched desperately for some thread of hope, the image of two mighty Malakian warriors standing beside the empty crypt vividly filled her mind. She stood straight and tall. "I don't know how to answer any of those questions. But I do know that there is no longer a dead body in that crypt. *Jeshu is alive!*"

As Brae proclaimed this impossible truth, a chill swept through her body that made all the hairs on her arms stand straight. Though all doors were closed and exterior portals turned off, a brisk wash of wind swept through the room—and then it happened.

"Why are you so dismayed? Don't be afraid." A powerful voice filled the room and shook the impuissant sectators until they trembled in fear.

The bodily form of Jeshu materialized in the middle of the room. As if pushed by some invisible force field, every sectator stumbled away from the vision, gasping in chilling fright.

"A hologram," someone dared whisper.

Jeshu looked directly at Lubin. "Not a hologram, Lubin. Come see for yourself and do not be dismayed."

Lubin swallowed hard then stepped forward toward Jeshu, his eyes full of wonder. When he was just a few feet away, Jeshu turned to look each of his followers in the eyes, ending with Brae. He smiled. "I am indeed alive." He held out his hand to her.

Brae stepped forward, daring to hope yet afraid of being tricked. She held out her hand to his, cautiously moving closer to the vision of her hero. As her fingers neared his hand, chills flashed across her whole body, nearly paralyzing her. The thought of her hand passing through the image of Jeshu, as it would if he were a hologram, albeit a perfect hologram, terrified her. This single touch would either elevate or utterly destroy everything she had come to believe in since she was a child.

One...single...touch. The entire room held its breath as Brae's fingers landed in the warm palm of Jeshu's hand. At first touch, tears burst from Brae's eyes as she gripped his hand then fell into his embrace. Jeshu wrapped his arms around her as others came near. He reached for them, offering the touch of truth.

"It is I, my beloved sectators. Don't be afraid."

After a few moments of joyful embraces, each of the sectators stepped away to make room for Jeshu, searching his face for future hope and meaning.

"Are you merely translated from the Ruah?" Cilla asked.

"No, Cilla, my body is as real as yours." Jeshu gazed lovingly into the eyes of his watcher. "Through the power of my father and the Protector, I am the first fully regenerated and immortal human that has ever lived. One day you will all be like me."

"But you appeared to us just as if a Malakian had translated into our dimension," Brae said. "And yet I don't see an interphasal translator." Brae scanned his body for Immortal tech that would allow such a thing.

"I am as real in the Ruah as I am here. Both dimensions of existence belong to me. Ell Yon has given me all power in the Ruah and in the realm of humanity."

Jeshu took a deep breath as if preparing to convey a message of extreme importance.

"You are the new Navis of this time. All of the galaxy must know of my sacrifice to save them from the death of Deitum Prime. The Protector used my blood as the catalyst to create an antidote for the perils of Deitum Prime. It is the only way to Sovereign Ell Yon. Every human being must be given the opportunity to be healed."

Jeshu paused, letting his words settle deeply into the hearts of his sectators. "Take heart, my friends—they will hunt you and terrorize you and kill you because you follow me, but do not be discouraged," he said, holding out his hands to his Navis. "Whether you live or die in this domain, you will live with me forever in a kingdom that has no end. Do you understand this?"

The words were heavy and joyful…frightening and yet encouraging. Brae always marveled at Jeshu's powerful and unapologetically truthful speech. His words were stunning to the ears of mortals. Slowly, each sectator nodded.

"Good. Then now is the time for power to be given to you," Jeshu said, lifting his hand to Brae. She stepped forward and took it.

Just as she had seen him do when teaching them how to commune with Ell Yon, Jeshu placed his left hand onto the Protector on his right forearm. He tilted his head forward slightly, gazing deeply into Brae's eyes. He lifted a replicated Protector from his original Protector and placed it above Brae's right forearm.

"Unlike before, your Protector will never leave you. From this day forward, you will be one with the Protector."

Jeshu pushed the pearl white Immortal device onto Brae's arm, and the synaptic interphase immediately overwhelmed her with the presence of Sovereign Ell Yon. The immersion consumed the entirety of her being yet seemed very different this time. Her mind shifted into the Ruah, and her body began to tingle from the inside out. She nearly collapsed to her knees, but Jeshu held her. This feeling was one she had never before experienced…a feeling of sheer purity. She opened her eyes, peering into the eternal fire of Jeshu's gaze.

"The Protector is using the antidote to purge the Deitum Prime from the innermost parts of your body. What you are experiencing is the beginning of your eventual complete regeneration."

Brae found the strength to stand on her own, rising up a new and powerful version of her former self…a version purged by the antidotal blood of Jeshu. She felt as if she could nearly fly.

"Jeshu," she whispered.

Jeshu smiled gently, putting a hand on her cheek. "Daughter."

Brae had no words for what she felt. Death itself held no threat for her now. Not even the great Navis of old, including her own father, had experienced the presence of Ell Yon like this. She heard the cry of a thousand generations pleading for the hope that she now carried in her bosom. She would go to the four corners of the galaxy if called to. She slowly backed away as Jeshu turned his eyes toward Rhett.

One by one, each of the sectators had their own Protector bestowed upon them, and like Brae, their faces glowed with the hope of a brilliant future...a hope that would never die and ultimately destroy the forces of Dracus.

Jeshu stayed and fellowshipped for a few hours, teaching them and answering their questions. When the time came for him to leave his sectators, he left them with a charge.

"You are just the beginning. Your mission is to make Navis of all people from all worlds. The rescue of souls from Deitum Prime is my final command to you."

"Jeshu, how will we know if others are willing to join us as Navis?" Brae asked.

"By their confession of this creed," Jeshu replied. "I believe in Sovereign Ell Yon, ruler of both realms, and in Jeshu the Merchant, his only Son, our Commander. Through the Protector he came to us and was persecuted by Subchancellor Pylok, tortured on the Ring, and died. He was translated to Gehenna, and three days later was regenerated from the dead and is alive forever. He will judge both realms in truth. I believe in the Protector, the order of the Navi, the purging of Deitum Prime, and the regeneration of all Navis into Immortality."

Jeshu scanned the faces of his eleven followers. "The Protectors you wear will guide you and determine the truth of another's words."

Jeshu stood and went to each sectator in turn, pouring love into their souls. Approaching each of his followers, he embraced them and whispered a personal message to each of them.

When Jeshu came to Brae, her heart began to break for there was a finality to his parting actions.

"Your joy will sustain you, and your sorrow will be the catalyst to save millions," he whispered as he embraced her. "Stay true and strong," he finished.

At last Jeshu came to the perfectly silent and still technological statue, standing forgotten near the far wall. Although Jeshu said nothing to Rivet, the android tilted his head forward in humble reverence. He then lifted a hand to his chest as if to swear to keep some secret promise that no human soul may ever know.

Jeshu then turned to address his sectators.

"From this day forward, you are sectators no more. You are my Navis. Keep heart. Sovereign Ell Yon is with you...as am I."

Just as he had appeared, Jeshu left, his body slowly dissolving out of their dimension. Brae and her companions stared at the empty space for thirty long seconds. No one was willing to shatter this precious experience with paltry words.

After a few weeks had passed, the Navis sensed a significant subsidence of tension among the Keepers, Builders, and even Terrok's Royal Guards. This allowed the Navis to disperse from *Arcton Hold* to find their own new dwelling places. Many remained in or close to Jalem, but a few took up residence in other nearby cities and towns. *Arcton Hold* remained a designated place of meeting when needed. Evidently with Jeshu's execution, the powers that ruled the planet had every impression that his influence on the people was over. Little did they know what was coming.

"The people at the Jalem sanctum are still talking about Jeshu," Quill said. "Quietly and in secret—but still talking."

Brae, Rhett, Bridger, Quill, and Cilla were eating a meal in Codemus's home not far from the sanctum. They had relayed in detail the things they had seen and heard regarding Jeshu. Codemus listened to each word with great anticipation.

"I wish I could see the excitement of the people," Codemus piped in. "But the guards won't let me even set foot in the outer courtyard without causing a ruckus."

Brae placed a hand on the elder gentleman's arm. "Your actions will be remembered for all time, my friend."

Codemus offered a slight smile, his gaze shifting to the Protector on her arm. "What's it like?" he asked.

Brae felt the Protector nudging her in the strangest of ways. "But, sir...you've worn a Protector. Haven't you experienced the presence of Ell Yon?"

Codemus looked a little sad. "I did don the Protector at the Joppik sanctum once. There was a brief moment when I felt I could see the entire galaxy, but it vanished as quickly as it had come upon me."

Brae looked into the seasoned eyes of the man. "Codemus, do you believe that Jeshu was the appointed Navi as foretold by the oracles...the promised Merchant?"

Codemus lifted his gaze from Brae's Protector to her eyes. The slight hesitation didn't feel like doubt to Brae. It felt as though he were giving such an impending confession the due honor it deserved. "I do, and I will commit the rest of my life to his service."

Brae felt chills flash up and down her spine as the room became silent, and she accepted the command of Ell Yon. She placed her left hand on her Protector as if to remove it.

"Brae, what are you doing?" Rhett asked. "To give up your Protector—"

But Rhett didn't finish his words because as Brae appeared to lift her Protector off her arm, it remained in place as a replica translated into existence. The other Navis gasped. Codemus's eyes opened wide as everyone present fully understood what was happening. In like fashion as Jeshu had bestowed the Protector to his Navis, Brae placed the replicated Protector onto Codemus's arm. His face instantly illuminated with the sheer joy and fear of entering into the presence of Sovereign Ell Yon. Rhett, Bridger, Quill, and Cilla could hardly contain themselves, reaching for and grasping both Brae and Codemus with great joy and affirmation.

"Incredible!" Cilla gasped.

"It is the way," Brae said. "The power of Jeshu will spread exponentially throughout the galaxy, just as the oracles of old foretold and none could understand. Today we see the fulfillment of Ell Yon's promise to end Deitum Prime!"

Rhett grabbed Bridger's shoulder. "Let's go to the sanctum. Surely there are thousands waiting to see the power of Ell Yon in such a way!"

CHAPTER

5

Vessels of Power

Within the hour, Rhett and Bridger were entering the outer courtyard of the Jalem sanctum. Brae and the others had elected to find and share their new Protector-duplication discovery with the rest of the Navis before joining them at the sanctum.

As Rhett walked through the courtyard with his brother, an anticipation hung in the air that Rhett couldn't describe. He was still trying to adapt to the connection with the Protector, doing his utmost to sense and respond to the subtle yet deeply piercing promptings now resident within him. A distinct sense fell on him that he could still choose his every action regardless of what he felt the Protector telling him, but a deeper understanding pierced him that if he walked his own chosen path, he would miss out on experiencing and participating in the dramatic power of Ell Yon in a very real and personal way.

Rhett and Bridger stood shoulder to shoulder in the middle of the courtyard, watching hundreds of fellow

Rayleans meander throughout the sanctum promenade. Rhett looked over at his brother, amazed at the changes he saw in this typically stolid man.

"Doesn't it feel as if we are standing on the edge of the galaxy, peering into eternity?" Bridger's eyes shone with a brightness Rhett had never seen.

"That is well said, brother," Rhett replied. Something caught Rhett's eye as he looked over Bridger's shoulder to the far side of the promenade. Between two of the many columns near one of the entrances into the sanctum proper, a lone boy seated in a chair intrigued him. Rhett tapped Bridger on the arm and began walking that way.

As they approached the entrance, Rhett diverted them slightly to the right, bringing them to the lad sitting in his chair hovering ten inches off the ground. Something about the boy felt off.

"It's a nice day to soak up some sunshine," Rhett said to the boy.

The boy looked to be about sixteen. He glanced up, offering a weak smile, then turned his head away.

"Do you come here often?" Bridger pressed.

The lad looked back up at both of them, scrutinizing them carefully.

"Nearly every day. When I'm finished with my studies, there's not much else to do. My father's a Keeper, and he thinks coming here does me some good." The boy's eyes saddened. "I suppose he's right."

Rhett then began to understand what the state of the boy was.

"How long have you had to rely on the hover chair to get you around?" Rhett asked.

The boy's forlorn countenance deepened. "I've never walked, sir."

"You look well taken care of. Haven't the medtechs been able to help you?" Bridger asked.

The lad's gaze fell to the ground. "The leading master medtechs on the planet have tried but—"

Rhett knelt down next to the boy. "May I?" he asked, reaching for the blanket covering the boy's legs. As he did so, Rhett's sleeve pulled upward just enough to expose the lower edge of the Protector.

"You're Jeshuans!" the lad exclaimed quietly.

Rhett wondered if the boy would alert the Keeper Order and have them dismissed from the sanctum courtyard...or worse. Rhett glanced up at Bridger. "Yes, we are."

The lad glanced from side to side, scanning to see who might hear him. "I heard him speak once, here at the sanctum." His eyes lit with enthusiasm.

"And what did you think of the man?" Bridger asked.

The boy scanned once more. "His words were life! I've never heard a man speak like him."

Rhett suddenly heard the whisper of Ell Yon, but it frightened him. He hesitated for just a moment, gazing into the revived eyes of the lad.

"What's your name?" Rhett asked.

"Harris."

"Harris, Jeshu was sent from Sovereign Ell Yon to save us from the death of Deitum Prime," Rhett said as he placed his hand on Harris's leg. The Protector began to glow in warm ribbons of blue light. "Do you want to walk?" Rhett asked, gazing straight into the lad's watering eyes.

Harris swallowed. "Yes," he whispered, hope lighting his face.

In that moment, the Protector began to pulse with life-giving power. Rhett felt its hot energy pouring from the hand of Ell Yon through the Protector and into the weak and frail limbs of Harris. For ten long seconds, Rhett, Bridger, and Harris watched in awestruck wonder as the Protector bathed the lad's legs in Immortal power. A dozen onlookers gathered nearby to see what was happening. When it was over, Rhett held up his hand for Harris to take.

"In the name of Jeshu, rise up and walk," Rhett commanded.

The hopeful face of the lad was an image Rhett would never forget. Harris reached for him then carefully stood, leaving his hover chair behind forever. At first, Harris seemed as wobbly as a new fawn, standing for the first time in his life. He looked up at Rhett, still clinging to his hand. His face beamed with anticipation. A number of people in the crowd gasped, having known the boy for years. Harris took his first step, and although it was but a stutter step, it was the first of a hundred thousand more. With each step, his legs seemed to grow stronger, and his steps widened until Harris began to run and jump into the air as if he could fly. The crowd gawked in wonder as word spread and people gathered around them. Rhett and Bridger smiled broadly as they watched the lad running to people he knew with unquenchable enthusiasm.

"Look...I'm walking...I'm running!" he screamed, grabbing the arms of each stunned spectator.

Rhett saw Brae coming toward them, pushing through the crowd to get closer.

"What is happening?" Brae asked, scanning the sanctum courtyard in the throes of stunned observation.

Rhett couldn't take his eyes off the boy. "Jeshu happened."

The clamor among the crowd spread quickly, not only throughout the courtyard but also into the chambers of the sanctum itself. As the crowd enlarged, so did the joyful enthusiasm of Harris until all at once the lad stopped, turned, and looked straight at Rhett. The crowd parted so Harris could fully set his eyes on Rhett. He slowly walked toward Rhett and Bridger. Each step he took pounded the truth of what Jeshu through the Protector had done in the life of the boy. His eyes filled with tears of great joy until he fell on his knees before Rhett, weeping in gratefulness.

"How can I ever thank you for what you have done?" Harris asked, his arms outstretched, reaching for Rhett.

Rhett leaned down to Harris, grasping his arms.

"Stand up, lad," Rhett said. "I have done nothing. Jeshu through the power of the Protector has healed you. Turn your thanks to him and to Ell Yon."

Rhett and Harris stood up together. Harris lifted his arms upward, slowly turning about, uninhibited by his public adoration for the man named Jeshu.

Just then, the Keepers and Builders of the Jalem sanctum appeared at the main entrance. Fasa Kylos marched toward Harris and the Navi with an entourage following close behind.

"What is the meaning of this?" Kylos demanded, his face fierce with indignation.

Harris spun about to see the Preeminent Keeper.

"The greatest Master Medtechs on Rayl could not help me, but through the power of Jeshu, I walk and I run!" Harris proclaimed.

Kylos stepped forward. "Do not profane this sanctum with the name of that heretic!" Kylos shouted. The crowd was stunned to silence by Kylos's words of fury.

Rhett glanced over at Brae and the other Navi that had gathered to witness this remarkable act of the Commander of the Immortals. He saw great apprehension in their faces. *Did Kylos have the power to detain and execute them just as he had conspired against the Son of Ell Yon?* Rhett wondered. It seemed to Rhett a much smaller thing to harm them.

Kylos glared at the boy, raising a finger toward him, but before he uttered further rebuke, Harris's father pushed through to the front of the Keepers. When he saw his son standing in the strength of his own legs, his mouth fell open, and his eyes filled with tears.

"My son?" he whispered.

"Father," Harris said, stepping toward his father. "Look what Sovereign Ell Yon through his son, Jeshu, has done for me this glorious day!"

As if waiting for a mirage to disappear, the man hesitated, then ran to Harris. Father and son embraced in shared tears of joy. The father then pushed Harris back, wanting to see the boy standing once more, as if to convince himself he wasn't imagining the miracle.

"Enough of this charade!" Kylos shouted. "What you are seeing here is trickery by the hand of this heretic's followers!" Kylos set his eyes on Rhett. "Don't think for a moment that we will allow you to bring that man's treacherous lies back into this sanctum...or any part of Jalem for that matter."

Rhett's Protector trembled with power. "And the Merchant will appear and will expose the mighty, destroying their power, which is of the darkness of Dracus. He will bring hope to the lowly and healing to the destitute. Of his dominion there will be no end!"

The words from an ancient oracle saturated the courtyard with condemning truth.

"Silence!" Kylos's face reddened with rage.

"Let the man speak!" shouted someone from the crowd.

"Yes, we want to hear him!" shouted a woman.

Before Kylos could respond with any measure of action, hundreds of people began to shout their affirmation to have Rhett speak to them. Not even the sanctum guards seemed to have any effect on the enthusiastic crowd. When it became clear there would be no recovering the masses, Kylos turned about and exited the outer court, returning to the inner chambers of the sanctum, his entourage of Keepers and Builders following close behind...all but one.

Rhett scanned the crowd that had now swelled to thousands, his gaze falling finally on Brae. She smiled with a warmth that revealed in him a courage he didn't know he had.

"People of Rayl," Rhett shouted, turning his attention back to the masses. "Why do you marvel at what you have seen here today? Why do you look at us as though by our own power we healed this lad? Sovereign Ell Yon has given power and honor to his own son, Jeshu, whom you delivered to Pylok to be killed, even though the Morian Subchancellor had intended to let him go. Instead, you killed the Prince of Life. But Ell Yon has raised him from the dead as we have witnessed. It is in the name of Jeshu that this young man was made strong in your very presence."

Rhett paused, seeing the great conviction his words were bringing to the hearts of the people.

"What you did to Jeshu you did in ignorance, for the words of ancient oracles were fulfilled by your hand. Repent of what you have done and turn your hearts to Jeshu, the author of life and of your future, and you will be purged from Deitum Prime. And Sovereign Ell Yon will send Jeshu once again to fully deliver us from the evil of Dracus. This has been foretold from the beginning of the Aurora Galaxy. And it will be so that anyone who does not hear this oracle...this Navi of modern day...will be destroyed from the people of Rayl. You are from the oracles of old who warned of the Merchant's arrival. Now, accept Jeshu as your Merchant who has purchased your future from the death of Deitum Prime!"

Rhett's words were filled with such Immortal power that thousands of Rayleans came in humility, begging to follow in the ways of Ell Yon through his son, Jeshu. The Navis received their confessions of wrong and then bestowed on all who asked a replicated Protector of their own.

After nearly an hour of such profound expansion of the Navi order, Kylos returned with reinforcements. Six sanctum guards accosted Rhett and Bridger, while 20 more began dispersing the crowds, expelling them from the outer court of the sanctum. Brae reached for Rhett, her eyes conveying deep angst, but the guards separated them, casting her, along with the rest of the crowd, out of the courtyard. Rhett and Bridger were briskly escorted into the sanctum and cast into a locked chamber.

After a Stabil retention field door was activated and they were left to themselves, Rhett paced to the far side of the room, thinking about what their fate might be.

"Well, brother," Bridger said, "it looks like we are certainly following in the footsteps of Jeshu." He smiled. "But it was worth it!"

Rhett stopped, glancing back at Bridger. "I'm glad you think so because I don't see a way out of this."

Bridger snorted. "For centuries oracles yearned to see what we have seen. I wouldn't change a thing."

Rhett nodded, realizing that Bridger was absolutely right. "Agreed."

The next morning Rhett and Bridger were brought into the oration chamber of the sanctum. Rhett instantly recognized the father of Harris sitting in the front row, his eyes cast down, avoiding Rhett's gaze. Next to him sat Harris, his face still glowing with gratitude. The two Navis were placed on the platform before the leaders of the Keepers and the Builders. Kylos glared at them, waiting.

"By what power and what authority have you done this thing?"

Rhett was more than surprised by the question. Then he realized that this was their way of officially recording a confession so the Navis could be convicted of heresy. He considered keeping silent, but once again the Protector would not allow it, compelling him to speak the words that were forming in his mind from Ell Yon himself.

"Keepers and Builders of Rayl, if you are asking of the good deed that was performed on this young man," Rhett answered, motioning to Harris, at which point the lad stood up. "Then let it be known to all that it is through the man Jeshu, whom you killed but Ell Yon brought back to life, that this young man is standing before you today. Jeshu is the Merchant, whom you have rejected. He is the cornerstone, and there is none other who can save us from Dracus and his Deitum Prime."

Kylos glared at Rhett and Bridger and then at Harris. The sheer evidence of his miraculous healing was incontestable. Kylos turned to consult with five other Keepers and Builders, including Krisha Monae, Master Builder of the Protectors. After a few minutes, Kylos left the chamber in a huff. Monae approached Rhett and Bridger.

"You will no longer speak of this false Navi named Jeshu. If you continue, we will arrest you and convict you of heresy."

Bridger then replied. "We will speak of those things which we have seen and heard."

Krisha Monae's eyes narrowed, fully understanding what Bridger's response meant. But in that moment, she flinched. Rhett sensed that the woman's ruthless logic may have given her one brief glimpse into the truth that stood before her.

"Release them," she ordered, then turned and exited the chamber with the other leaders.

Within the walls of Jalem's sovereign sanctum, a secret chamber meeting was about to begin. Preeminent Keeper Fasa Kylos and Master Builder Krisha Monae were sitting in the middle of a large, arcing semi-circular conference table. The six chairs to their left and five chairs to their right were occupied by the Master Keepers of the other eleven cities with sanctums. The rest of the chairs in the room were occupied by the sanctum Builder Order masters. Although these two orders now had nothing to keep and nothing to build since the heretic

Jeshu had sabotaged all existing Protectors and the omeganite collectors, a desperate urgency surged through the room.

"Master Builder Monae and I have called you here to discuss how we ought to deal with the persistent and vexing followers of the false Navi named Jeshu—Jeshuans I believe they are now called." Kylos sneered as he spoke the name. "In Jalem they are becoming increasingly bold about spreading their propaganda, and I fear they will soon be adding to their numbers."

"Not only in Jalem, Preeminent!" the Master Keeper from Zareth interjected. "The disturbances in our sanctum and in the rest of the city by the Jeshuans is increasing every day. Something must be done!"

"In our sanctum," the Master Keeper from the Rea sanctum began, "there have been reports of multiple healings, or rather false healings, and they continue to insult us, calling us puppets of the evil Lord Dracus!"

Other Keepers and Builders voiced their affirmation of the charges. Kylos held up his hand to regain order.

"That is why we are here," Kylos said calmly. "I would like to hear your opinions as to how we not only contain this—this heresy—but eliminate it once and for all."

The ensuing silence testified to the dark thoughts that ran through the minds of every single member of the chamber. Kylos waited to see if any would be brave enough to voice what needed to be said. It was the Master Keeper from the Rea sanctum that finally spoke.

"Everyone here knows there is only one way to stop fanatics such as these. But we don't have the authority, especially with Subchancellor Pylok looking over our shoulders."

Kylos slowly nodded. "You speak truth, Keeper Voller."

For the next thirty minutes, nearly every member of the two orders offered many ideas...all but one—Krisha Monae. Kylos imagined her shrewd and brilliant mind was formulating the perfect plan. Kylos patiently listened until he became frustrated as the ideas grew increasingly absurd. The volume and discord mounted. At last, he stood up.

"Silence!" he shouted. The chamber became quiet. He scanned the room until at last he turned to look at Monae to his right.

"I would like to hear if Master Builder Monae has anything to offer."

As leader of the Builder order, Krisha Monae had proven her resourcefulness throughout the many challenges both the Keeper and the Builder orders had recently faced. She was a reliable and intelligent counselor to Kylos, often when there seemed no path forward. Monae seemed hesitant to speak. Lately, Kylos was often beginning to doubt her resolve in the more serious matters of the sanctums.

"Come, Krisha—speak!" Kylos insisted.

Monae leaned forward, her eyes narrowing. The rest of the chamber members were waiting, knowing that every word she spoke would be measured and calculated.

"We are not the only ones that find the Jeshuans to be a threatening menace. What is it that the Morians want from Rayl?" Monae asked.

"Our resources!" shouted a fellow Builder.

"Yes," Monae said. "But they also want our resources without turmoil—Pylok most of all."

Kylos was intrigued. "Please continue."

"Just as we convinced Pylok of the real and imminent threat that Jeshu was to the peace of Rayl, we return to the Subchancellor and convince him of the same regarding the Jeshuan remnant followers. We remind Pylok that we all want the same thing...peace on this planet. We will draft an edict for him to sign granting us the authority to deal with the threat of the Jeshuan insurrectionists."

"Yes," Kylos's face illuminated. "By any means necessary."

Monae's countenance darkened, but her ingenious plan quickly gained approval from the entire chamber. Kylos remained thoughtful then turned to face the entire chamber.

"I will draft the Peace Preservation Edict," he announced, nodding Monae's direction. "I charge all of you to keep the affairs of this meeting confidential. Swear by the honor of our orders that you will do so."

"We so swear!" declared all 24 members of the chamber in unison.

Brae glanced over at Rhett, seeing the concern on his face as she, Rhett, Mazon, and Cilla navigated the streets of Jalem. Each of them had received a prompting from their Protector to journey into the city for no apparent reason. She knew there would be some measure of risk, but they all had come to accept and abide in the will of Ell Yon through the Protectors' call.

Rhett was a fearless man except when it came to his perceived responsibility to protect everyone he cherished. He never feared for himself. But his fierce sense of loyalty, which was wired within his soul, would never change. This protective loyalty annoyed Brae at times, but it was also what caused her to love him so much. She reached for his hand. Her touch seemed to instantly release the tension manifested in his countenance.

"We'll be okay, Rhett."

Rhett flashed his signature crooked grin then continued to scan the city.

Morian commando patrols had resumed their normal schedule. Ironically, Brae wasn't as concerned about the commandos as she was Kylos's sanctum guards and, to a lesser degree, Terrok's personal royal guards.

As they approached Jalem's city square, Brae too became uneasy. She tried to quell the rising apprehension, but it simply would not release her. The others were so preoccupied with keeping an eye out that only after thirty minutes did Rhett realize something was up.

"What's wrong, Brae?" Rhett asked, halting Mazon and Cilla.

Brae shook her head, scanning the surrounding buildings as if looking for something or someone.

"I'm not sure, but something's happening right here and right now."

Rhett pulled the other three out of the main thoroughfare and into a triangular nook formed by the base of two sky-high buildings.

"I don't see anything," Mazon said. The special ground assault training he'd received from Jeshu at Olea Station made him an excellent choice for this excursion.

Brae touched the Protector on her arm. The intensity of her connection with it was increasing. "Not in our realm. I think we need to commune."

The other three Navis stopped scanning to look at her. Once she had spoken it, they also seemed to sense the call.

"We need a quiet place to isolate ourselves," Cilla offered.

After a short search, they located an empty conference room on the second floor of a nearby building. They formed a circle, kneeling just as Jeshu had taught them. Brae felt the Protector surging as wisps of blue power shimmied up and down the length of the vambrace. Brae closed her eyes as she submitted herself to the Protector's call. Within a few seconds, the fabric of her reality melted away to transcend her being into the Ruah. The first indication that she had left the realm of humanity was the fierce sound of advanced battle. Brae opened her eyes to a world of war. She stood up, then moved away from her communing body and toward a window just to her left. Seconds later, Rhett, Mazon, and Cilla joined her. From this vantage point, they could see intense clashes between Malakians and Torians at three different locations not far from their position. Brae felt extremely vulnerable here in this land of warrior giants and especially so since they had no tactical gear to protect them.

"What is this battle for? Why now?" Mazon asked.

Just then, the door to the conference room burst open, and the four of them turned, instinctively reaching for their blasters. But weapons from their realm could not translate into the Ruah. They were defenseless.

A Malakian female of authority and two accompanying warriors entered the room then hesitated. She tapped her com band.

"Found them. We'll be at your location in 60 seconds."

The woman's eyes narrowed as she scrutinized the four translated Navis. She then approached, walking right through their four communing bodies kneeling on the floor. She stopped a few paces in front of them, placing her hands on her hips. The tactical combat suit she was wearing was similar to what they had seen Jeshu don.

"You're late, and now we don't have time to properly acquaint you with your tactical gear."

"You were expecting us?" Rhett asked.

The woman tapped a quick sequence on her com band. A 3-D image filled with data and navigation information appeared briefly.

"Yes...thirty minutes ago," she said as she swiped the data page twice before making it disappear. "Follow me. We don't have much time, and there's much at stake."

The woman turned about, leading them out of the room. The two warriors waiting at the door followed behind them, ever vigilant with weapons in hand.

Outside the room, the woman led them back down to the main floor and into a large auditorium filled with a hundred Malakian warriors, tactical instrumentation, and displays that pulsed with activity. Brae instantly recognized the fervent but coordinated actions of a war room. Brae, Rhett, Mazon, and Cilla were all overwhelmed at what they saw. Brae began to wonder if they had made a mistake by communing. Surely, the only thing they would be capable of here was to impede the Malakian effort against the Torians, whatever that was. Once again, she felt like a child among giants.

In short order, they were led to the central part of the auditorium, where a Malakian commanding officer was issuing orders while analyzing multiple holographic representations of a nearby section of Jalem. Their escort held up her hand to indicate they should approach no closer—they silently waited and watched. The commander's back was to them. The Malakian female warrior waited for a five-second break in the commander's actions.

"Colonel Ruger, here is the Navi contingent."

The colonel turned to address them. Brae thought she recognized the warrior from their brief encounter in the Ruah when Jeshu had first taught them how to commune. Ruger frowned, further confirming Brae's doubt about their presence here. Instead of addressing them, he turned to the woman warrior.

"Major Ki, I don't have the time or the resources to deal with this. We have less than an hour to make our assault and keep Pylok from signing that decree. The Torians are amassing a sizable response." Colonel Ruger flashed a despairing glance their way. "Besides, they'll certainly not be of any help to us."

The female warrior didn't respond immediately. She joined Ruger in gazing their way.

"I wouldn't dismiss them so quickly, sir. One is a Starlore, and I saw how the Protector empowered both her parents in remarkable ways."

Colonel Ruger looked unimpressed. "You get them ready. They're your responsibility."

"Yes, sir."

Brae peered reverently at the female warrior. This was the Malakian warrior of her father's stories. She repressed the smile that wanted to form on her lips. She felt as if she was jumping into the pages of a legend.

Colonel Ruger turned back to address an incoming communique while Major Ki motioned for them to follow her.

"Grab their tactical equipment," she ordered. The two accompanying warriors diverted as Ki led the four Navis out of the auditorium and toward the back of the building. Once outside, Ki led them to a small courtyard that gave a measure of isolation from the conflict with the Torians just a couple of city blocks in the other direction. The two warriors soon appeared, setting a tactical bag in front of each of them.

"I'm told you've been in the Ruah before. What you do here and how effective you are will depend on your connection with the Protector and the courage in your heart. Don your combat suits and your headgear."

Brae, Rhett, Mazon, and Cilla all exchanged glances. Although there was a measure of demur in each of them, Brae also saw the spark of resolve in their eyes.

Just as before, the advanced combat suits form-fit perfectly to each of their physiques. But unlike before, these suits were imbued with multiple facets of weaponry and defense systems Brae could only guess at. She noticed that the back of her combat suit was thicker than before. There were also slight bulges near her wrists and ankles. She donned the included black padded gloves and self-binding combat boots that joined seamlessly with the suit. Inside her tactical bag she discovered an extremely advanced class-one blaster and a Talon-style weapon. Both clung via some invisible tether when placed in close proximity to her belt and would instantly release when her hand encircled the grips. Brae also discovered a sleek force field power module that she slipped onto her left hand. The last piece of equipment in the tactical bag was a light-weight helmet that resized itself to fit her head perfectly. Once the helmet was set, the visor seemed to appear out of nowhere. The transparent fisheye visor hosted a plethora of display information. Brae sensed a presence that accompanied the donning of the helmet, almost as if something was knocking on the door to her mind.

Brae turned to face her fellow Navis. Though hardly the stature of a Malakian, she had to admit that these combat suits certainly projected a warrior-like appearance.

"Your visor display will present all pertinent information for any combat scenario you may encounter." Major Ki's voice was now heard in perfect clarity through the helmet audio. They all turned to face her. "Including friendly and enemy locations, weapon status, enhanced combat suit status, and any other information you want to custom configure. Your combat suit and gear provide defensive and offensive weapons, communication and navigation, and assisted maneuverability."

Major Ki drew her blaster. "Your blaster is three times as powerful as any class-one blaster in your realm." She spent ten seconds demonstrating the functions and indicators of the weapon then moved on.

"The Talon is a silent close-range weapon with an enhanced stasis field generator," Ki explained as she extended and charged the Talon. "What sets this weapon apart from your version of the Talon is its ability to cast an expanding stasis burst wave up to 20 feet. It's slower than a plasma shot and dissipates with distance, but there's very little that can stop it. This talon does not double as a blaster." Ki retracted the Talon's blade and set it to its position on her belt. "If you haven't had Talon training, I recommend postponing your use of it for now."

Although the weapon had different capabilities than the Talon her father had trained her on years ago, Brae was excited to dust off her skills and give it a try.

Ki secured the force field power module on her left hand. "This is the Emuna Shield," she said, simultaneously pushing her hand forward while opening her fingers wide. Instantly an oval-shaped force field appeared two inches in front of her hand, projecting upward and downward far enough to cover her body. "It is your best and first level of defensive protection. Your body armor has a micro field protection array and is a second level of protection against an energy weapon. But believe me, you'll still feel the impact if a blaster hits you. Your shield can withstand two class-one hits then needs fifteen seconds to recharge. Your body armor can take one. The Torians know this and have set their weapons for a four-burst rapid fire—the first three to take out your shield and body armor and the fourth to kill you."

Rhett extended his hand just as Major Ki had, but nothing happened. "Do I have to activate it somehow?"

"The Emuna Shield is always on," Ki said, retracting her hand as her shield simultaneously retracted. "The reason it's not working for you is because you haven't gained control of your combat suit through the neural connection in your helmet. You'll not survive here if you aren't able to master this." Ki looked Brae and the others over carefully, a wisp of concern on her face. "Close your eyes and concentrate. Feel the combat suit on your body. Every point of contact provides a pathway for the neural connection. Now follow those pressure points up and into your mind. Allow the helmet to access those sensations. The Protector will guide you."

Brae concentrated as Major Ki had instructed. At first it seemed impossible, but over the course of the next few seconds, it felt as if she were gathering data points and delivering them to a new place in her mind. Continuing to focus, she waited, then joined the synaptic connection with the Protector in this neural space. Almost as if she had touched a bare power cord, her entire body felt the zing of the helmet's neural connection bond with her mind in a moment. She opened her eyes and felt empowered like she had never experienced before. She held out her hand, imagining the Emuna Shield, and it instantly appeared.

"Good, Starlore. You've made the connection," Ki said. "Now for the rest of you."

Major Ki refused to move on until they had all mastered the technique. Much to Rhett's frustration, it took each of them a couple of tries, but within a few minutes all four Navis had made the connection.

"Now that you've all connected to your combat suits, you'll have information access, weapons control, and the maneuverability necessary to survive and be effective in combat. With practice, your connection will get stronger and more efficient. In time, you will hardly have to think a thought—the suit will nearly anticipate your commands. The suit and its advanced capabilities will feel like an extension of your own body."

Brae smiled. It felt as if there were a host of capabilities just waiting for her to discover them.

"The Protector can work in harmony with you and your combat suit." Ki placed her hand on the vambrace encircling her right forearm, glancing down at it. Her Protector looked slightly different than theirs—shorter and positioned close to the wrist. "Just realize that unlike the weapons you carry, you do not control the Protector—it controls you...if you let it. The Protector will always bring you to a better outcome than you could ever accomplish on your own, even in conjunction with your weapons and suit. If you try to control the Protector, you will fail. Do you understand?"

Ki hesitated, apparently wanting to make sure they understood how important this was. Each of the Navis nodded.

"I can't even begin to elucidate how the Protector can defend or attack an enemy, for its abilities are enumerable. Only Sovereign Ell Yon and the Commander understand it. When in combat with the Scourge, lean into the power of the Protector to guide you."

Brae remembered the valiant tales her father had told her about the Protector. This was a new manifestation of the Protector that the oracles and Navis of old had only dreamed of.

"As you gain mastery of the neural connection with your combat suit, your ability to fight in the Ruah will be supremely enhanced." Major Ki hesitated, apparently preoccupied with a thought. "I suspect perhaps in ways that may even surprise a Malakian."

Brae held out her arms, looking the suit over more closely. Her hand touched the slight bulge near her wrist. Something new was there. Major Ki watched Brae closely, intrigued.

"What are these?" Brae asked.

"Those are part of the suit maneuverability enhancements. Within the suit near your hands and feet are molecular cohesion field generators that work in concert with your gloves and boots."

"I don't understand," Mazon said. "Cohesion field generators?"

"Yes...CFGs. This may take some time to master, but your CFGs activate a sophisticated, thin monomer layer on the surface of your gloves and boots that bind with nearly any material at the molecular level," Ki explained.

The four Navis stared blankly at each other. Ki looked slightly disappointed.

"Watch," she said and walked over to stand next to one of the walls of a building in the courtyard. She placed the toe of her right foot on the wall then stepped up while placing the flat of her right hand above her head on the wall. She hung suspended, turning outward to address the four stunned Navis.

"You can walk on walls?" Cilla exclaimed.

Major Ki crawled up the wall a couple of feet, then jumped away while spinning about, landing just in front of them. Brae had yet to see Major Ki or any of the Malakians smile, but there was the subtlest hint of such on her face.

"You can do a lot more than walk on walls," Ki said. She turned back to the wall, which was about ten feet away. She crouched then launched herself upward with a leap that carried her thirty feet into the air. At the pinnacle of her leap, she clung to the side of the building with both hands and both feet. She then released her left hand and foot, rotating to face outward. Ki jumped out from the wall while performing a flip in the air. Brae cringed at the thought of her hitting the ground from such a fall, but a few feet from the ground, she slowed midair as if she had merely jumped from a two-foot stool, landing perfectly in a poised and ready position.

"Impossible!" Rhett exclaimed.

"Your cohesion field generators can bond to just about any surface that isn't loose, so be careful," Ki warned. "The pack on your back is a surge anti-grav engine, meaning it can provide concentrated but brief bursts of anti-gravity force. This is useful for vertical jumps and landings. There is also a quark propulsion micro engine that can provide some horizontal thrust when you need it. The coordination of all maneuverability features of your combat suit will take a long time to master, so be patient and cautious."

With every new feature of the combat suit Major Ki introduced, Brae felt like another piece of the puzzle was put in place through the neural connection. Oddly, the link felt quite natural. She glanced at her fellow Navis, wondering if they felt the same.

"As marvelous as this may seem, improper use can get you killed in seconds," Ki continued. "I've discovered that the best place to fight is with your feet on solid ground, so don't be lured into thinking the extra maneuverability the suit can perform will give you an advantage. Every warrior in the Ruah has similar capabilities, Malakian or Torian, but there are different varieties depending on mission requirements, like full jet packs for sustained flight."

"Alert!" Brae's helmet com clamored in her ears. "Target action initiated. All squad commanders and their tactical teams report for the final briefing."
Ki's head snapped back toward the doors of the command building. "Training's over." She looked circumspectly at her green recruits. "Your training was rushed and incomplete, so you'd best stay low and observe only. This is going to be brutal. I can't have you on a casualty list the first day."

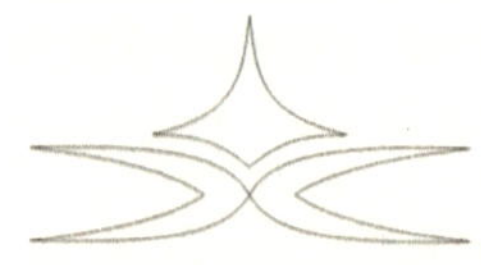

CHAPTER

7

The Fire of the Scourge

Ki led the four Navis back to headquarters, where the level of activity within had swelled to a feverish pitch. At least 200 Malakian warriors had gathered before Colonel Ruger for the briefing. The warriors were divided into 14 squads of 14 warriors each.

"The four of you will join my squad as observers only," Ki said as they joined a group of 13 other warriors. She turned to one of the warriors. "Is the team briefed and ready?"

"Yes, major," came the quick reply.

"Squad leaders, position your teams at these locations," Ruger announced, pointing to a 3-D image of a section of Jalem that appeared above them for all to see. Brae instantly recognized the area as Skyburough, the headquarters for Morian Subchancellor Pylok. Squad designations appeared at 14 locations in a semi-circle around Pylok's palace.

"Why are they defending Pylok?" Mazon whispered.

Brae had the same thought, confused by the directive. The answer came quickly.

"Kylos will be bringing his proposed Preservation Edict to Pylok to sign. If he is successful, this edict will give the Keepers authority to search out and kill all Jeshuans without excuse or due process. Every attempt we have made to thwart Dracus's move through Kylos has failed. This is our last chance!"

Brae glanced toward Rhett, Mazon, and Cilla, seeing shock on their faces. The gravity of this engagement fully hit them.

Ruger took a moment to scan the faces of these mighty men and women of war. "Kylos is traveling to Pylok's palace in an anti-grav hover transport, so this will be a ground assault with limited air support. Intelligence reports that Dracus has assigned nearly 100 Torian warriors to escort Kylos. If Dracus is successful, the impact on the distribution of the Commander's Solution to humanity will be severe. This mission is of the utmost importance. Squads Alpha through Foxtrot, move out. Squads Golf through November get to your troop carriers and prepare to engage!"

All at once, every Malakian warrior pounded a fist into an open palm, then turned to face their fate in the crucible of war.

"Bravo Squad, let's move!" Major Ki commanded.

It was evident that each squad had its own com frequency. Brae tested her ability to jump frequencies using the neural connection. She effortlessly tapped into three other squads and then back to Bravo's frequency in just a few seconds. She began analyzing the visor data, organizing it to an arrangement she was familiar with. She cued up a menu of all possible data that could be displayed and was stunned by the endless options. She prioritized squad member locations, a city map with a two-mile radius, and enemy locations, along with three other data sets she thought might be useful.

As Bravo Squad moved toward the front exit of the building, Brae mentally activated the cohesion field generator for her right boot. She tried to lift her leg but couldn't.

Hmm…that's easier than I thought.

She released the CFG then fell in step with her squad. She noticed that most of the squad members carried a class-one rapid fire plasma rifle. Major Ki, her first sergeant, and the four Navis were the only ones carrying handheld blasters. According to the positions Colonel Ruger had displayed, Bravo Squad was to take up a position one-half mile east of their current location. Exiting the headquarters building served as the Navis' cue to draw their blasters and don their Emuna Shields. They had to work hard to keep up with the fast-moving Malakian warriors. Brae noticed that Major Ki would occasionally check on their progress, which quietly annoyed Brae since she knew that their presence could distract Ki and ultimately jeopardize the mission.

The streets and structures of Jalem were wet with the rainfall from a small, isolated thunderstorm directly overhead. The low angle of a late afternoon sun illumined the wet surfaces, causing bright reflections beneath a brief cloudy sky that resulted in a peculiar combination of darkness and light. As Brae jogged, she continued to strengthen the neural connection with her combat suit and the Protector by testing access to suit and weapons status, intelligence reports, and targeting modes.

Within a few minutes, Bravo Squad was taking up positions to guard the approach to Pylok's palace via Accolade Thoroughfare, a high-traffic route. They were assigned to the north side of the route, and Charlie Squad was across the way protecting the south side of the route. The elaborate buildings of Jalem on each side of Accolade Thoroughfare towered overhead like massive marble statues. Multiple anti-grav transports raced across the cityscape on elevated rails while hundreds of personal transports swished to-and-fro at three different flight levels. Brae had to remind herself that she was invisible to the world of humanity. It was the first time she realized how distracting the visual noise from her realm would be in a conflict with the Torians.

"Koran, Chi, and Porvik, third floor vantage in that building," Major Ki ordered.

Three Malakians turned, leapt 30 feet into the air and onto an open-air terrace on the third floor of an adjacent building.

"Malin and Vry, cover that corridor," Ki continued, pointing to a space between two buildings. "Everyone else take up positions on ground level. Intel expects Torian forces to escort Kylos with support from the northwest. Any breaches in our line and we fall back to checkpoint Alpha to regroup. The east side of the palace is our retreat line if everything falls apart."

Major Ki turned to face Brae, Rhett, Mazon, and Cilla. "I want you four back 100 yards and behind cover. If we can't disrupt Kylos and the Torians break through, you'll only have seconds to exit east before they're on you. Listen close for my call to bug out. Is that clear?"

All four Navis nodded. Ki seemed satisfied. "Move out."

Brae cued up a private com channel between herself and the other Navis while continuing to monitor the Bravo Squad channel.

"I didn't expect this when I said we should commune," Brae radioed.

The other three snapped their heads her direction. "Is this a private channel?" Rhett asked.

"Yes. Designation Navi 4.128," Brae replied. "I've reserved this channel for us."

"How did you figure that out so quickly?" Cilla asked.

Brae was surprised by the question. "It just...I'm not really sure. It was intuitive." She tried to explain but realized she couldn't. She caught Rhett looking at her quizzically.

"How do you all feel about watching from the sidelines?" Mazon asked.

"Not cool!" Cilla piped up.

"Agreed," Rhett said as Brae nodded.

They had all experienced some actual combat with the Torians the night Jeshu was taken by Kylos—Brae and Rhett in the Starstreaks and Mazon and Cilla on the ground, but Brae had a feeling that this mission might be a whole other level.

"I say we look for an opportunity to engage—" Mazon began, but then the world around them exploded.

Four Torian fighters decloaked just a mile out and began bombarding the Malakian positions with phaser bursts and plasma cannon fire at the same time that six Torian squads began executing a preemptive strike. The Torians were supported by tactical ground assault vehicles with dual-mounted class-two plasma cannons. Brae could see Kylos's transport coming down Accolade Thoroughfare a half mile from Major Ki and her warriors' positions with another four squads in escort.

"Bravo Squad requesting air support!" Brae heard Ki radio headquarters. "Multiple Torian fighters and assault vehicles are attacking from Sector Lima. Need additional support immediately!"

Similar requests filled the com channel from other Malakian squad leaders, also under attack. Brae instantly recognized that the Malakian intel had grossly underestimated the strength of Torian forces for this engagement. Wherever additional Malakian support troops and air support were, they were too far away, considering the speed with which the Torians were attacking.

Brae, Rhett, Mazon, and Cilla took cover behind a concrete support beneath an elevated grav-railway as the doom of a massacre enveloped them.

"What do we do? Can we help them?" Cilla radioed as the com channels filled with chatter from a dozen Malakian squads in dire situations.

Just one hundred yards away, the Navis watched as Bravo Squad took a beating from above and from the ground forces ahead. It was a battle for survival. After two minutes of relentless assault, three Malakian Starstreaks engaged the Torian fighters, allowing Bravo and Charlie Squads a chance to regroup and start returning fire. But more Torian squads were coming.

"Bravo Squad, these are overwhelming forces we didn't expect," Ki's voice bellowed over the squad com channel. "Backup is too far out, so command is ordering our retreat. Fall back to checkpoint Alpha. I want you four Navis to hold tight until we recover to your position. You'll be too exposed to retreat without our cover support."

Brae exchanged dour looks with her fellow Navis. They watched as Major Ki and eight of their remaining warriors began a methodical step-by-step retreat. One of the warriors on the elevated platform attempted to descend to ground level but was blasted by a class-two plasma burst from an assault vehicle trained on their location. The warrior's lifeless body careened through the air, impacting the ground just a couple of feet before the Navis. The fallen warrior's class-one rapid-fire plasma rifle skidded to a halt at Brae's feet.

"Major, we're taking fire from inside the building, and the assault vehicle has us pinned down from below," one of the two remaining warriors on the platform radioed. "We have no avenue of retreat."

"Hold tight. We're coming," Ki called back, but now the additional escort squads accompanying Kylos's transport were nearly on them, doubling the Torian fire power.

"This is a massacre," Rhett radioed on the private Navi channel. "They're not getting out alive."

As Brae watched the impending doom of Major Ki and her squad, a fierce resolve began to swell within her. An eternal fire she could not understand ignited within her heart, its flames born out of the ancient stories she had listened to as a little girl. Something unstoppable compelled her to rise up. Although she didn't see it, the Protector on her arm had begun glowing hot blue with the power of Ell Yon.

"I can't watch this happen," Brae exclaimed as she readied to leave the protection of their concrete cover.

Rhett grabbed hold of her arm.

Brae looked back at him with fire in her eyes. "There's no stopping me."

Rhett's gaze steeled. "Oh, I know, but you're not the only one who feels it. This is why we're here."

Rhett, Mazon, and Cilla all held up their Protectors to show the same powerful glow emanating from Ell Yon's Immortal weapon.

"What's the plan?" Mazon asked.

"Kill the bad guys and save the good guys," Brae replied as she holstered her blaster then picked up the rapid-fire plasma rifle at her feet, slinging it over her shoulder.

Kylos's transport was now just a quarter of a mile away and approaching fast. The Torians were engaged with a mission not only to ensure his safe passage to Pylok's palace but also to systematically eliminate every Malakian squad position as they went, allowing no avenue of retreat. The squad com channels were populated with urgent calls for additional support and emergency response. Brae could sit still no longer.

"Cover me until I reach our closest squad members," Brae said, launching herself into the fiery fray that surrounded them. The cacophony of laser bursts and plasma cannon fire was deafening as the space around them filled with brilliant flashes of deadly weapon fire. But Brae was unafraid. In some surreal state of mind, the

Protector and her combat suit lifted her neural connection and mental acuity to a level she had never even imagined possible.

She sprinted toward Major Ki's trapped squad members with her Emuna Shield in place while pinpointing rapid-fire bursts from her plasma rifle on the closest three attacking Torians. Since they weren't expecting her attack, she decimated them in seconds. This won her the vicious attention of multiple other Torian warriors, and they unleashed on her. The onslaught of weapon fire from multiple positions looked to be an impossible thing to survive.

"No, Starlore! Retreat!" Brae heard Ki's urgent command on the com channel.

As the barrage of vicious fire rained down on Brae, time seemed to slow to such a degree that she could see each ribbon of plasma and move to avoid each one. Brae dodged, twisted, turned, and shield-deflected every single burst while simultaneously firing precision return salvos. At one point, she activated her surge anti-grav engine and leapt twenty feet into the air, clinging to the wall of a nearby building using her CFGs. She was now positioned directly overhead of Major Ki and her eight warriors. Brae disengaged the cohesion field generators on her right foot and right hand just long enough to spin her body around to leap forward and over the top of an approaching squad of Torians intent on eliminating Ki and her warriors. In one lightning-fast fluid motion, Brae drew her Talon and shot an expanding stasis burst wave directly down on top of the Torian squad. The move was executed so quickly that the Torians couldn't react in time to defend themselves and were obliterated in seconds.

Before Brae's feet touched the ground, she holstered her Talon and reacquired her rifle. As her feet hit the ground, she began laying down cover fire for Ki's warriors, who were attempting to evacuate the raised platform. The synchronized capabilities of Brae's mind with her combat suit, while submitting to the superb direction of the Protector, were revealing the presence of Ell Yon in the battle with the Torians. These were capabilities never witnessed before.

A few seconds later, a Torian assault vehicle trained its class-two plasma cannon on her position. With nowhere to take immediate cover, it looked as though this would be the end of Brae. She dropped her rifle to its sling position then lifted her right hand toward the cannon just as it unleashed its first deadly salvo. In similar fashion as Jeshu's, the power of Ell Yon burst forth from the Protector in a flash of consuming fire, swallowing up the stream of deadly Torian plasma fire while ripping through the assault vehicle with a pulverizing energy that instantly destroyed it and its occupants.

This sequence of Brae's interfering actions was accomplished in less than sixty seconds, and it stunned every warrior present, both Malakian and Torian. It was as if Sovereign Ell Yon was just now revealing a secret weapon hidden from the foundation of the galaxy. The five seconds of eerie reprieve were brief, however, as the Torians doubled down on their response to this new threat.

By now, Kylos's transport was nearly on them, and along with him came four more squads of Torian reinforcements. But Brae was not alone. With newfound skill and courage, Rhett, Mazon, and Cilla took up positions near her with rifles recovered from the wounded and the dead. The scene unfolded in the most epic of intense battles the realm of the Ruah had ever seen. Four bold Navis took on the overwhelming forces of Dracus in a fight for survival. And although their valor and skill were unmatched, the sheer number of Torian warriors and assault vehicles was too much. Brae and her Navi warriors strategically fought to buy enough time for the Malakian forces to retreat to safety. By day's end, the Navis had helped four Malakian squads in dire situations to recover back to headquarters. Rhett and Cilla had each taken hits, but their body armor's micro field protection array had saved them.

When the four Navis finally made it back to headquarters, everything felt different. As they entered the auditorium, every Malakian warrior turned their eyes on them. The silence of the room was strange and unreadable as they took in the gaze of a hundred of Ell Yon's mighty warriors. Major Ki and Colonel Ruger approached, faces stern and sober.

Have we offended them? Brae wondered.

They stepped to within a few feet of Brae. Oddly, Brae was able to look Major Ki eye to eye, their statures now nearly equal. After a few seconds of an awkward silent exchange, Major Ki held out her arm to Brae. Brae slowly reached out her arm in response. Ki embraced her forearm, a look of extreme respect in her eyes.

"You saved many Malakians today," Ki said, glancing at all four Navis. "We are indebted."

Colonel Ruger stepped forward. "Welcome to the Ruah, warriors of Ell Yon."

Instantly the auditorium erupted in a unified chant of 100 voices. "Warriors of Ell Yon!"

Although Brae was honored by the response of such a mighty force, there was little to celebrate. Kylos had made it to Pylok's palace with hundreds of Torians to secure Dracus's evil plan to destroy all Jeshuans in the realm of humanity. This defeat in the Ruah would have profound and far-reaching consequences for the followers of Jeshu on Rayl. It was a dark day indeed.

Brae was still processing everything that had happened. The rush of battle was still coursing through her veins, and the mix of emotions was complicated and confusing.

"We need to return and warn the others," Brae said.

Ruger's face turned dour. "From this day forward, the battle in both realms will be great."

Brae nodded, then the four Navis turned to recover themselves, each of them changed by the crucible of war in the Ruah. Despite their newfound skills as warriors of the Ruah, Brae felt severely vulnerable. How would they survive the overwhelming forces of Kylos and the Morian Empire?

CHAPTER

8

The Edict of Kylos

They persecuted me, so they will also persecute you. You will be cast out of the sanctums and imprisoned. They will make false accusations against you and kill you. When these things come to pass, know that your reward in Tsiyyon will be great. – Jeshu, Son of Ell Yon

When Brae, Rhett, Mazon, and Cilla returned to the realm of humanity, they all collapsed to the floor, each one bearing the intense aftereffects of such a lengthy and perilous exposure to warfare in the Ruah. Rhett was the first to recover, helping each of the others gain their feet in turn. When he came to Brae, he gently lifted her up, but she fell into him. She glanced at the others, sensing that her exhaustion seemed to be the most severe.

"What did we just see in there?" Rhett asked, his gaze never leaving Brae's face.

Brae shook her head. "Nothing I expected—that's for sure. Us actually being effective in the battle with the Torians."

"I'm not talking about us," Rhett replied. "I'm talking about you…what was that?"

Brae glanced from face to face. "I don't know what you mean. We all played a significant role in helping to save those trapped warriors."

"Not like you, Brae," Cilla replied.

"I've never seen anything like it," Mazon added. "You morphed into some super warrior—and with almost no training at all!"

Brae considered denying the claim, but by the look on Rhett's face, that would be pointless. Her gaze fell to the floor as she tried to replay those few seconds that pushed her to action against all odds.

"I'm not sure," she said, continuing to stare blankly at the floor. "I'm sorry for putting you all in danger."

"That's not what any of us are thinking," Cilla said. "We're just trying to sort out what this means and how it will affect what we do as Navis for Jeshu."

Brae looked up at them, her gaze landing on Rhett. "I don't think I can answer that. I just know that here in our realm, life for every Jeshuan is going to quickly become perilous."

After a few more minutes, the four Navis made their way down to the main floor and out onto the walkway of Accolade Thoroughfare. No assault vehicles or Torian attack fighters or warriors were firing plasma cannons…just the peaceful humdrum of Jalem on a sunny late afternoon. For Brae, it seemed as though she had just woken up from an intense dream. *Did it really happen?* she wondered.

"They're all blind to the reality of the war all around them," Mazon said.

"Yes. Blind, ignorant, and happy, and yet their very futures hang in the balance," Cilla added.

Sequences of the recent battle rushed in on Brae's mind as the four Navis walked beneath the raised platform where an hour earlier Malakian Warriors were fighting for their lives. She could almost hear the roar of a rapid-fire class-two plasma cannon tearing through the concrete terrace structure above them.

"You okay?" Rhett asked.

Brae sensed that something was different with Rhett. He was quiet and very focused on her.

"Yeah…I'm okay. Just still trying to recover."

The four Navis called for an urgent meeting of the Jeshuan Council at *Arcton Hold* to warn about the edict that Kylos had successfully presented to Subchancellor Pylok.

Preeminent Keeper of the Protectors, Fasa Kylos, stood before Subchancellor Pylok's large chamber door, waiting to be summoned by the Morian leader. The last time he had met with Pylok, Kylos had petitioned for commandos to be granted to guard the crypt of the anarchist and false Navi, Jeshu. With each encounter, Pylok's patience seemed to wear thinner. Although Pylok was clearly perturbed by every interruption of his governance, Kylos was hopeful the man's demeanor would be one of—dare he say—gratitude for eliminating a substantive threat to both the Morian Empire and the legacy of the Keeper and Builder Orders of the Rayleans.

Kylos regretted not having Krisha Monae accompany him for this request. Her smooth rapport often had a way of tempering any rising emotions exhibited by Pylok. But for some reason, the leader of the Builder Order seemed hesitant to join him, even though the original idea was hers. Perhaps it was because of the boldness of the edict Kylos had written and planned to propose. Even though he was alone, Kylos didn't feel alone. A powerful presence seemed to surround him and propel him forward in this noble quest to purge Rayl once and for all of the remnant factions of the followers of this Jeshu character.

Two sleek but massive doors slid effortlessly away from their center positions to reveal Pylok's inner court. Two commandos stood guard just inside the entrance. Kylos straightened his shoulders, lifted his chin, then proceeded into the chamber to stand before the most powerful man on Rayl. Pylok was seated in his raised throne-like chair with his back to Kylos, gazing out a massive circular window. The lofty, majestic view of the city of Jalem was a sight to behold. Slowly, Pylok's chair rotated one hundred eighty degrees until he was facing Kylos. At first glance, Kylos was surprised at the apparent morose state of the man. Pylok stared at Kylos in silence for a moment. Finally, the Morian leader rubbed a weary hand across his face.

"Lystra told me I should have nothing to do with the man you brought to me." Kylos frowned. "Plagued with distressing dreams and sleepless nights, she's left me and returned to Moria."

Kylos fidgeted. This was not a good start. "Your excellency, that man was causing global unrest that would have soon become uncontrollable. His execution has restored order to the planet you so benevolently govern. At least, nearly restored…"

Pylok leaned forward, frowning. "Nearly? What do you mean…nearly?"

"After the unfortunate incident at the crypt," Kylos began, not daring to levy too much fault on the Morian commandos, "the followers of this anarchist became emboldened in their efforts to keep his rebellious movement alive."

Pylok's eyes narrowed. "You assured me that his death would end these disturbances."

"Yes, your excellency, and it has to a large degree. But there are always a few embers that remain that must be dealt with after any fire." Kylos took a step forward to emphasize his earnestness. "I am here to facilitate the final elimination of those embers so that you do not need to be concerned with the petty affairs of our traditions."

Kylos presented a thin glass display. "This is an edict that, with your approval, would grant me the authority to quell any disturbances rising from the followers of this dead anarchist. Our goal is to maintain a peaceful and orderly population without the Morian Empire having to expend any resources."

Pylok glared at Kylos, then motioned for the edict to be transferred to his virtual display. A moment later, the edict lit up in front of Pylok, the words floating in the air before him. The man quickly read the succinct edict.

"Exacting authoritative force commensurate with the duty of eliminating threats to the established governance of the region," Pylok voiced as he finished reading the edict. "And what exactly does that mean?"

Kylos took a deep breath. "It means that our Keeper Defense Force will police all Raylean districts to ensure that the followers of this dead Navi will not create any disturbances that will disrupt your rule."

Pylok turned his head away from the floating display and toward Kylos. "You always make your requests sound so favorable to the Morian Empire, Kylos. Your loyalty and devotion are an exemplary model for every Raylean citizen."

Kylos chose not to respond to Pylok's obvious sarcasm. He waited.

Pylok lifted his hand to the displayed edict which then captured the imprint of the subchancellor's bio identity.

"Do as you must. I don't want to hear another word regarding this man named Jeshu. I want this planet to be as if the man never existed. Am I clear?"

Kylos smiled. "Perfectly."

⬦⬦

Once all the Navis had gathered at *Arcton Hold*, Rhett, Brae, Mazon, and Cilla explained what had happened regarding the coming edict proposed by Kylos to Pylok.

"What does this mean for us?" Kase asked. "Are we to flee the planet?"

"I don't believe that's what Jeshu wanted," Jaym replied. "All of us have a Protector now. Does anyone sense that Sovereign Ell Yon wants us to flee?"

No one offered a rebuttal.

"No," Kase offered. "So what do we do? Get in line to be executed by Kylos and his evil henchmen?"

"Kase has a point," Salara added. "I have news that Kylos plans to create a Keeper Defense Force, dubbed the KDF. The whole purpose for this miltech force is to seek out and eliminate all the followers of Jeshu."

"There's only one thing we *can* do," Bridger piped up. "We go underground, and everything is conducted in secret."

The room became silent as they all processed what this would mean for them.

"It's going to make our mission to bring others to Jeshu very difficult," Rhett said. "But then again, Jeshu never promised easy."

By early evening, they were all in agreement and had preliminary plans on how to continue to be effective as followers of Jeshu and yet remain undetected by the newly forged KDF.

Later that night, when everyone except Rhett and Brae had left *Arcton Hold*, Rhett insisted on preparing a meal for her while she reclined on a sofa in the main hall. Although she had refused at first to be pampered, the rush of the day had taken a greater toll on her than she realized, and she acquiesced. The next thing she knew, Rhett was gently stroking her cheek, trying to wake her up to eat.

"Would you rather sleep?" Rhett asked. "The food will keep."

"No...no, I'm sorry. I just dozed off for a minute. I'm starved."

The delightful smell of roasted meat with sautéed spices and herbs was intoxicating, causing her stomach to rumble in anticipation. Having lived with Rhett while raising Jeshu, Brae knew that Rhett could cook quite well, but she hadn't yet had the pleasure of experiencing his full culinary prowess. Rhett pulled out her chair to seat her as she took in the pleasing sight and aroma of the meal. She was duly impressed.

Once she finished her last bite, she leaned back in her chair with a wide grin on her face.

"Well, Mr. Stryker, I had no idea you could prepare a meal that delicious."

"I think you're just extra hungry after your excursion into the Ruah," Rhett offered with a crooked grin. "Hunger is an amateur cook's best friend."

Brae chuckled but became still as she considered Rhett's searching gaze. She waited for a question, but none came. Finally, she tilted her head, narrowing her eyes.

"What is it, Rhett?" Brae asked. "Ever since our communing, you've been different."

Rhett continued to stare at Brae for a moment longer as he prepared his response. "What you did in the Ruah was extraordinary, Brae. I'm not sure how to process what I saw."

"But all of us did some pretty remarkable fighting in that battle," Brae replied.

"Perhaps...but not like you." Rhett looked almost troubled as he readied an additional response. "I think Major Ki was right. There's something unique in the Starlore bloodline. Sovereign Ell Yon seems to have placed his special favor on you."

"You seem troubled by that," Brae said, becoming a bit concerned with Rhett's reaction.

"To be honest...I am."

If Rhett was nothing else, he was honest. Brae couldn't help the rising ire within her. *Was Rhett jealous?* she wondered. She shook her head at the thought of how this would damage their relationship and possible future together. Up until now, Rhett's flying, combat, and leadership skills were at such a level that he had naturally led the way. She didn't like the feelings stirring within her as she considered his response. She decided to address it straight up.

"I'm confused, Rhett. Why are you troubled by such a thing?" Brae asked, squinting slightly to emphasize her concern.

Rhett stood up and circled around the table to come to Brae. He pulled up a chair so he could sit face to face, gazing into her eyes. He gently took her hand in his.

"It isn't Ell Yon's favor on you that troubles me. In my limited understanding of his ways, when he favors one in such a dramatic way, he also calls that one to action that transcends our understanding or even our courage." Rhett became still and sober. "Often such a calling ends in tragedy, at least from our simple perspective. It burdens me to consider such an end for you. I love you too much to bear such thoughts with indifference."

Brae's false judgment of Rhett crumbled in a moment as she considered his heart. She stood up, holding her hands out to him. When he stood, she wrapped her arms around him, clinging to him as if her future happiness depended on it.

"I love you too, Rhett...with all my heart. And although what you say may be true, can you imagine shrinking back from the call Ell Yon has placed on both of us...after what we've seen?"

Rhett shook his head. "No, but the truth is that you scare me...you always have, and even more so now."

Brae leaned back to look at Rhett's face. "How's that?"

"You have the moxie to charge into any fight that's noble, even if it's dangerous and the odds are against you.

These new skills of yours in the Ruah are only going to make that worse." Rhett stroked her cheek with his thumb. "How am I going to keep you safe?"

Brae melted at the touch of his hand. "When we weren't friends, my father actually tried to help me see what a sterling guy you were."

"Really?" Rhett's eyebrows lifted.

"Yes, but I wouldn't have it," she said with a sheepish smile. "He told me that in spite of your not fully believing everything about Jeshu, you never left us...your loyalty was unique and admirable."

"Well, I didn't give you much to like about me. From the first day I met you, I didn't like you—until I loved you," Rhett said with a smile.

"And what was it that caused you to fall in love with me?" Brae asked. "I have a feeling it wasn't my witty charm."

"No," Rhett replied. "Actually, it was seeing how you dealt with the intense pain of losing your father. That's when I saw what a beautiful soul you had."

Brae had never imagined that such deep pain could also bring such purpose and blessing. She remembered an oracle's words regarding such a promise from Ell Yon. She searched Rhett's eyes, but his gaze was distant, and he seemed lost in thought. He then looked at Brae with a glow in his eyes.

"So...if your father thought I was a pretty decent guy, do you think he would approve if I were to ask for you to be bonded to me?"

Brae's heart began to race as she searched Rhett's eyes for any subtle measure of insincerity.

"I would imagine he would approve of such a thing," she said slowly...cautiously.

"Brae Starlore, will you be bonded to me?"

Brae tilted her head ever so slightly. "Are you sure you can handle a girl like me?"

Rhett's lips formed a broad grin. "No...no, I'm not, but I'd sure like to try."

Brae couldn't help the silly grin that spread across her face. "Yes, Rhett Stryker, I will be bonded to you."

Rhett looked as happy as Brae had ever seen him. "Do you think you can handle a guy like me?" he asked.

Brae chuckled then leaned in to his chest as he wrapped his arms completely around her. Her heart glowed in his loving embrace. Despite what might come because of Kylos's evil edict, for this brief slice of time, everything seemed right in the galaxy.

Ever since the moment when Brae had broken down after the tragedy at the Magnifical Festival and clung on to Rhett like her life depended on him, deep down Rhett knew his destiny would be bound to hers. That it would culminate in a bonded relationship with her was a secret his heart knew but only revealed slowly to his mind over the span of two years. Even though Rhett could make instant life and death decisions in a space fighter, the final decision to ask Brae to be bonded to him was one that had taken months to arrive at.

The mind and the heart can often be on different paths, but once they align, there is no outcome that will ever truly satisfy the soul but the targeted destiny. Once Rhett had decided Brae was the one, he discovered an apprehension when considering if being bonded to him was what Brae truly wanted. Would she say "Yes"? The intensity of their encounter in the Ruah had in some fashion motivated and therefore accelerated his proposal. The smile on her face when he asked her would be an image he would treasure forever. There was now a joy and a newfound confidence he didn't realize he had been missing.

After significant discussion, Rhett and Brae decided to seek out Codemus and ask him to perform their bonding ceremony. This time Codemus's wife, Voletta, was with him. She was wearing a Protector and a warm smile as they greeted Rhett and Brae into their home. After pleasantries were exchanged, Rhett and Brae sat across from the older couple. Rhett reached for Brae's hand, perhaps looking for final confirmation that she truly wanted this. She squeezed his hand, and it was all he needed.

"Sir," Rhett began. "Brae and I would be honored if you would consider performing the bonding ceremony for us."

Codemus sat up straight, a look of bewilderment on his face.

"But I've renounced my position as a Keeper and don't have the official credentials to perform the ceremony," Codemus argued.

"Knowing what you know now about Jeshu being the true Son of Ell Yon and having been accepted as a Navi with your own Protector, can you imagine having any higher credentials to perform this ceremony under the eyes of Sovereign Ell Yon?" Brae asked.

Codemus closed his eyes and nodded as if being reminded of a fundamental truth he should never forget. When he opened his eyes, he smiled. "The ways of Jeshu are so new. I must shed the old and fully embrace the new. I would be honored to perform your bonding ceremony. When would you like this to occur?"

"We want this to be a quiet and small ceremony and as soon as possible," Brae said as she placed her other hand on top of Rhett's. "Would tomorrow be okay?"

Codemus's eyes opened wide, followed by a broad smile. "Certainly. And the location?"

Rhett realized that in all their discussion regarding who would or could officiate the ceremony, they hadn't discussed where it would occur. Brae turned toward

Rhett. There was a sparkle in her eyes that caused his heart to skip a beat. The delight he saw in that gaze was supremely satisfying.

"I've been thinking, Rhett. There's a special place that has great meaning to me."

"Of course, Brae. Anyplace you want," Rhett said.

"We've been there. It's where Jeshu took us to commune the night he was taken by Kylos—the Navi's Hall of Meditation."

Rhett was a bit perplexed by Brae's suggestion. That place held a painful memory for both of them. Brae seemed to understand that an explanation was needed.

"Very few people know that the Navi's Hall of Meditation was built by my father to protect my mother when she was experiencing the spacetime anomaly that transported her centuries into the future. When she reappeared hundreds of years later, Daeson traveled through time to find her. His love for her was literally timeless." Brae paused. "I think ours will be too, regardless of the pain we may endure at the hand of Kylos."

Rhett offered Brae a gentle smile. "I think it's perfect."

The next day, Rhett and Brae led a small entourage of their closest friends in a couple of speeders up the Serula Valley to the ancient place of forgotten memories, its marble floor and columns cracked and shattered. It held the ambiance of a once-significant-but-now-abandoned structure. Bridger, Kase, Shayde, and Cilla all agreed to stand as witnesses for Rhett and Brae. Included in this exclusive band of friends was Brae's mechanical companion, Rivet. Codemus stood in his ceremonial robe and stole as he began to position each of the attendants. Before the ceremony began, Rivet came to Rhett and Brae.

"My lady, you may not know this, but many centuries ago, I stood as a witness for the bonding ceremony of your mother and your father, just as I am for you today.

Although the ceremony of bonding a male and female human perplexes me, I have come to appreciate how powerful such a relationship can be in forging the futures of each of you. I am honored to be here. My duty to serve and protect you both is as indelible as the bond between you will be."

Rivet then bowed his head. Rhett was stunned by the eloquence of the android's speech and also his depth of understanding, even if he was limited by the lack of his own emotions. He glanced toward Brae and could see that she was deeply moved. She reached for Rivet and hugged him. Rivet gently returned the hug. When Brae released him, the bot stepped back and away to allow Codemus to begin. Rivet's opening remarks had set a perfect tone for the beauty of the bonding ceremony about to take place.

Rhett's com band quietly vibrated to alert him to an incoming message. One quick glance told him it was from his old friend, Major Kamp. It would have to wait a few minutes.

Codemus began by reading a blessing from the ancient Raylean oracle, Darnullay. The reading was typical of Raylean writings, holding a poetic charm that was both forlorn and hopeful at the same time.

"May the light of Ell Yon shine upon you, guiding your hearts and souls as you embark on this sacred journey together. May your bonding be blessed with the strength and wisdom of the ages, and may your love grow ever deeper with each passing day.

"As you stand before the stars and the heavens, know that Ell Yon watches over you, bestowing upon you the gifts of joy, peace, and eternal love. May your lives be filled with the harmony and grace that only the Sovereign can provide.

"In times of trial, may you find solace in each other's arms, and in moments of joy, may your hearts soar together as one. Let the bond you share be a testament to the power of love and the Immortal blessing of Sovereign Ell Yon.

"May your days be long and your nights filled with the warmth of each other's embrace. And may you always walk in the light of Ell Yon, forever united in love and purpose."

After Codemus finished reading the blessing, he fixed his gaze on Brae and Rhett.

"This covenant bond between you, Rhett Stryker, and you, Brae Starlore, is unbreakable and is witnessed here in our presence and by the watchful eyes of Sovereign Ell Yon. It is an indelible bond, not broken by tragedy or prosperity...by man or beast...by space or time. Do you make this covenant freely and with full understanding of this bond?"

"We do," Rhett and Brae spoke in unison.

Codemus took the ceremonial stole, embroidered with the mark of Ell Yon, from around his neck and held it before Rhett and Brae. Brae set the back of her hand on top of the stole, and Rhett rested his hand on top of hers, palm to palm. Codemus then wrapped the stole around both of their hands and wrists. Rhett felt Brae interlock her fingers with his, and his heart skipped a beat.

"Then by the authority granted to me," Codemus paused. "As a Navi of the Son of Ell Yon and of the Raylean people, I hereby proclaim you bonded. May the Sovereign Ell Yon ever be with you and prosper you."

Codemus then slid the stole off their hands, completing the ceremony.

Rhett turned to Brae and she to him. He leaned down and kissed her.

"Ell Yon Yevareh!" Codemus proclaimed.

"Ell Yon Yevareh!" the witnesses voiced in unison...all but Rivet.

"Armed forces are approaching quickly!" Rivet interrupted while taking up a defensive position with his arms extended.

Rhett and everyone else except Codemus drew their blasters, but in just a few seconds, three Raylean Guard assault vehicles swooped in from above, surrounding them.

"This is the Keeper Defense Force. Drop your weapons, or you will be fired upon," came an amplified voice from one of the assault vehicles as ground troops descended and surrounded them. Their dark gray tactical uniforms were emblazoned with the letters "KDF" on their fronts and backs.

Rhett lowered his blaster then dropped it.

"Stand down," Rhett ordered. "There's no escaping this."

Slowly, everyone followed suit except for Rivet.

"Rivet, stand down," Brae commanded.

Rivet hesitated a moment longer, apparently finding it difficult to submit to his lack of ability to protect them.

"I'm sorry, my lady," Rivet said, lowering his arms and standing straight. "I should have deciphered their jamming signal as a significant threat."

The captain of the KDF assault team stepped forward.

"You are under arrest for crimes of treason against the Raylean government, the Raylean orders of the Keepers and the Builders, and the Morian High Command. Place your hands behind your heads and kneel."

"There are no treasonous acts here," Codemus rebutted. "We are only conducting a bonding—"

Codemus's appeal was cut short when a KDF operative stepped forward and struck him across his face with the butt of a plasma rifle.

Rhett immediately jumped to his aid, but a dozen more guards threw him to the ground, placing knees on his back and fetters about his wrists.

"Silence, traitors!" the captain barked. "By order of Preeminent Fasa Kylos, you will be detained until your trial. Secure them and load them up!"

Rhett turned his head up and out of the dirt to look up at Brae as the guards gruffly pushed her into a kneeling position, pulling her arms behind her. The angst in her countenance tore his heart.

"Sir, what about the android?" one of the KDF operatives asked, his rifle leveled at Rivet's head.

"Deactivate it," the captain ordered.

The operative drew a decoupling phaser from his belt and shot Rivet. The broad beam energy weapon hit Rivet, and he instantly collapsed into a pile of mangled mechanical arms and legs.

"Rivet!" Brae screamed.

The KDF operative grabbed Brae by her locked arms and the back of her neck, yanking her to a standing position.

"Quiet, traitor!" he shouted.

"Take it to the KDF scitechs and have them download its memory before wiping it," the captain added. "We may get names and locations out of the thing."

Two KDF operatives threw the jumbled form of Rivet into an anti-grav container and then guided it back to one of the assault vehicles as Rhett, Brae, and the rest of their bonding ceremony attendants were marshaled off to another.

It became very apparent that Kylos's Peace Preservation Edict had nothing to do with preserving peace and that the newly formed Keeper Defense Force had the authority and the audacity to use whatever brute force was necessary to carry the edict out. Kylos's edict was no longer just a threat...it was reality.

CHAPTER

9

Dark Horizon

Intergalactic Radio Alphabet – a set of words used to represent the letters of the alphabet. Each word is chosen for its distinct sound to help ensure clear communication in challenging conditions.

A: Alpha, **B**: Bravo, **C**: Charlie, **D**: Delta, **E**: Echo, **F**: Foxtrot, **G**: Golf, **H**: Hotel, **I**: India, **J**: Juliet, **K**: Hilo, **L**: Lima, **M**: Mike, **N**: November, **O**: Oscar, **P**: Papa, **Q**: Quebec, **R**: Romeo, **S**: Sierra, **T**: Tango, **U**: Uniform, **V**: Victor, **W**: Whiskey, **X**: H-Ray, **Y**: Yankee, **Z**: Zulu

Brae, Rhett and the rest of their bonding party were returned to Jalem under a heavily armed KDF operative escort. They were taken to the Jalem Sanctum and ushered down the anti-grav lift to the lowest section of the facility. This level was large and nearly empty except for six internment cells located on the far side of the massive chamber. Their footsteps echoed as the seven Navis and eight armed KDF operatives walked toward the cells. Brae wondered if they would be placed in different cells, but that was not the case. Each cell was large enough to hold up to twelve prisoners. Evidently, Kylos planned on filling the rest of the cells quickly. The KDF operatives placed them all in one cell, activated an impassable Stabil retention field which comprised the fourth wall of their cell, and left.

Brae was still stunned by the brutality of the KDF. Even the Morian commandos rarely used such measures on peaceful Raylean citizens. If it was any indication of what was to come, their prospects didn't look good.

"I didn't even know this level existed," Codemus said. "This is lower than the Builders section."

"By the look of it, I'd say these cells are a recent addition," Bridger added as he inspected the Stabil retention field generators just outside their cell.

Shayde was trying to attend to Codemus, but she had little in the way of medicine and bandages to help him. The left side of his face was bruised, swollen, and bleeding.

"How are you doing?" Rhett asked Codemus as he joined Shayde.

"I'll be fine." Codemus winced as Shayde tried to wipe away some of the blood. "I never imagined our sanctum orders would exact such violence on our own people, regardless of what they believed."

"It's because there are much darker forces at play here than just Fasa Kylos," Brae replied.

Codemus nodded. "I suppose you're right. I remember the day Jeshu laid that claim against the Keeper and Builder Orders. How could we have lost our way to such a degree that the Keepers and Builders now serve the enemy of Ell Yon...the very one they claim to serve. The irony is painful."

"Looks like the butt of that plasma rifle must have been even more painful," Shayde said, trying to be careful.

"Those thugs didn't even have an invitation to the ceremony," Kase said with a straight face.

Everyone looked at Kase for a second, then they all began to chuckle. Bridger put an arm across his younger brother's shoulder. "Sometimes you're just what everyone needs."

Rhett went to Brae.

"This isn't how I imagined our ceremony would go," Rhett said quietly, taking her hand in his. "Not a great way to start our bonded life together."

"No…not what I was hoping for either." Brae sighed. "What do you think is going to happen to us? Any chance they'll let us go with another warning like last time?"

The anti-grav lift suddenly opened across the chamber, and Kylos stepped out with four armed KDF operatives.

"I think we're about to find out," Rhett replied.

Kylos's approach was slow and deliberate. He stopped a few feet away, glaring at each of his prisoners in turn until at last his gaze landed on Codemus.

"Well, Codemus," Kylos began, his voice thick with condescension. "See what your traitorous deeds have won you? What an embarrassment you are to the Keeper Order." Kylos's indignant gaze lingered. He huffed, turning his attention to Brae and the other Navis.

"I see we have more than one traitor in the group," Kylos continued. "Rhett Stryker, former Raylean Guard pilot, now one of the premier followers of that dead heretic." Kylos slowly shook his head. "What a fool," he said with a frown. His eyes turned toward Brae.

"And alas, I have captured the aloof Brae Thornton, daughter of the false Navi, Elias Thornton—the man who won the fierce chagrin and eventual execution from Prefect Terrok." Kylos took a moment to sneer at the lot of them. "In accordance with the Peace Preservation Edict sanctioned by Subchancellor Pylok himself, you all will be quickly tried and sentenced tomorrow morning. If you are found guilty of sedition by continuing to pervert the good people of Rayl and propagating the heretical beliefs and practices of Jeshu Starlore, your sentence will be execution."

Kylos stopped to soak in the stunned and frightened faces of his prisoners. Brae watched the man who had caused her such suffering already as he appeared to revel in his power over her and the others. Anger rose in her heart, taking her to the brink of rage.

Be still, daughter of Ell Yon. Vengeance is mine.

The quiet voice was not her own, and she instantly found peace in the power of Sovereign Ell Yon.

Kylos tilted his head back so he could appear to look down on them. "Make no mistake...this is the end of your feeble rebel movement. Every last one of you will be eliminated, and there is no one to stop me!" Kylos turned and left.

Once the anti-grav lift door rotated closed and disappeared upward through the ceiling of this dungeon, Brae and all of her companions turned to face one another, sorrow etched in each face.

"He's right," Cilla said. "No one can stop him now that he has an edict approved by Pylok."

"Sovereign Ell Yon has not forgotten us," Brae quietly offered.

It was just enough encouragement to soften the hard lines of worry in their faces.

After a couple of hours of rest, Brae and Rhett checked on each of their friends. "I think we need to commune with Sovereign Ell Yon," Rhett suggested.

Brae smiled. "Yes...that's exactly what we need to do."

Within a few minutes, all seven Navis awakened in the Ruah, still kneeling. Brae glanced toward Codemus, seeing a look of utter astonishment on the older gentleman's face. Across the chamber, two large and formidable warriors were standing near the anti-grav lift. Something about them told Brae they did not belong to Sovereign Ell Yon.

"We're still prisoners in this cell," Shayde whispered as she looked toward the Stabil retention field.

"And we don't have any tactical suits or weapons in here," Rhett added.

"Yes, but here in the Ruah, our Protectors speak clearly to us, and we can see what we're up against," Brae quietly replied. "There's always a powerful influence from the dimension of the Ruah in our reality."

"Dracus is at work here," Bridger said, eyeing the two dark warriors across the chamber.

One of the warriors seemed to notice their arrival. He said something unintelligible to the other warrior then approached their cell. The seven Navis all slowly stood. Brae's heart began to race. *What could they do to us here behind the Stabil retention field?* she wondered.

As the massive warrior approached, a scowl filled his countenance, and he lifted his plasma rifle into a ready position. Strangely, as he came closer, all seven of the Protectors on the forearms of the Navis began to glow in the blue power of Ell Yon. It caused the warrior of Dracus to halt in his approach. He was clearly affected by such a display.

"You all die tomorrow, regardless of your pathetic Protectors," the warrior hissed. He turned and walked back to his accomplice.

Prepare yourselves.

The voice of the Protector was distinct in Brae's mind. She looked at her fellow Navis. She could instantly tell that they too had heard the Sovereign's voice. Suddenly, the anti-grav lift opened again, and the chamber filled with rapid bursts of plasma rifle fire. All of the Navis fell to the floor to avoid being hit by a random shot. The assault lasted only a few seconds, just long enough for a four-member Malakian extraction team to eliminate the two Torian warriors. Once they had verified the rest of the chamber was clear, they vigilantly approached Brae and her fellow Navis.

Brae and Rhett were the first to stand up.

"Major Ki!" Brae exclaimed.

The resolve in Major Ki's expression said everything.

"Sovereign Ell Yon dispatched us to get you out of here. Other Torian warriors are close, so we have to move quickly."

Ki nodded to the Stabil retention field generator. One of her warriors blasted it with one shot, and the field collapsed.

"Return to your bodies so we can vacate the premises," Ki ordered. "Laem, you and I will interphase into their realm and operate the cloaking shields. Trace and Welcott, cover us in the Ruah until we can rejoin the rest of our squad on the main level. Once we clear the sanctum outer court gate, a transport will clear us out, and the Navis will be on their own."

"Copy, major," Trace replied.

Ki looked at Brae and her companions. "Now."

Brae, Rhett, Bridger, Kase, Shayde, Cilla, and Codemus all returned to their bodies and exited the Ruah. When they had recovered, Major Ki and the warrior named Laem were standing with them.

"Let's move," Ki said, directing them toward the lift. "Once we make ground level, you all need to stay close and stay quiet. Our cloaking shields have a limited range and will reduce sound but not completely eliminate it. Understood?"

All the Navis nodded.

Ki and Laem escorted them to the anti-grav lift. Within a few seconds the lift was slowing as it approached ground level. Major Ki and her warrior each drew a saucer-shaped device from their tactical belts that slipped over their hand like a small shield. Ki positioned herself on the right side of the group while Laem took the left side.

"We move quickly and quietly," Ki said, activating her cloaking shield. Laem followed suit.

From Brae's limited perspective, a silent and seamless translucent energy cocoon seemed to be created by the two cloaking shield devices on their left and right sides. Outside the shield cocoon, a bystander would see right through the shielded Navis and their rescuers as if they weren't there. Brae imagined they were surrounded by another six warriors in the Ruah...perhaps engaged in a firefight to enable their escape. She wished she could join them, but such a notion was unreasonable in this situation.

The anti-grav lift door opened and they quickly exited. Off to their right, two KDF operatives were standing guard. The opening of the anti-grav lift door caused a bit of stir when no one appeared to exit. One of the guards came to investigate, but by the time he arrived, Major Ki and her cloaked Navis were well clear. Since it was now far into the night, very few people were in the sanctum. An occasional Keeper assistant and a few KDF operatives stationed at the entrances were all that were present. Just as Major Ki and the rest of the group were about to exit the main door of the sanctum, three KDF operatives came from around the palisade. They walked through the main door and straight toward the cloaked Navis. Major Ki motioned for the Navis to all move to the left to avoid detection, but they would never all make it out of range in time. Brae watched as Major Ki drew a Talon in a short sword configuration. The operatives were now just a few steps away and on a collision course with the cloaked group.

Brae felt someone grab her arm. She turned.

"What I have seen...thank you!" Codemus whispered. The Keeper turned Navi then ran out of the cloaking shield and away from Brae and the rest of the group.

The sudden appearance of Codemus stunned the three operatives so completely that they were slow to react.

"Keep moving!" Major Ki urged, but Brae was fully intent on helping Codemus.

"Don't make his sacrifice count for nothing," Ki reprimanded.

Brae looked to Rhett for support, but he nodded toward the rest of the group, indicating that anything they did now would jeopardize everyone else. Brae's heart broke as she saw the three operatives begin pursuing Codemus. The distraction gave Major Ki and Warrior Laem enough time to maneuver the group away and out through the sanctum entrance. Outside, Ki accelerated their pace across the sanctum courtyard to the outer gate. Once they were clear, Major Ki and her warrior dropped their cloaking shields and disappeared without another word.

Brae looked back at the sanctum where she could hear the faint sounds of a commotion inside.

"Come on, Brae," Rhett urged. "Codemus knew exactly what he was doing, and Major Ki was right—let's not waste his sacrifice."

Begrudgingly, Brae allowed Rhett to guide her toward a waiting eight-passenger speeder. All six of the Navis took their seats as a familiar face powered up the craft.

"It's good to see you, Major Kamp," Rhett said as the speeder lifted up and away.

"Always seems to be during some state of emergency," Kamp replied with a crooked grin. "I was told there were seven of you."

Brae looked toward Rhett. He just shook his head slightly. It told Major Kamp everything. Brae stared out the window of the speeder, the buildings swishing by in a line of blurred structures. There was every sense that despite their high and lofty call to save the galaxy, the cost would be great, and the sacrifice of Codemus was just the beginning.

Major Kamp delivered the escaped Navis to a regional spaceport where the *Aviel* was waiting for them. Rhett piloted the *Aviel* back to *Arcton Hold* where the other five Navis were communing together to plead with Ell Yon for some miracle rescue of their fellow Jeshuans. When the rescued Navis stepped out of the *Aviel*, Jaym, Mason, Quill, Salara and Lubin eagerly greeted them. Brae noticed that Quill's first concern was for Cilla.

"We heard that Kylos had captured all of you. How in the name of Ell Yon did you escape?" Jaym asked.

"While we were communing, a Malakian warrior extraction team rescued us," Rhett replied. "But we don't have time to share details. Rivet was captured, and they are extracting his memory as we speak. He was here, so it's just a matter of time before they discover our location. We need to evacuate *Arcton Hold* immediately."

"Where do we go?" Salara asked.

"I know a place," Jaym offered. "A man who recently joined us is wealthy and has a lodge in the Cresswood Mountains. He offered it in case of emergency. I think this qualifies."

"Good, everyone memorize the coordinates. Don't leave any coordinate history in any ship in case the KDF somehow accesses them," Rhett ordered. "We need to be launching in 40 minutes."

In less than 30 minutes, the *Aviel* and eight *Spacehawks* were lifting off to leave *Arcton Hold*, never to return.

Brae selected a private channel to talk to Rhett as *Arcton Hold* disappeared in the clouds below them. She clicked her mic on. "I'm sorry, Rhett. I thought this might be our home together."

"I knew the risk. I just didn't think it would come so soon," Rhett replied. "I don't have much of a bonding present to offer you now."

"I don't need one," Brae replied. "I just need you." She cringed. *That was corny*, she thought, even though the words captured her deepest emotion.

"Thanks and ditto," Rhett replied.

Two hours later, the eleven Navis set down their nine craft wherever they could find an opening large enough. Although the lodge was much more than Brae had expected, it certainly wasn't designed to hangar nine spacecraft. Three *Spacehawks* had to land over one-half mile away.

Once they had recovered and entered the lodge, it became apparent that Jaym's associate was wealthy indeed. There was ample room for all of them with a massive great room and dining hall that could seat sixteen people. A meal was quickly prepared, and the eleven Navis gathered in the dining hall around the large banquet table where there was a lengthy retelling of the events that had unfolded. After eating some of the delicious food and drink that had been prepared, Brae felt exhausted. And yet there was too much to discuss and consider before she could rest. She felt guilty for wishing away all these troubles so that she and Rhett could enjoy their new life together. She felt cheated, yet others were already suffering or would soon suffer much more than a missed celebration. Although there was profound gratitude for the intervention of Ell Yon on behalf of the Navis, there was also a foreboding spirit that settled on the group as they considered the future.

"Even the Morian commandos aren't as brutal as Kylos's KDF operatives," Shayde said with a distant stare. Brae was certain she was thinking of Codemus's bloodied face.

"It's true," Kase added. "And it seems that their methods are sanctioned by Pylok, so we have no avenue for appeal."

"We have to warn all new Jeshuans immediately," Quill said.

"Yes," Bridger agreed. "Our efforts will have to shift from the sanctums and go underground."

"Do we fight back?" Lubin asked the question everyone was thinking. "We are warriors by our own right—trained to fight by Jeshu himself."

Many of them turned to Brae for a response. Her powerful presence as a warrior in the Ruah was well known. Brae hesitated, but she knew the answer to Lubin's question.

"Jeshu said that our fight is not with Kylos or even the Morians."

Her blunt answer was hard for all to hear, but there were no arguments.

"Then what does this really mean for us...for all Jeshuans?" Mazon asked. "People living every minute of every day looking over their shoulders—waiting for Kylos to arrest and execute them? This is what we offer?"

The silence in the room was telltale. Brae wanted to respond and rally them with some heroic speech, but it wasn't in her. Her mind turned to Codemus, knowing his execution was imminent. She thought of Rivet lying in a heap on the shattered marble floor of the Navi's Hall of Meditation. Despite all her effort to restore the beloved bot, Kylos had destroyed him in a moment. Brae tried to push through this collapsing wall of oppression but could not muster up a way to do it. It was Jaym who spoke up, his steadfast perspective offering encouragement to everyone.

"Let us all remember that Dracus through Kylos offers fear, but Jeshu offers hope and a future to *all* Rayleans. As Kylos tightens his grip, the unquenchable truth of Jeshu will slip through his fingers. Jalem is Kylos's focal point right now because that's where we are. We must take our mission to every city and homestead on the planet before Kylos can stop us."

Rhett stood up from the table where they were all seated. "Jaym is absolutely right. Kylos has limited resources. We can gather thousands of Jeshuans to our cause in an hour...as we have already seen. It will take

Kylos weeks to prepare KDF forces for other cities like he's done here in Jalem. We have the advantage!" Rhett said, leaning forward to offer strength through his determined gaze.

Brae looked up at Rhett with a warmth in her heart that spread throughout her entire being. When she and Rhett were raising young Jeshu, she would have never imagined Rhett would arrive at such faith in the Sovereign Ell Yon. *I chose well,* she thought, a gentle smile settling on her lips.

Within just a few moments, the dark and oppressive cloud lifted from their hearts, and they all became hopeful and energized to press on. They agreed to spend the next few days planning and strategizing just how they would accomplish this new global mission.

When all retired, Brae was grateful she didn't have to leave Rhett's side. With such a monumental mission before them, there was a satisfaction in her soul that reassured her she could endure, now that they would forever have each other as bonded mates.

CHAPTER

10

Death's Door

Creed (the statement) – a statement of profession that concisely defines the beliefs of all who follow Jeshu, Son of Ell Yon.

Creed (the organization) – the global federation of all people who proclaim to believe in and follow the ways of Jeshu, Son of Ell Yon.

Creed haven – the physical location or building that houses the organization of the Creed.

Jeshuan – a follower of the ways of Jeshu, the Merchant and Son of Ell Yon.

Navi – a devoted follower of Sovereign Ell Yon, often used interchangeably with Jeshuan. Typically, a Navi is a Jeshuan who is in leadership at a Creed haven.

In the weeks and months that followed the rescue of the Navis at the Hall of Meditation, the mission to take the hope of Jeshu to the rest of the planet became a reality. The eleven Navis of Jeshu chose an honorable and committed Jeshuan named Hiam to replace Dahj. Hiam subsequently teamed up with Jaym. Six teams of two Navi each launched out from the Cresswood Lodge to bring the cause of Jeshu to the entire planet. And although their efforts to thwart Kylos's plan to crush the spread of

Jeshu's message were successful, that success came at great cost. Kylos grew more ruthless in his pursuit and persecution of anyone claiming to follow Jeshu. KDF operatives were the hunter-killers of Jeshuans everywhere, initiating what Kylos called "instant judgment protocol" and justifying the immediate execution of punishment by twisting the intent of the Peace Preservation Edict authorized by Morian Subchancellor Pylok. With all his plans falling into place, the Preeminent Keeper was anticipating the eradication of the Jeshuan heretics. However, he became concerned when Subchancellor Pylok called him to his palace at Skyburough.

Kylos entered Pylok's Hall of Judgment with great apprehension. *Have I gone too far in the implementation of the Peace Preservation Edict?* he wondered. His footsteps echoed as he approached. Pylok's judgment seat slowly rotated away toward the massive circular window that looked out over Jalem until he was facing Kylos directly.

"Preeminent Pylok," Kylos said a little too joyfully. "I am glad to see you are well."

Pylok smirked. "So, Kylos, I see you have wasted no time in executing the edict you enticed me to sign."

"I try to be efficient in all of my efforts, especially those that are sanctioned by the Morian Empire and its governors," Kylos said with a fake smile.

"I'm sure," Pylok replied. "So how go your efforts to eradicate Rayl of the Jeshuans? I hear it's proving to be a bit more daunting than you imagined."

Kylos eased slightly as he sensed Pylok's shift from his stiff, formal tone to one somewhat more casual.

"They have proven to be resourceful, but my KDF operatives are rooting them out bit by bit," Kylos answered.

Pylok didn't offer his usual contemptuous response. "I also hear that you have enlisted some of the new androids the tech companies are producing. Are they proving useful?"

The question seemed genuine, and Kylos wasn't sure how to manage his response.

"Actually, yes, they are." He decided to extend his answer to test this new familiar tone Pylok was offering. "We captured one of the Jeshuan bots. Extracting its memory proved very useful. I had our scitechs reprogram it since its construct was quite advanced, and it has proven to be extremely helpful. It has prompted me to expand the use of other bots in our cause."

Kylos waited, wondering if he had ventured too far. Pylok seemed lost in thought.

"I won't have one around here. They make me nervous," Pylok confessed. "You never know when some rogue coder will decide to ignore all the anti-AI code rules and we find ourselves back in the fight for humanity. Just be sure the code in your bots at least abides by the first rule of human non-violence, or the Morian Empire will shut you down and lock you away forever."

"Of course, Subchancellor," Kylos said with a slight bow. "Their primary duty is to analyze data and provide security until judgment is given."

That last sentence seemed to pique Pylok's interest. He leaned forward, eyeing Kylos carefully.

"Don't think I don't know the liberties you've taken regarding the authority of the edict, Kylos." Pylok's expression lightened. "However, I understand that our goal is mutual. Just be careful. Morian law dictates due process for every person, regardless of their crime. From what I'm hearing, your 'due process' is rather instantaneous."

Kylos squirmed a bit, knowing exactly what Pylok was referring to. Kylos's operatives had been implementing his instant judgment protocol more frequently than he had anticipated. He was about to respond when Pylok continued.

"Let me just say that how you execute your interpretation of the edict is your business. But if Morian commandos see a clear violation of Morian law, they will respond, and you will be held accountable." Pylok hesitated. "We don't want this reflecting badly on either of us. Am I clear, Kylos?"

Kylos smiled. "Perfectly."

Pylok seemed satisfied.

"Is there anything else, Subchancellor?" Kylos asked.

"Yes." Pylok frowned. "My commandos have started to have more frequent encounters with a group of Rayleans that call themselves Partisans. Unlike your Jeshuans, these people are violent and well-armed. What is your association with them?"

"Subchancellor, I and my Keeper and Builder Orders have no association with that group of radicals whatsoever—you can be assured of that!" Kylos said emphatically.

Pylok lifted his chin slightly. "And you would give me any information regarding their organization?"

"Without hesitation, Subchancellor. The Partisans' anti-Morian stance is reprehensible. My people understand and accept the mutual benefit of having the Morian Empire manage the affairs of Rayl."

Pylok's frown remained. "Very well, Kylos. You are dismissed."

Kylos exited Pylok's Hall of Judgment, his obsession to rid the planet of all Jeshuans bolstered by this meeting. He was more than willing to oblige the Morian Empire in its efforts to subjugate the Raylean people if it won him the eradication of the Jeshuans. The trade-off was well worth it. They could deal with the Morian Empire later. Besides this, Kylos did enjoy the position of power he had been granted by Pylok. Prefect Terrok, the Morian Empire's puppet Raylean governor, had become little more than a side note in the political landscape of Rayl. Terrok seemed more than happy to acquiesce political influence to Kylos as long as his palace remained well equipped with the pleasures of Deitum Prime and other indulgences Terrok was accustomed to.

As Kylos considered the warning from Pylok regarding his operatives' adherence to Morian law, he realized that the implementation of his instant judgment protocol needed to be handled in a stealthier manner by his KDF operatives. He made a stop at the research division of the Raylean forcetech facility.

Forcetech Master Olickgard greeted him. "Preeminent Keeper Kylos...this is a rare occasion. To what do we owe the pleasure?"

"It's my understanding that you have variants of the archaic Talon that I might be interested in," Kylos replied.

Olickgard's look of shock transformed into one of interest. "Does this have to do with the KDF operatives I keep hearing about?"

Kylos scrutinized Olickgard, wondering if the man might be sympathetic to the Jeshuans. "Yes. Let's just say I need a quiet method of subduing the rebels. And they never fight back, so a Talon-style weapon might solve everything."

Olickgard smiled, which pleased Kylos. "Come with me," the forcetech master said.

Kylos followed Olickgard through multiple chambers and levels until they reached an armory of ancient weapons. The smile on Olickgard's face was akin to a father bragging about his children.

"This is my favorite chamber in the entire facility," Olickgard said, placing his hand on the bio scan reader.

The door opened just as ribbon lights flashed on, illuminating hundreds of weapons on display. Although Kylos wasn't typically a fan of such miltech hardware, the artifacts dazzled his eyes with grisly splendor. Olickgard escorted Kylos down an aisle for a few feet until they came to a display of multiple variants of the Talon.

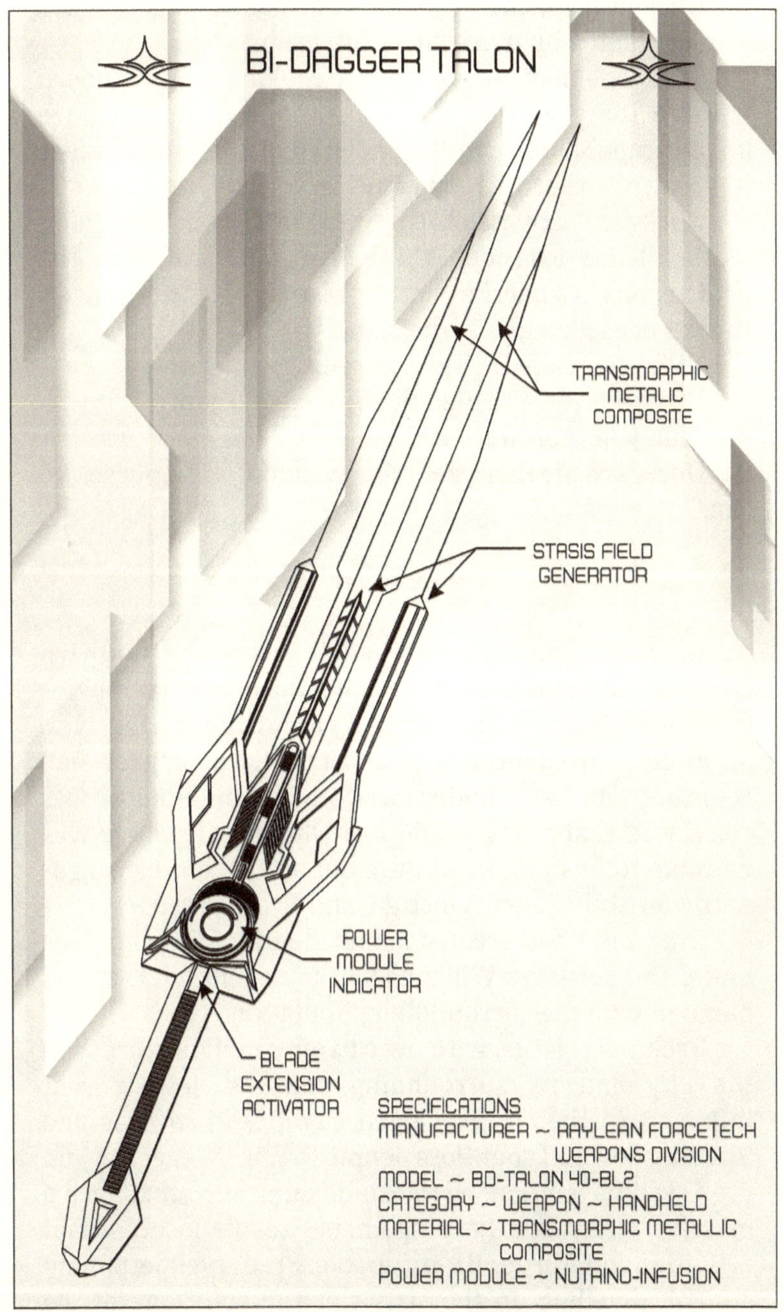
BI-DAGGER TALON
TRANSMORPHIC METALIC COMPOSITE
STASIS FIELD GENERATOR
POWER MODULE INDICATOR
BLADE EXTENSION ACTIVATOR
SPECIFICATIONS
MANUFACTURER ~ RAYLEAN FORCETECH WEAPONS DIVISION
MODEL ~ BD-TALON 40-BL2
CATEGORY ~ WEAPON ~ HANDHELD
MATERIAL ~ TRANSMORPHIC METALLIC COMPOSITE
POWER MODULE ~ NUTRINO-INFUSION

Olickgard reached for one that had a single center grip bracketed by two sharp protrusions.

"This one may be what you're looking for. In modern warfare there is little use for it since it doesn't have blaster capabilities, but the sheer sight of it invokes fear in a way no other weapon can."

Olickgard activated the power button, and two Talon stasis blades extended three feet outward from the protrusions in a parallel sizzling display of cutting power. Kylos's eyes gleamed at the sight.

"What's it called?" Kylos asked.

"I believe it was called the Bi-dagger Talon."

"Can you reproduce it?"

Olickgard deenergized the weapon. "Of course we can."

Brae and Rhett had agreed to make the southern continent of Korsika their mission. One of the major cities there was Brohn, where Rhett's parents lived. However, at Rhett's insistence, Wescott and Kara Stryker had relocated to an undisclosed location. Rhett was convinced that Kylos would use whatever leverage was possible to flush him and Brae out after their exchanges with him at the Jalem Sanctum, and Brae agreed.

Brae and Rhett created a new identity for themselves under the surname Williams so they could interact and blend in with the surrounding population.

Brohn was large, with over twenty million citizens in the city and its surrounding suburbs. Jeshu's past influence in the city had been significant, so Brae and Rhett discovered countless people that were eager to join the Creed haven they were establishing at Brohn. Such a massive city made keeping their Creed's location and activities underground very doable. Brae and Rhett found a small dwelling on the sixty-third floor of one of the massive residential sky towers. Although both of them preferred the open country life, this arrangement allowed for anonymity and proximity to the masses. The location of the Brohn Creed haven was literally underground. A new Jeshuan to the Creed owned a medtech supply company with a basement that housed its excess supplies. Half of the lower floor was segmented by a concrete wall and was a perfect location for clandestine Creed meetings for the Brohn Jeshuans.

Brae and Rhett had arranged secure communication channels with each of the other Navis' Creed havens so aid could be rendered whenever possible. Despite the severe persecution and oppression experienced at the hands of Kylos and his KDF operatives, the number of Jeshuans increased exponentially, just as Jaym had predicted. Jeshuans on each of the different continents, in numerous regions and cities of Rayl, began to organize themselves, adapting to varied customs and cultures as necessary, but the universal bond between them all was the Creed Jeshu had given the original Navis.

One development that took most Jeshuans in the global Creed by surprise was that several off-worlders came to believe in Jeshu and received the honor of a Protector from Sovereign Ell Yon and the purging of Deitum Prime because of it. Intense discussions arose among Raylean Jeshuans everywhere. In the near future, a council of the twelve original Navis had planned to convene at the lodge in the Cresswood Mountains to discuss the implications and a potential path forward.

Through all the changes, Brae's love for Rhett deepened with each passing day as they labored together for a cause that transcended any mission in the history of humanity. Together they rejoiced for each new Jeshuan that joined the Creed and mourned the lives that were lost for the same cause.

Brae did everything within reason to find out what had happened to Rivet, but her investigation came up empty. Rumors swirled that Kylos had been seen with an android that looked much like Rivet. However, over the past few years, robotic tech companies had begun producing more and more of the humanoid androids, apparently disregarding many of the anti-AI code rules. Therefore, Brae had convinced herself that Rivet had been destroyed rather than re-programmed as an accomplice to Kylos and the KDF.

Brae and Rhett, along with many other courageous Jeshuans, frequently entered the Ruah to join in battle with the mighty Malakian warriors against Dracus and the Torians. Brae's combat prowess became legendary among her fellow Jeshuans, as well as among the Malakian warriors. The efforts of Jeshuan warriors in the Ruah altered the outcome of many crucial battles.

One evening Brae and Rhett were taking a walk in one of Brohn's central city gardens, one place they could feel like they weren't being suffocated by glass and concrete. Rhett's com band alerted him to an encrypted incoming message. It was Major Kamp. Brae and Rhett found a secluded area of the garden, deep beneath the covering of some large trees.

"Major, it's good to see you," Rhett began, but it was clear Kamp had no time for pleasantries.

"A couple of fellow Raylean Guard pilots were recruited into Kylos's Keeper Defense Force," Kamp said. "I now have access to some intelligence within the KDF. When I call, you need to know that my information is extremely time sensitive."

"We understand, Major. What do you have?" Rhett asked.

Major Kamp's holo image looked left and right before revealing the information. "The Creed haven at Joppik has been identified by the KDF. They are less than one hour from raiding it."

"There are two havens there," Brae said. "Which one?"

"I don't know," Kamp said. "You'd better warn them both."

Major Kamp's holo image immediately disappeared.

Brae looked at Rhett. "That's Quill and Cilla. I'll take the eastern haven. You take the western," Brae said before walking a few feet away so their warning messages wouldn't interfere with each other.

Once the calls were made, Brae paced anxiously waiting for word. They both appealed to Sovereign Ell Yon through their Protectors for the safety of both havens in Joppik. Forty-five minutes later, Brae received a two-word message from Cilla— "Havens clear."

Brae breathed a sigh of relief.

"Thanks to Ell Yon for Major Kamp's asset," Brae said, wrapping her arms around Rhett. "Whoever he or she is, they just saved many lives."

Rhett wrapped his arms around Brae, resting his cheek on her head. "Yes. Perhaps one day we can thank them."

As the Creed havens grew in number across the planet, so did the size of Kylos's KDF forces. And although the Creed havens and their Navis became more adept at avoiding detection, the warning calls from Major Kamp's asset proved to be critical in that regard.

Each major city on Rayl now had at least one Creed haven. Brae and Rhett had grown the Creed haven at Brohn to over 4200 Jeshuans. Multiple smaller meeting places existed throughout the city, but the location of the primary haven was still in the basement of the medtech supply facility and had become a critical center of operation for the entire city.

Late in the afternoon on a crisp fall day, Rhett made a supply run to a haven in a small city named Soverville, 180 miles to the northwest of Brohn. Too much cargo was involved for him to take his *Spacehawk,* so he rented a small six-person transport that was slower but tripled the amount of supplies he could carry. Brae and three fellow Navis by the names of Trace, Keirsa, and Frall were attempting to set up another haven location on the southeastern edge of Brohn.

"The location we've identified is now in the process of being purchased by a transport company," Trace reported. "This is the third location we've lost in that region of the city."

"There's more going on here than just some commerce decision," Brae responded. "It's time we commune and get a better read on what's happening."

Trace, Keirsa, and Frall all agreed. They decided the safest place to do so was back at the main Creed haven, where a room was dedicated to communing. Within the hour, all four had entered the Ruah and had traveled some distance to where they had hoped to establish their next Creed haven. Once they arrived, they discovered that the Torians were certainly the cause for the disruption of their plans. They joined forces with two Malakian squads in order to secure the fourth attempted location.

Brae, Trace, Keirsa, and Frall were assisting the first Malakian squad when a Torian assault vehicle descended nearly on top of them. The vehicle hovered fifty feet off the ground just long enough for eight warriors to jet out of the ramp, taking up strategic locations that boxed in Brae's team and the Malakians.

"We need air support at sector three delta," the Malakian squad leader radioed.

"Navi Bravo One, this is Navi Romeo One, do you copy?" Brae heard Rhett radio on a secure com channel. Within the Ruah, the Navi's designation was "Navi" followed by the Intergalactic Radio Alphabet corresponding to the first letter of the Navi's name and a numeric identifier. Brae's designation was "Navi Bravo One."

"Navi Bravo One here," Brae replied, wondering why Rhett was in the Ruah when he was supposed to be transporting supplies to Soverville.

"I have a critical alert for Brohn Creed Haven One. ETA of KDF forces is 20 minutes. What's your status?"

"Twenty minutes!" Brae exclaimed as she ducked behind the corner of a wall to avoid the rapid-fire plasma rounds coming from the assault vehicle that had relocated after its warrior drop. "We'll never get everything out in time."

"Copy that Navi Bravo One. Forget equipment and supplies. You need to exit the Ruah and get our people out of there!" Rhett replied, his voice ripe with tension.

The angle of fire from the assault vehicle was now making their current cover extremely hazardous.

"Navi Romeo One, we are pinned down by two squads of Torian warriors. Help is on the way, but we are too far out to make it in time. Can you assist?" Brae radioed back while returning fire with her fellow Navis.

"Brae...you have to stop communing and get out of there!" Rhett urged.

What do you think we're trying to do? Brae thought but didn't speak. Brae and her fellow Navis would be completely vulnerable to KDF operatives if they couldn't return to their bodies before the operatives arrived. When Brae didn't respond, Rhett radioed again.

"I'm returning to Creed Haven One. My ETA is fifteen minutes."

"Copy, see you there," Brae radioed—hoped.

The firefight with the Torians intensified, causing Brae to wonder if this was part of a Torian strategy to trap them while the raid in her realm was happening. She became angry with herself for not seeing the danger of taking on such a distant mission. She tried to quell rising angst so she could focus on finding a timely way back to the creed haven, but she feared greatly for the safety of her companions.

"Squad leader, we need to get back to the haven ASAP. A raid from KDF forces is imminent," Brae radioed.

"Copy Navi Bravo One. We've just received the same intel. Reinforcements are enroute. As soon as you see a break, go for it, and we'll cover you," the Malakian squad leader replied.

"Navis, be ready. On my signal," Brae radioed to Trace, Keirsa, and Frall.

They each nodded. Brae could tell they were overwhelmed and rattled, having never seen such intense battle in the Ruah like this before.

"Cover me," Brae said. "I'm taking out that assault vehicle."

Brae broke from her cover, firing her rapid-fire plasma rifle at one of the hovering Torian warriors. Trace, Keirsa, and Frall all unloaded on the assault vehicle and two other warriors as Brae jumped forty feet into the air, latching onto the side of the building across the street using the cohesion field generators on her feet and hands. She pivoted, narrowly deflecting a burst of plasma fire by using her Emuna Shield. She lifted her right hand in the direction of the assault vehicle just as it was repositioning to lock onto her location. Her neural connection synchronized with her Protector, and the power of Ell Yon unleashed an energy burst that ripped into the front quarter of the vehicle, causing it to collide with the closest building in a fiery explosion.

"Navis, move out now!" Brae ordered. "I'll cover you from up here."

As her team navigated back toward central Brohn, Brae leapt from building to building to provide cover from any hovering Torian warriors. From her perch, there was every indication that Torian forces were descending on them with the exclusive purpose of cutting them off from reaching their Creed haven. When the Navis were pinned down again and all seemed lost, two Malakian Starstreak fighters wreaked havoc on the encroaching Torian forces, blazing a way for Brae and her team to resume their retreat to the haven. Brae joined the team on the ground as they sprinted toward home—fourteen minutes since Rhett's warning transmission. Brae was leading them as they turned the last corner to the haven. What Brae saw terrified her. Two KDF vehicles were positioned outside the entrance to the medtech supply facility—they were too late.

"Brae!" Keirsa called out.

Brae turned about to see a look of abject horror on the face of her fellow Navi. She had stopped running and was holding her abdomen. Keirsa fell to her knees just as her Ruah body dissolved to dust and disappeared.

"No!" Brae screamed, but despite all her super abilities in the Ruah, she could not stop what was happening in her own realm.

The faces of Trace and Frall both turned ashen, then they too fell to their knees and dissolved away to dust. Brae knew death was upon her. From the same corner they had just turned, Rhett came running. But he could not see her for he was in the realm of humanity. He froze as he too beheld the KDF transports in front of the building. Brae wrapped her arms around him, her arms passing through his body.

"I'm sorry, my love," she whispered into his ear. Then it came—the searing, white-hot dual spear of death piercing through her abdomen. The pain was excruciating, as the world of the Ruah faded away.

Momentarily reentering the realm of humanity, Brae realized she was lying on the floor of the communing room looking up, her hands grasping the bloody wounds in her stomach.

Three KDF operatives were standing above them with energized Bi-dagger Talons. The bodies of Trace, Keirsa, and Frall were collapsed and motionless beside her.

"Morian commandos are enroute," one of the operatives announced, at the exact moment an android entered the room. "We need to exit now!"

The android came to Brae, kneeling down by her side. Brae felt consciousness slipping away as her blood spilled onto the floor. Brae looked into the hollow eyes of the android, but she knew who he was.

"Rivet!" Brae whispered. She lifted her bloody hand to touch the bot's face. "What have they done to you?" she asked, tears running down her cheek.

"KDF Bot R32, evacuate premises now!" The KDF captain ordered as he and the other operatives exited the room.

Rivet remained motionless as he looked down on Brae. As she lost consciousness, her hand slipped down Rivet's torso, leaving a trail of her blood on his armored white chest. Then the world went black.

Rhett's legs ached with adrenaline the closer he came to the haven. Violating multiple flight ordinances, he flew the transport directly into the lower level of the city in the vicinity of the haven. A courtyard where he figured he could set the craft down was just a block away. Before the engines were fully spooled down, Rhett had the transport door open and was running the final block to the haven. All he needed was three minutes. He rounded the corner of the building and became witness to the end of hope. He froze in his tracks when he saw two KDF vehicles positioned at the main entrance of the medtech supply facility. *What can I do? How many people made it out...how many died?* As these thoughts of horror flooded his mind, Rhett had the strangest sense that Brae was close by, but the feeling quickly faded.

Morian commando alert sirens began to fill the air as Rhett abandoned reason and ran toward the facility entrance, heedless of the likelihood of nearby KDF operatives. Just as he arrived at the door, eight KDF operatives exited the facility with urgency. Rhett came face to face with the captain of the operatives. The captain sneered as he glanced up the street where Morian commando transports were speedily coming at them.

"We'll be back to get the rest of you," the captain scowled. He turned and entered the second vehicle. Seconds later they were gone.

Rhett turned to enter but instead locked eyes on the lifeless gaze of a KDF bot as it exited the facility, its face and torso stained with the blood of a Navi.

"Rivet!" Rhett screamed. "What have you done!?"

The bot came right up to Rhett, its icy-cold eyes piercing his soul. Morian vehicles arrived, settling to the ground to allow the commandos to exit and investigate. Rivet silently turned his eyes toward the retreating KDF vehicles in the distance and sprinted after them.

Rhett ran into the facility and down to the basement where his heart utterly fractured at the sight of evil's handiwork. Twelve bodies were strewn about the room. Rhett quickly checked for signs of life, inwardly hoping against hope but knowing Brae would be among them. He sprinted to their designated communing room. As the door swished open, Rhett's nightmare became reality. He went to the limp and blood-stained body of his bonded mate, raging against the truth of what he saw.

"Brae!....Brae!" he cried, kneeling down next to her. Tears streamed down his face, falling onto the beautiful and rare daughter of Ell Yon. He leaned over next to her beautiful face.

"Four more in here!" shouted a Morian commando as he entered the room with Rhett. "Who did this?" he asked.

Rhett looked up at the man, sorrow permeating every fiber of his soul. "Kylos did this!" Rhett shouted. "You know he did this!"

The commando frowned. "Without first account witness by a commando, we have no recourse to pursue," he said emotionlessly.

The rage within Rhett began to rise...fury waiting to unleash on the complicit Morian commandos and their hypocritical facade of justice.

"Rhett!" Brae gasped.

That singular raspy whisper from Brae's lips pulled Rhett back from the brink of self-destruction. His heart found reason to beat once more, even if it was but a wisp of hope that coaxed him onward.

"Brae!" Rhett exclaimed, coming close to her face once more. "Stay with me, Brae...please stay with me!"

Rhett scooped Brae up in his arms and ran out of the room, frantically asking for help from the Morian commandos. It was a foolish endeavor, for there was an obvious reticence to help emanating from all of them. Rhett was fraught with fear at the thought of losing Brae. Her abdominal wound was serious...too serious to consider anything except immediate treatment regardless of any other risk. He decided to take her to Brohn's major medtech facility just two blocks north of the haven. Pleading out to Ell Yon for help, Rhett carried Brae as quickly as he dared, hoping that someone who truly cared about saving lives would help her.

Fasa Kylos wrestled within himself regarding the sulky mood that seemed to preoccupy his mind as of late. The heretic named Jeshu had been eliminated, the Keeper Order had been purged of the radical and misguided men and women that were swayed by the enticing words of the false Navi, and Subchancellor Pylok of the Morian Empire seemed at least appeased with the restored order that had been such a longstanding element of their political arrangement. In fact, Kylos had every reason to celebrate. Earlier this same day he had received word that his newly appointed Keeper Defense Force, fully authorized by the Morian Empire under the Peace

Preservation Edict, had discovered and eliminated a major cell of Jeshuan followers in Brohn, which included the elusive Brae Thornton, daughter of the man who had started the insurrection against the Keeper Order years earlier.

All of Kylos's trouble had begun with the false Navi Elias Thornton and subsequently his daughter, who had become one of Jeshu's most ardent followers, causing serious dissension among the people. The search for her had been extensive but fruitless...until now. Her discovery and elimination could finalize his solution for ending the influence of this heretic named Jeshu once and for all.

There was much to celebrate indeed, yet something nagged in the corner of his mind. Sure, the occasional disturbance by a few of the heretic's remaining disbanded followers was frustrating, but they would be dealt with very soon. Besides this, Kylos was absolutely certain that time would quell and finally extinguish the fanatical words of the dead false Navi.

Kylos tapped on the portal side post of his home to make the invisible force field dissolve away. He stepped onto a beautiful, serene terrace, where the lush trees and fragrant flowers surrounding his personal sanctuary seemed to soothe his unsettled spirit. He closed his eyes, breathing in the delicious fresh air. The evening sounds were enchanting as the songs of two different species of birds mixed in a delightful but dissonant melody.

Yes...this is all I needed, he thought then opened his eyes. His gaze landed on the small grouping of his own carefully nurtured Wild Crimson Roses. In a moment the peace he had so desperately sought was shattered by the sight of the brilliant white flowers. Without the once vibrant red color, the traditional reclamation ritual practiced throughout Rayl among his people had stopped. All of his previous anger and frustration instantly returned. He tried to assuage his rising fury by remembering that the finality of his exacted justice would take time. He was extremely grateful that Ell Yon had given him the enhanced protector to overcome the masterful and deceptive heretic. Kylos had to admit that whatever this Jeshu character had been, he was very near to a real-life wizard. How he had engineered and manipulated the genomes of the Wild Crimson Rose to globally manifest as white flowers instead of red ones was still a mystery, but his special biotech team would soon reverse the damage.

Kylos's mind flitted from one staged mystery of the false Navi to another until it landed on the greatest trick of all—making all the Protectors dissolve away at once. This was perhaps the most devastating of Jeshu's vandal acts on his beloved order of the Keepers. Rage filled Kylos's heart at the thought of it. He arrived at one certain conclusion—Jeshu was a masterful technological terrorist. Olea Station was certainly not the innocent base the heretic and his followers had claimed it to be.

I will not rest until every follower, memory, and trace of that heretic has been erased from the minds of my people. Kylos lifted his eyes upward. *To you I swear, Sovereign Ell Yon!*

Kylos's com band softly alerted him to an incoming message. He tapped on a small icon, and the holographic image of one of his assistants appeared.

"What is it, Garon?" Kylos asked, making no attempt to hide his annoyance at the interruption.

"Master Keeper, there's an urgent message from Medtech Master Trayl at the Brohn primary medtech facility."

"I can't imagine that anything happening in a Brohn medtech facility is urgent enough to require my attention. You take care of it, Garon, and don't disturb me again until tomorrow." Kylos reached for the disconnect icon.

"If I may be so bold, Preeminent, you will want to hear him," Garon persisted.

Kylos huffed. "If you're wrong, I'll be sending you to Karack Island for another remote duty."

Garon didn't seem dissuaded.

"Connect him," Kylos ordered.

Garon reached to transfer the messenger, and a second later his image dissolved away, replaced by that of a medtech master.

"Master Kylos, I am Medtech Master Trayl. I am loyal to our Keeper and Builder Orders, and therefore—"

"Master Trayl," Kylos cut in. "It's late, and I'm tired. I was told this matter is urgent. What is so important?"

"Of course. Thirty minutes ago, I was called to treat the serious abdominal wound of a young woman. I will be able to save her life, but I thought you might be interested in knowing her identity." Trayl paused as if waiting to tell some grand secret.

Kylos waited a few seconds. "Out with it, man!"

"The woman is a Jeshuan," Trayl continued. "She currently goes by the name of Brae Williams, but a genetic scan identifies her as Brae Thornton, daughter of the late Elias Thornton."

Kylos froze. He had been told about the recent raid and that the Jeshuan hideout had been eliminated. To discover that Brae Thornton was alive and within his power to capture could give him an advantage he didn't think possible.

"What would you like me to do, sir?" Trayl asked.

Kylos's shrewd mind immediately began to formulate a plan as to how he could turn this botched execution to his advantage. "Sedate her and don't let her leave. Is anyone with her?"

"Yes, her bonded. I believe his name is Rhett Stryker."

The corner of Kylos's mouth turned upward.

"There is one more thing you should know," Medtech Master Trayl began.

CHAPTER

11

A Legacy in Peril

Rhett paced the waiting area at the primary medtech facility in Brohn. With hardly a word, Brae was whisked away as soon as the medtechs understood how serious her wounds were. The medtech staff at the facility seemed extremely competent, but Rhett was gravely concerned about how loyal the people here were to Prefect Terrok and, more importantly, Fasa Kylos. The Protector on Brae's arm was an indicator as to her allegiance, even though the Protector might pass as a standard com band worn by nearly every Raylean. Some of the more tech-savvy Jeshuans had even fabricated pseudo displays that were attached to the Protector to disguise its unique origins. Rhett and Brae had both adopted the displays in an effort to maintain the secrecy of their Creed haven sand their fellow Jeshuans, but would it be enough?

After two hours of agonizing waiting, Rhett rose to meet with Medtech Master Trayl when he exited the operation room. Rhett could hardly contain himself as

Master Trayl seemed to linger too long in relaying the outcome of Brae's surgery.

"Her injuries were very serious, but I'm hopeful she'll recover," Trayl said with a weary voice. "The next 24 hours will be critical...we'll know then."

Rhett closed his eyes. Trayl's words were enough to give Rhett hope.

"Thank Ell Yon," he said quietly. "Thank you, Master Trayl. When can I see her?"

"In a few hours. We need to closely monitor her. If she makes it through, she should regain consciousness tomorrow. One of my assistants will take you to her when she's ready."

Master Trayl nodded then returned through the door by which he'd entered, seemingly in a hurry to move on. Rhett didn't care though—Brae was alive.

Rhett needed to walk off some of the anxiety that had dismantled him over the last two hours, so he left the room and wandered around the facility. Although Brae was alive and fighting for her life, Rhett's next greatest fear began to occupy his mind...KDF operatives coming to take them away. As he perused the facility and its campus, he was ever watchful for the enemies of Jeshu. But after nearly two hours and a bit of food, he saw nothing to indicate that the KDF was coming for them.

When Rhett was finally allowed to be with Brae, he came to her bedside and carefully lifted her hand into his. When the medtech staff left him with her, he gently kissed her forehead. The warmth of her skin on his lips unleashed an avalanche of emotion that he didn't know was inside of him. He began to weep and couldn't seem to stop. Brae had become so entwined with his life that her close brush with death shattered his psyche. He needed her. Rhett realized he had never truly known fear until today.

Rhett wiped his eyes. He kissed the back of Brae's hand, holding on for dear life.

When Brae first opened her eyes, she was extremely confused. She wallowed in blurry images and fuzzy memories for what seemed an eternity, trying to make sense of what it all meant. As her vision cleared, so did her mind, and she snapped into a reality that was frightful in every way. She tried to speak, but her lips only mumbled unintelligible sounds. She tried to move, but it felt like her entire body was tethered down.

"Brae...Brae!" a familiar voice called.

Brae turned her head in the direction of the voice. "Rhett...we have to get out of here...the KDF—"

"Ssshh." Rhett hushed. "You're okay, Brae...thank Ell Yon you're okay."

Rhett's voice soothed her as did the warmth of his eyes. It was then that she felt his warm hands holding hers. She focused more clearly on his face. His smile was broad and his eyes moist.

"I thought I'd lost you," Rhett said, stroking her cheek.

"Where are we?" Brae asked.

"You're at the Brohn primary medtech facility."

Brae's eyes opened wide. "We can't be here! Kylos will find us."

"Brae," Rhett said, his smile fading. "You were going to die. I had no choice."

Brae's memory of her last conscious moments came back to her. Excruciating pain in the Ruah...return to reality...KDF operatives...

"Trace, Keirsa, and Frall...are they okay?"

Rhett pursed his lips, his silence proclaiming everything. Brae felt the crushing weight of intense guilt sweeping through her being. She leaned her head back, closing her eyes as tears fell down her cheeks. Then her mind remembered the last image she'd seen. She opened her eyes to look at Rhett again.

"Rivet!" Brae exclaimed.

Rhett's eyebrows furrowed. "He's one of them now."

"No," Brae languished. Centuries of devoted service by Rivet to the protection of her family had been undone in a moment. Intense sadness and anger flooded her soul. She glanced toward the door. "Is the KDF outside?"

Rhett hesitated. "Actually...no."

At that moment, the door slid open, startling Brae, but it was just a medtech assistant. When she saw that Brae was awake, her eyes softened, and she offered a slight smile.

"You've awakened," the woman said. "How do you feel?"

Brae looked past the woman to the door, again trying to see if anyone else was waiting outside. The woman also glanced back at the door as it closed and came straight to the side of the bed opposite of Rhett. She leaned forward to speak, as if to share a secret, her smile exchanged for a solemn look.

"I know who you are...the daughter of the Navi Elias and sectator of Jeshu."

Brae swallowed hard, trying not to panic just yet.

"It's not safe for you here," the woman continued, briefly pulling up the sleeve on her right arm to show the edge of a disguised Protector. "I'm Adina."

Brae exhaled in relief.

"What do we do?" Rhett asked. "She's not well enough to leave yet."

Adina was about to respond when the door behind her opened again. Medtech Master Trayl entered.

"Adina...you were supposed to inform me when our patient revived," the man said with a smile as he came to the foot of the bed.

"Yes, sir. I only just discovered she was awake," Adina replied.

"I see. And how are we feeling?" Trayl asked Brae.

"Rough," Brae answered.

"I'm sure," Trayl replied, glancing toward Adina. "How much have you told her?"

"Nothing at all, Master Trayl. She's literally just awakened."

"Hmm," Trayl murmured. "Whoever it was that attacked you certainly didn't plan on leaving you alive. There were two stasis blade piercings. Fortunately, neither of them severed any major arteries, and I was able to repair most of the damage to your internal organs."

"Most?" Rhett asked.

Adina gently touched Brae's hand. "I'm afraid we couldn't repair the damage to your reproductive organs...children won't be an option for you," she said tenderly.

Considering their current situation, Brae responded rather numbly. She was more concerned with Rhett and herself making it out of the facility without the KDF discovering them. She turned to look at Rhett. There was sorrow in his eyes.

"I'm sorry, Rhett," she whispered.

Rhett shook his head. "I'm so grateful you're alive, Brae. That's all that matters to me."

"Yes...well, a fair trade to be able to live your life out," Trayl offered with a forced smile. "You'll need to stay with us for a couple of weeks until your wounds have healed. Adina and her staff will take good care of you."

"Thank you, Master Trayl," Rhett said, standing up to shake the man's hand.

Trayl thrust his hand out then promptly exited the room. Adina stayed silent, occupying herself with monitoring Brae's vitals until it appeared no one else would enter the room. She then looked at Rhett.

"It would be wise not to wait the full two weeks," Adina said quietly.

"How quickly can I leave?" Brae asked.

"As serious as those wounds are, five to six days would be the absolute minimum, but even still you'll have to be extremely careful. Wounds like these take six to eight weeks to fully heal."

"I'll leave in four days," Brae said. Adina looked skeptical. "Every day I stay here increases the chance that Kylos will find us. I'll risk bleeding out before letting his thugs capture us."

Adina still looked concerned.

"I'll secretly arrange for an early release. We'll transport her using an anti-grav gurney." Adina looked at Rhett. "Can you get a speeder large enough to accommodate that?"

"Yes," Rhett replied. "Just tell me the time and place to have it."

"I'll let you know," Adina said as she prepared to leave.

Brae grabbed her hand. "Thank you!"

Adina squeezed Brae's hand. "Jeshu be with you," she said then quickly exited the room.

Medtech Master Trayl never returned to check on Brae. Late in the evening four days later, Adina and Rhett successfully transported Brae from her room to a speeder where Bridger was waiting in back of the medtech facility. As soon as Brae was loaded into the speeder, Rhett thanked Adina, jumped in, and closed the door. Bridger immediately accelerated up to speed. Although the anti-grav gurney helped immensely, the slightest movement was still incredibly painful for Brae.

"How are you doing?" Rhett asked, holding her hand as Bridger carefully but quickly navigated the thoroughfares of downtown Brohn.

Brae winced as Bridger made a turn and elevated the speeder one level. "I'm fine, although I may have been a little optimistic," she confessed, holding her arm across the wounds in her stomach.

Rhett looked toward Bridger in the cockpit. "Any tails?"

Bridger shook his head. "Clear." Bridger made a sudden unexpected turn into a building with an open portal. As soon as they entered, the portal closed to disguise them from the world.

"What's going on?" Brae asked.

Rhett squeezed her hand as Bridger brought the speeder to rest in the middle of four personnel with specialized equipment.

"We have to check you over," Rhett said reassuringly.

"What do you mean?" Brae instantly became concerned.

The doors on both sides of the speeder opened so the techs, or whatever they were, could have clear access to Brae.

Bridger turned around in the cockpit to face Brae. "I'm the one that arranged this, Brae. It's just too peculiar that the KDF didn't find you at the medtech facility. Knowing Kylos, there's a good chance he's implanted a tracking device inside you."

As the four techs powered up their equipment, Brae's rage with Kylos revived. Bridger's reasoning made perfect sense. She and Rhett had talked at length about the risk of her being at the medtech facility, and Adina had confirmed it. It was the perfect opportunity for Kylos to use her to get to the rest of the Creed havens. *Will Kylos's evil persecution of my family never end?* she wondered.

"You have to leave me," she urged as she considered Bridger's speculation. "They could be coming for us right now!"

Rhett put a hand to her cheek. "No matter what they find, I'll never leave you, Brae. And let's not jump to conclusions just yet."

Brae closed her eyes, leaning her head back onto the gurney. Her mind ran wild with horrible possibilities.

"What if it's some sort of bio micro quantum tracker?" Brae asked. "There would be no way of detecting it."

One of the techs stopped his work and looked directly at Brae. He was clearly the leader and the brains behind the work they were doing.

"Fascinating idea," he said thoughtfully. "But it doesn't exist...I would know about it." The man continued to scan Brae with a device she had never seen before.

"Yelson is a scitech master from my region...the best on the planet," Bridger said. "If there's anything that's not supposed to be inside you, he'll find it."

Brae waited patiently for over two hours as Yelson and his tech team performed a hundred scans over every inch of her body. When the ordeal was over, Yelson looked at Bridger.

"There's not a single molecule inside her that would indicate any tracking tech whatsoever. She's clean."

Brae and Rhett both breathed a big sigh of relief. Bridger didn't seem quite as relieved.

"What is it, brother?" Rhett asked.

Bridger paused, appearing to choose his words carefully as he often did.

"Kylos is too well-connected, at least in the major cities like Brohn. Something doesn't make sense."

Brae and Rhett considered his words.

"Adina was a surprise secret Jeshuan. Maybe there are more than we realize," Rhett suggested. "It's possible that even Master Trayl is a Jeshuan who considered it too risky to reveal himself to us."

Bridger slowly nodded. "I suppose that's a possibility." He looked at Brae, offering a subtle smile. "Let's get you home."

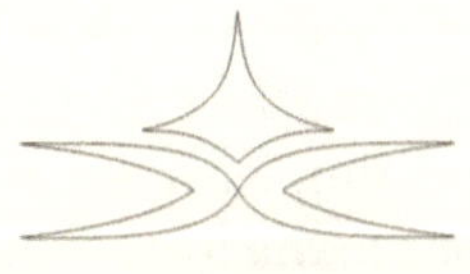

CHAPTER

12

Intersection

Within four weeks, Brae's wounds were mostly healed. She felt as though something inside her had been rearranged, and she didn't like the feeling. Strange twinges of pain would appear out of nowhere, but all in all, she was grateful to start returning to a normal life. Rhett hardly left her side, and she lovingly scolded him for it, which he promptly ignored.

Upon regaining her strength, Brae returned to the Ruah and discovered an extraordinary phenomenon—any pain or weakness she experienced in the human realm was conspicuously absent in the Ruah. In fact, she found herself stronger than before, engaging in numerous valiant battles on behalf of the Creed and the expansion of Jeshu's global mission.

Together with Rhett, Brae trained many new Navis in the art of combat within the Ruah. She observed that each dedicated warrior of the Ruah possessed unique abilities that were natural for them to adopt. Some excelled as exceptional Starstreak pilots, others in ground tactical combat, and some became expert strategists and tacticians. A select few were invaluable reconnaissance assets, often collaborating with the elite Malakian Recon Teams. Their missions in the Ruah significantly disrupted

Dracus's plans to dominate Rayl, which consequently led to increased persecution in the human realm by the Torians, who utilized their human agents, notably Fasa Kylos, to great effect.

Brae and Rhett stayed in close contact with as many of the other burgeoning Creeds across the planet as possible without compromising their secrecy, often sharing training techniques and encouragement. As new Jeshuans joined their ranks, an underground network of skilled people in every tech field was formed so that the Creeds didn't need to rely so heavily on those businesses and services loyal to the Keepers and Builders. But as they expanded and grew, so did Kylos's Keeper Defense Forces and their use of brutal tactics to suppress the Jeshuans.

One day a few months after her injury, Brae worked up her courage to discuss something of great importance with Rhett. She had prepared a favorite seafood dish of Rhett's in their small yet cozy dwelling on the outskirts of Brohn. They had become accustomed to moving every few months to thwart any attempts by Kylos to locate and arrest them. This cottage, with a brook running through their property, was Brae's favorite dwelling by far. She could see the vast open spaces of the surrounding terrain, reminding her of her childhood days with her father at their country home. As Brae was standing on their back patio gazing at the gorgeous orange, yellow, and blue hues of Rayl's setting sun, Rhett came to her, wrapping his arms around her from behind.

"Thank you for that delicious meal," he whispered into her ear. "Now...what is that you want from me?"

Brae turned around to face him. "Why would you think I want something?" she asked, lifting an eyebrow.

Rhett stifled a laugh. "You should know by now that you can't hide things from me."

Brae smiled as she held him, leaning her head on his chest. "I suppose you're right, but I actually don't want anything from you."

Rhett leaned away so he could see her face more clearly as if to scrutinize her more closely.

"Really?"

Brae looked up at him, gazing deeply into his eyes.

"What would you say if I told you that another Jeshuan was added to our ranks today?"

Rhett looked confused. "I would say, 'Thank Ell Yon,' just as I always do. Is that what happened?"

Brae nodded.

"Who is he? Can I meet him?" Rhett asked.

Brae nodded again, then slowly brought her hands to her stomach.

Rhett tilted his head, further confused. Slowly his countenance transformed. His eyes opened wide, questioning, as if not daring to say what Brae was inferring. His lips moved, but no words came out. Brae waited, herself stunned by what this meant.

"Are you sure?" Rhett finally asked.

Brae nodded. "Quite. I know it's not—" Brae began, but her words were cut short when Rhett grabbed her, lifting and spinning her about.

Brae nearly laughed, having never seen Rhett respond like this to anything. His jubilant reaction and giddy look on his face were certainly something new.

"Brae! This is incredible...I can't believe it!" Rhett said, setting her down. He brought his hands to her face. "I don't know what to say...I'm so happy!"

Brae realized that she was smiling ear to ear. Rhett's response was exactly what she had secretly hoped for. She teared up.

"I'm so glad you're happy about this," she said, wiping her eyes.

"Oh, darling...I'm more than happy. But how? We were told this was impossible."

Brae shook her head. "I honestly don't know. After the attack, I felt as though something was different...wrong inside me. It must have just been the wounds healing. I have no explanation."

Some of Rhett's enthusiasm waned. "We need to find a trusted medtech and a birth attendant right away. I'll start canvassing the Creed havens."

"No need, Rhett. Layal from the Gershite Creed is a certified medtech who has delivered countless babies and has agreed."

"She's already scanned you? Everything is normal?" he asked.

Brae nodded again. Rhett's full smile returned. He knelt down so his face was at the same level as Brae's stomach. He placed a hand over her abdomen.

"A child," he said quietly. "Welcome to the world, little warrior."

Nine months later, on the eve of the anniversary of Jeshu Starlore's regeneration, Stone Stryker, aka Stone Williams, was born. Brae and Rhett were overcome with joy. The child represented hope, promise, and a future.

Although Brae and Rhett had already experienced the raising of a child together when they were called to care for the infant Merchant years earlier, this time their experience was wildly different. At first Brae was cautious, but to her pleasant surprise, Rhett quickly proved to be a fully engaged and willing father. As the boy grew, Brae and Rhett discovered things about themselves and each other that surprised and delighted them in ways they couldn't imagine. The taste of brief parenting they had shared when raising Jeshu was certainly a glimpse of this new kind of deep sacrificial love, but now with a child that was of their own flesh and blood, it just felt different...it felt more.

Stone Williams was of fair complexion with a joyful and content spirit. Brae and Rhett delighted in him and he in them. By the time the lad was ten years old, it was evident that he had inherited not only the physical aptitude of both of his parents, but also the deep love for Sovereign Ell Yon and his Son, Jeshu. Hearing her son speak of his heart for Ell Yon filled Brae's heart with joy and also with wonder. If she were completely honest, Brae had moments of anxiety as she considered the destiny of the child. After all...he was a Starlore by blood. The call of the Immortal on her child's life was both thrilling and frightening at the same time. But Brae trusted in the Sovereign, realizing that this sweet and fragile child would one day be a strong and confident man. *Perhaps then I'll feel different*, Brae thought to herself.

"Mother...tell me a story about my grandfather," Stone would ask nearly every night. Although too young to fully grasp the journey of Daeson Starlore, Stone reveled at each telling, and Brae was more than willing to oblige such requests.

Brae and Rhett hoped they would add to their family, but each year that passed it seemed as though their one and only special gift would be that of their precious son.

Over the next few years, the number of Creed havens continued to increase throughout Rayl, despite the aggressive efforts of Fasa Kylos, Preeminent Keeper of the sovereign sanctums. The harder he tried to stop them, the more the Navis thrived, but the cost in Jeshuan blood and tears was significant. Morian Subchancellor Pylok seemed to become preoccupied with the rising sentiments of the rebel group known as the Partisans and therefore continued to allow Kylos great latitude in the execution of the Peace Preservation Edict, which he carried out without discretion. The Jeshuans grew savvy in the operation of their Creeds and in the training that was conducted. An entire underground network of communication and support was established throughout the planet as the global Creed increased in number and effectiveness. In one realm, this new breed of Navis was as harmless as doves. In the realm of the Ruah, many became fearless warriors of valor. Through it all, Kylos's obsession with ridding Rayl of these Jeshuan heretics only intensified.

Brae and Rhett's passion for following in the ways of Jeshu was passed on to their only child. As Stone entered his teen years, he waxed strong in the ways of Jeshu and his Navis. Beginning at the age of fourteen, Brae and Rhett started equipping him with piloting and hand-to-hand combat skills, knowing that one day he would face the same threats and missions in the Ruah that were now common among all dedicated Navis. Now at the age of seventeen, Stone was on the cusp of becoming a Navi himself. With a little over a year left at the Brohn Academy, the call of Ell Yon began to resound in his heart. He anticipated receiving his own Protector and joining the battle for humanity in the Ruah. But for another year, he would need to abide in the awkward world of adolescence.

"Stone, there's a fireball game tonight at sunset," a friend named Briggs said over Stone's holo com band. "You in? We really need you."

Stone smiled, his blond hair and bright blue eyes magnifying his enthusiasm. If Briggs was using the holo com, it must be urgent. He checked the time—he could make it. "Of course. Who are we up against?"

"A street team from the east side," Briggs replied. "I hear they're pretty good, so bring your A-game."

"See you soon," Stone finished, swiping away the holo image.

Just then Brae entered the room. "I'm not so sure I like you participating in that dreadful game."

"I have the feeling fireball is child's play compared to what you and Dad used to do," Stone said with a smile.

"Used to?" Rhett said, following Brae. He grabbed his son and mock-wrestled him for a few seconds.

Stone was a strong lad with a nearly constant cheerful disposition. He pushed back, recognizing his dad's dominant strength…but maybe someday.

"I think it's good for him," Rhett said, leaving Stone's side to wrap an arm around Brae. "There's a lot of crossover in the Navi skills we teach him…as long as you stay away from the official league play," Rhett added, pointing a finger at Stone. "It's too conspicuous."

"I will," Stone promised.

His mother didn't seem convinced.

"The origins of that game are horrid," Brae said with a frown.

There were a dozen other athletic activities that the youth of the day participated in, but the lure of fireball garnered most of the enthusiasm. The modern-day version of fireball was a tame revival of the original game invented thousands of years ago when the Rayleans were space nomads without a home world. The original game was a savage way to occupy the idle time of a people with little to look forward to, often ending in maimed or dead contestants. Over the last few decades, fireball had morphed into a competition of athletic skill and strategic prowess, especially for Raylean youth. It had become so popular that entire leagues with hundreds of teams were created, with tournaments hosted in all the major cities. Some tournaments drew thousands of spectators into arenas dedicated to the sport. But for many aspiring fireball enthusiasts like Stone and his friends, street fireball was satisfying enough. Occasionally, an extremely talented street player would debut into the world of the elite league play and win great popularity. For a Jeshuan youth, that was never really an option, however, simply because of the risk of exposure to those in power who despised them.

Stone realized that his dad was right—a lot of the Navi hand-to-hand combat skills he had been taught by his parents certainly helped him master the game of fireball to the point that he was a well-respected player among many Brohn street teams.

"Mom, the fireballs today aren't designed to kill people. We don't even intentionally throw them at each other," Stone petitioned.

Brae looked at Stone, her frown easing. "Just remember who we are and what we stand for...okay? The KDF has been known to come after young Jeshuans from time to time."

Jeshuan youth were carefully counseled to only reveal their affiliation as a Jeshuan with other youth they personally knew from their local Creed. Outside of that, they kept their Jeshuan status secret, allowing the adults to determine risk versus authentic interest in a questioning individual. With the unrelenting hunt of the KDF, lives were at stake, and extreme caution was exercised by all Jeshuan youth.

Stone grabbed his fireball gear and headed for the door. "I will," he shouted over his shoulder.

Nearly a young adult, Stone was eager for life. The galaxy seemed too small to hold all his dreams and ambitions. His optimism and subtle charm won friends quickly and the respect of peers and adults alike. While some Jeshuan youths questioned the difficult path set before them because of their parents, Stone did not. It was easy for him to believe and walk in the ways of Jeshu. Becoming a Navi and joining the warrior cause in the Ruah was something he greatly anticipated. His infectious faith was unique, and he bore any ridicule because of it with ease.

Stone pulled up on his open-air one-man speeder, a vehicle he found a little too thrilling at speeds above those allowed by his parents and the Morian city patrols. His friends were already gathered at the usual spot, a wide-open plaza flanked by towering buildings and minimal activity as the setting sun ushered in the evening. The lights about the periphery of the plaza all illuminated in sync, softening the departing day. Stone's arrival was met with cheers and friendly jabs as he greeted each of his teammates. Briggs was the team captain and strategic mastermind who could predict opponents' moves with uncanny accuracy. Then came Tish, whose agility and quick reflexes made her the best dodger in their crew. Brendal and Sayash, the inseparable twins, were known for their synchronized plays and flawless teamwork. Kal was a powerhouse who could hurl a fireball with such force that it seemed to create its own shockwaves. And finally there was Zandi, the silent observer who often came up with the most ingenious tricks when least expected. Together, this diverse group of friends formed a skilled fireball team, each contributing their unique talents to the game they loved. They called themselves the Vanguards.

At the far end of the plaza, seven fireball players gathered to face off.

"Well, boys and girls, here come the east side Torches," Kal said looking their way.

"They don't look like much," Brendal said, scrutinizing the opponents, still a fair distance away.

"Nobody looks like much when they're 200 feet away," his sister scolded.

Sayash was right, for the closer the Torches came, the more formidable they appeared.

"Nobody get scared and run off now," Briggs said only loud enough for his team to hear.

In the revived game of fireball, much of the original equipment was the same. Each player controlled an arc glove capable of generating various sizes of energy plasma spheres, aka fireballs, that could be thrown at a target and opponents. Players also operated double-ended TalonX weapons minus the razor-sharp metallic composite. The stasis field was also replaced by a less fatal glowing Stabil retention field so that the effect on a struck opponent was painful but not lethal.

The TalonX could also generate a two-foot diameter energy repulsion shield that could be activated for a few seconds at a time. The most significant addition to the fireball equipment was the use of anti-grav hover boards that each player operated and played from. Maneuvering a hover board while managing the arc glove and TalonX took an incredible amount of balance and skill. It had the effect of ramping up the tempo of the entire match.

Another key difference between the modern and ancient versions of fireball was the scoring. No longer was the goal to cripple or kill the opponents. A slot-shaped target hovered ten feet in the air at each end of the arena. A fireball entering the slot was a hit. A predetermined number of hits would win a match. The defending team had a variety of options to keep an opponent's fireball from entering the slot. Despite the taming of the original game of fireball, there were still enough energized plasma balls and enough TalonX blade energy to inflict significant pain if a player wasn't careful to defend himself or herself properly. Although there were various team configurations, the typical match was five versus five with substitutions as needed.

After a brief introduction, the match between the Torches and the Vanguards began. It took two scores by the Torches before Stone and his team found their rhythm. Although Briggs was the captain, Stone was the one everyone looked to when it came down to the wire. When he was in the zone, Stone possessed a situational awareness of the arena that was unparalleled. He had the ability to see opportunities and the perception to know what every player was doing in a moment. Stone made the final goal to finish the game with a 5-3 win.

After the two teams parted and the Torches left the area, Briggs turned to face his team.

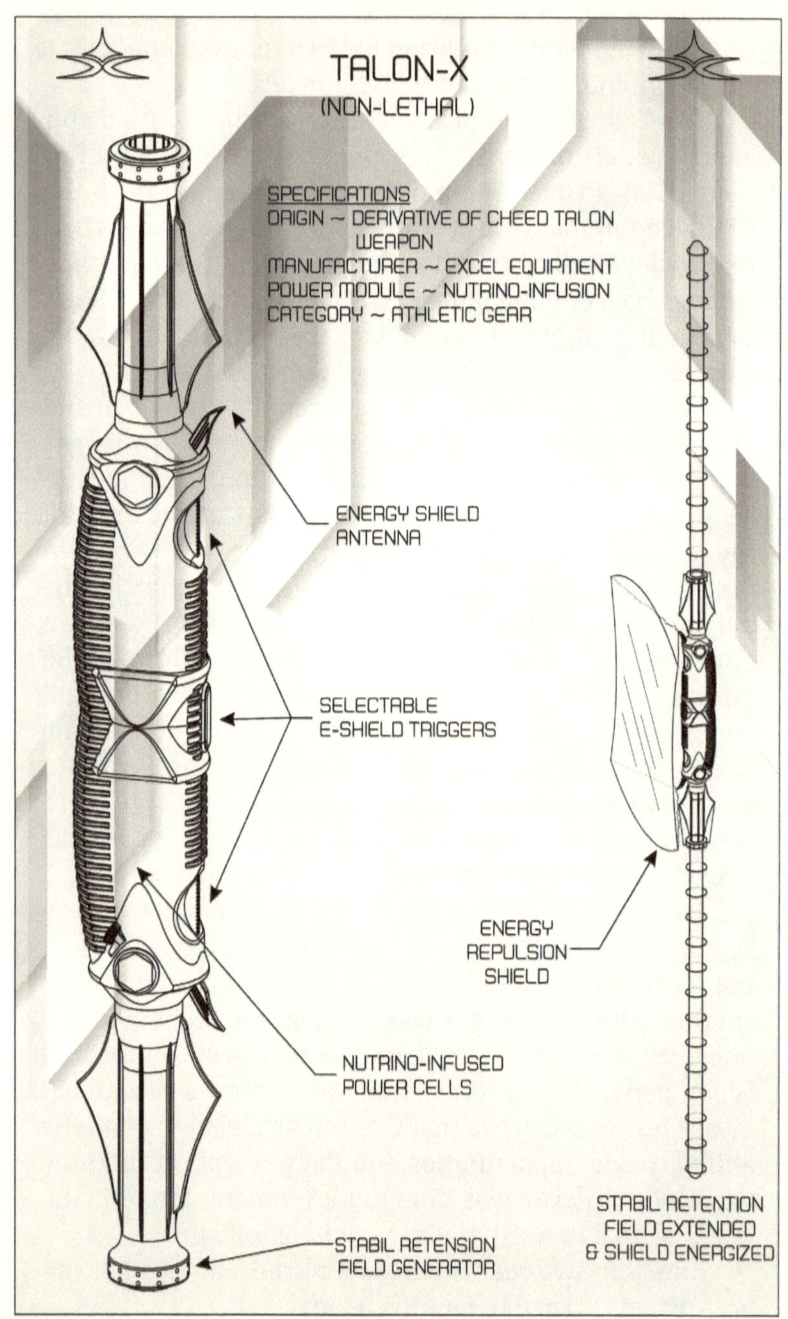

TALON-X
(NON-LETHAL)

SPECIFICATIONS
ORIGIN ~ DERIVATIVE OF CHEED TALON
WEAPON
MANUFACTURER ~ EXCEL EQUIPMENT
POWER MODULE ~ NUTRINO-INFUSION
CATEGORY ~ ATHLETIC GEAR

ENERGY SHIELD
ANTENNA

SELECTABLE
E-SHIELD TRIGGERS

ENERGY
REPULSION
SHIELD

NUTRINO-INFUSED
POWER CELLS

STABIL RETENSION
FIELD GENERATOR

STABIL RETENTION
FIELD EXTENDED
& SHIELD ENERGIZED

"Hey, there's a sanctioned fireball league game at the Brohn Academy tomorrow night," Briggs announced as they gathered their fireball arena tech. "Two top teams going at it!"

"I heard," Kal replied. "The Brohn Infernos take on the Jalem Juggernauts."

"We should go," Brendal posited. "I hear the Juggernauts have a guy on their team who's a shoo-in for the Global Fireball Champion Team."

"I'm in," Tish offered.

One by one, each of Stone's friends agreed to attend the match—all but Stone. He knew that getting his parents to agree would be nearly impossible.

"What do you say, Stone?" Briggs urged. "You in?"

"I doubt my parents will let me," he replied. "You guys fill me in when it's over."

Stone's rejection of the invitation brought a relentless barrage of jibes, insults, and reconsideration appeals.

"Okay…okay…I'll ask, but don't expect to see me there," Stone decreed. "Just getting permission to hang out with you hoodlums is a miracle."

That night, Stone lay awake rehearsing how he could appeal to his parents to let him go to the league match. He figured his dad would be an easy win, but his mother— that would be the challenge. In his own right, Stone was an outstanding fireball player. At times he could almost recognize what was going to occur before it actually happened. Those surreal moments of clarity were almost an out-of-body experience, as if he were looking down from above like a hover drone. However, Stone had once seen a top-tier fireball athlete play in a tournament and was mesmerized by the skill of the player. Stone knew that fireball was just a game that added little, if any, real value to the life of a budding Navi, but he couldn't help becoming enthralled with the thrill of the sport. Getting a chance to see a rising fireball star play was something he would thoroughly enjoy.

By midafternoon of the following day, Stone gathered enough nerve to pitch the idea of attending the fireball league game to his mother, making sure his dad was present to lend support.

"It's just for a couple of hours," Stone added.

Brae shook her head. "It's too risky, Stone. I'm sorry, but your father and I are on the KDF's target list."

Stone glanced at his dad with a "Please help" look.

"Brae, he won't be alone, and the KDF squads wouldn't risk arresting a youth in public. Kylos still needs the support of the masses, and it doesn't get any more public than a sanctioned league fireball match."

Stone saw the fire in his mother's eyes light at hearing his dad's comment. He instantly regretted even asking.

Brae turned to face Rhett. "You can't keep defending his risky requests when you know full well what's at stake!"

"We also can't keep him hemmed in like some sheltered pet!" Rhett returned.

Rarely did Stone see his parents fight, but when he did, he hated it. He was fortunate enough to have parents that were bonded and still together. Many of his friends didn't have that.

"Hey," Stone interrupted. "It's okay. I don't need to go. Please don't fight."

Stone's comment instantly diffused the tension between his parents. Brae's eyes softened. She looked at Rhett sympathetically then back to Stone.

"Is your whole street team going?"

Stone pursed his lips and nodded.

Brae took a deep breath. "All right, but you stay together, and com us at least twice to let us know everything is okay...got it?"

Stone went to his mother. "Really?"

Brae nodded.

Stone wrapped his arms around his mom. "Thank you!" he said with a grin on his face. He then hugged his dad and quickly exited the room just in case they recanted.

A few hours later, Stone was sitting at the Brohn Academy arena with his six Fireball teammates.

"How many teams does Jalem have now?" Tish asked.

"Thirty-four," Kal piped up. "But the Juggernauts are their top team this year."

"There he is," Briggs said. "They call him Lethal Ledger. I hear he has an ego that's as big as he is good."

Stone watched as ten Juggernaut players entered the fireball arena, their captain leading the way. Even from a distance, the guy looked formidable. Stone could tell just by the way he walked that he was strong, agile, and skilled. Something about the gait of a superior athlete exuded respect. *That's not ego*, Stone thought, seeing no strut in his walk.

For the next hour and a half, Stone and his teammates cheered for their home Brohn Infernos, to no avail. The Juggernauts were too powerful, and they were led by the best fireball player Stone had ever seen play the game. It was hard not to cheer for Lethal Ledger just out of respect for his skill.

When the match was over, Stone, Briggs, and the rest of the team made their way back to their sector of the city on speeders. Although it was already well into the evening, they were so enthused by the rousing game between the Infernos and the Juggernauts that they had to play a couple of rounds themselves just to try out a few of the moves they had seen.

Once the arena tech was set and operating, they faced off in a 4 vs. 3 match. But just as Briggs was about to signal the start, three speeders pulled up and shut down. Stone noticed them first.

"Hey...you ready Stone," Briggs asked.

Stone pointed to the three figures dismounting their speeders. They started walking their way, and Stone knew immediately who one of them was.

"What do we have here?" Kal exclaimed as he turned to watch the approach of the trio with the rest of his teammates.

A street fireball match typically drew a few onlookers, especially aspiring young players, but it was unusual this late in the day. Briggs and his six teammates approached the three. At 20 feet away, it was clear Stone's suspicion was right. Lethal Ledger and two of his teammates, a large brutish player named Rax and a girl named Vayna, who was an excellent fireball caster, watched them skeptically.

"Great match," Briggs said.

Ledger gave a subtle nod to acknowledge the compliment. "You got a match going?"

Briggs glanced over at Stone with a look of surprise.

"Just about to start," Briggs replied. "We're the Vanguards."

"You up for a 3 v 3 with us?" Ledger asked.

"Any time," Kal responded with a slight sneer.

Brendal stepped forward. "Sayash and I can play on their team. That way no one sits out."

Ledger eyed Brendal and Sayash. "That works. Full up then."

"Full up," Briggs said. "Three hits is a kill, five fireballs in the slot is a match. Two fireballs max active at a time and energy at 50 percent. The right center retention field generator puck is weak, so if any fireballs exit there, we reset."

Rax huffed. "Come on, Ledge...what are we doing here? These chumps don't even play at full power."

Ledger turned to his Juggernaut teammates. "Our fireball master says some of the best talent is in the street...I want to see if he's right, so shut up and play."

Kal stepped toward Rax and faced off just inches from him. He raised his arc glove, activated it, then ran the power setting up to 100 percent.

"Game on, chump!" Kal said, glaring into the eyes of his large opponent. This ignited a private war between the two that was soon to play out in the arena.

The other eight players matched up. Ledger initially squared off with Briggs, and Vayna paired up against Tish. Brendal took Stone, and Sayash guarded Zandi. Two minutes into the match, Tish cast a fireball toward their slot goal, which went wide by a few feet. It deflected off the perimeter retention field wall and back into the active play area. Before the fireball could dissipate, Stone broke from Brendal's defense, activated his TalonX's shield and deflected the fireball into their target for the first score of the game.

"Weak!" Rax snapped at Brendal, sneering at his new teammate.

But Vayna scoffed at Rax. "You're just lucky you weren't guarding him." She glanced toward Stone. "Nice move."

It quickly became obvious that Stone was the one to contend with, so Ledger switched to cover him. From that point on, the match ramped up to an intense game of street fireball.

Stone had been duly impressed while watching Lethal Ledger play in his league game earlier in the evening, but guarding him one-on-one in their own street match generated another level of respect for the guy. He was quick, strong, and clever in his use of the arc glove and TalonX. Stone had to play at the top of his game. If he let up for even a few seconds, Ledger took advantage of him. And yet, Stone noticed that Ledger didn't take a single cheap shot, which fireball is notorious for allowing. Ledger played an honorable game, and Stone even suspected that he had won Ledger's respect following a couple of tough plays. After 45 minutes of intense fireball action, the score was four to four—the next score would win the match.

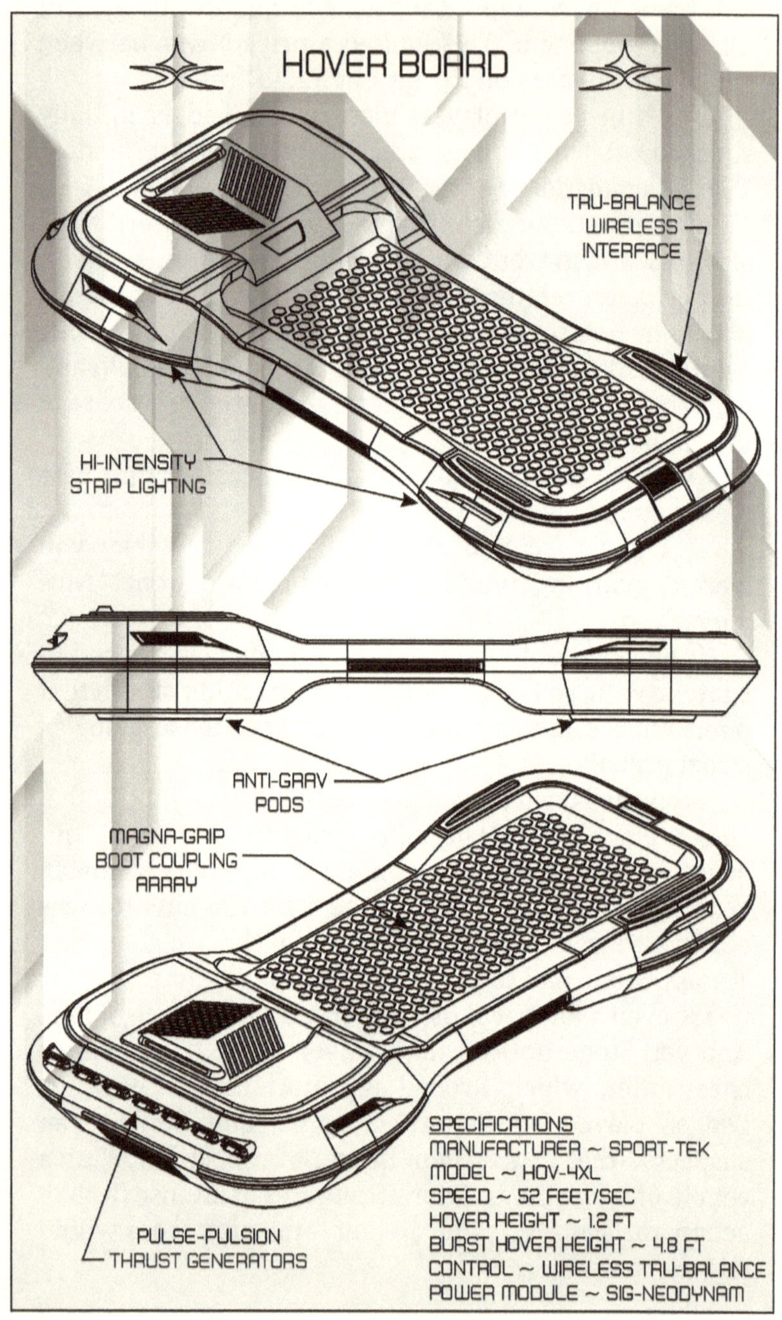

HOVER BOARD
TRU-BALANCE WIRELESS INTERFACE
HI-INTENSITY STRIP LIGHTING
ANTI-GRAV PODS
MAGNA-GRIP BOOT COUPLING ARRAY
PULSE-PULSION THRUST GENERATORS
SPECIFICATIONS
MANUFACTURER ~ SPORT-TEK
MODEL ~ HOV-4XL
SPEED ~ 52 FEET/SEC
HOVER HEIGHT ~ 1.2 FT
BURST HOVER HEIGHT ~ 4.8 FT
CONTROL ~ WIRELESS TRU-BALANCE
POWER MODULE ~ SIG-NEODYNAM

Ledger's team began an offensive play for a final goal. Out of the corner of his eye, Stone saw Rax attempt a shot on Kal, but Kal was able to deflect it just enough with a wild TalonX slice. Simultaneously, Zandi had formed a fireball and was in a perfect position to make a shot on Sayash. Stone considered helping her out, but that's when Ledger made his move. He made a fake drive toward the goal then circled back to pick up Rax's deflected fireball just as Zandi threw his fireball Ledger's direction. Stone knew Ledger was going to attempt a double shot, so he activated his energy shield, lunging forward to block the first fireball. Now he was over-extended and out of position, such that Ledger had a clear shot at the target slot. Stone made a gutsy move midair by flipping over close to the ground so he could quickly reverse his direction on his hover board and stop the second fireball that Ledger had captured from Zandi. The problem was that Stone's energy shield had expired and didn't have enough time to recharge to stop the shot. Stone gambled and lunged at the fast-moving fireball just two feet in front of the target slot, hoping he could use his TalonX to cut it short. He barely missed, and the only thing stopping the 100 percent energy-charged fireball was Stone's body. Rather than turning to avoid the hit, Stone took it straight on, hoping that he had bought enough time for one of his teammates to make a score on the opponents' end and that his protective chest armor would absorb most of the force of the fully charged fireball.

WHAM! The fireball collided into Stone's body with bruising force. It knocked him into the retention wall energy field and completely off his anti-grav hover board. He fell four feet to the concrete floor with a thud. Excruciating pain riddled his body for the first ten seconds, and its diminishing was entirely too slow. He didn't dare move until he could think straight and analyze if he had any serious injuries. Every muscle and joint in Stone's body was screaming in rebellion for the abuse he had just inflicted on them. At this point he didn't care who won the game...he was done regardless.

That was really stupid, he thought, trying to muster the intestinal fortitude to regain his feet. The pavement beneath him seemed to refuse to let go of him. He opened his eyes to see Lethal Ledger jump off his hover board and stand over him like a conqueror, his feet wide and his hands on his hips.

So now he's going to lord his victory over me? Stone thought.

Then the unexpected happened. Ledger bent over and reached out a hand to Stone. "Gutsy move. I don't think I would've tried it. Unfortunately for you, Vayna made the final score for us."

Stone wasn't sure what to make of Ledger's affable offer. He hesitated, but Ledger didn't retreat. Stone finally grabbed his hand, hoping it was a genuine offer to help— he needed it. Once Stone was vertical, the world began to spin, and he stumbled. Ledger grabbed his arm to steady him.

"A full energy fireball packs a punch. You okay?" Ledger asked, releasing his grip once Stone was steady.

"Yeah...I'm good. Thanks."

Stone saw his teammates respectfully shaking hands with their opponents. Even Kal and the brute from Ledger's team seemed to find a place of respect for each other.

Stone offered his hand to Ledger. "Good game. I can see why the Juggernauts are contenders for the championship."

"You gave a go of it," Ledger replied. "You should come play for us."

Stone scrambled for a reason that wouldn't sound fake. "Brohn's a fair distance from Jalem. I don't think my parents would allow it."

The two young men were now face to face. Ledger's dark hair and chiseled jaw line were a stark contrast to

Stone's fair complexion, yet there was a warmth and strange familiarity in Ledger's gaze.

"Too bad. You're a good fireballer. We could use a guy like you," Ledger said.

Stone was flattered by the offer. He gave a slight smile and a nod as thanks.

"What's your com ID?" Ledger asked. "I'd like to stay in touch."

Now Stone was really unsure what to do. The Jeshuan scitechs had devised a way for each of their com bands to have two different IDs—a public ID that was used for business operations and for youth at the academy, a second private ID that was used only between trusted Jeshuan followers. But even if Stone gave his public com ID to the Jalem star fireball captain, his parents would be concerned. They would certainly consider it reckless and dangerous since they were the leaders of multiple Creed havens in this region of the country. As Stone searched for an excuse, a thought landed on his mind. *What if Ledger is a secret Jeshuan?* It was just enough of an excuse to do what he did.

"Yeah…sure…that would be great," Stone replied. "3679Victor2."

Ledger tapped on his com band. A second later, a 3D image of Ledger displayed on Stone's com holo port.

"You've got mine too," Ledger said just as the other players gathered around. His demeanor instantly changed to one of indifference.

"Thanks for the match, Vanguards," he said stepping away from Stone. He looked over Stone's six teammates, pursed his lips and slowly nodded. "Not bad," he acknowledged, turning to leave, his two mates following close behind.

Stone, Briggs, and the others watched as they mounted their speeders and left.

"Hot quasar!" Briggs said. "I never thought we'd ever see that. We did great!"

"Yeah," Kal agreed. "And that Ledger guy isn't the tool I thought he was."

Stone rubbed his chest, still feeling the aftereffects of the fireball hit.

"You don't look so good, buddy," Briggs said. "That last hit must have really taken it out of you."

"Yeah…I need to go home and lie down," Stone said. "You guys got the gear?"

"Sure thing…see you tomorrow," Briggs offered.

CHAPTER

13

An Unlikely Friend

As Stone made his way home, he began second-guessing his decision to give his com ID to Ledger. But after thinking it through many times, he reasoned that Ledger was just another student like the thousands he encountered every day at the Brohn Academy. Besides that, the chance that Ledger would actually connect with him was pretty much nil.

He parked his speeder around the back of their home and secured it. When he entered, the place was dark and silent.

"Mom...Dad," he called out, but there was no answer. Stone carefully searched, but there was no sign of them. He was immediately tempted to think the worst.

"Lights," he spoke as he entered the kitchen.

His gaze landed on a note on the table—*Visiting friends...be home late. Love, Dad and Mom.*

Whew.

Stone went to bed earlier than usual. It seemed to him that a good night's rest would help him recover from the fireball hit.

The next morning Stone woke up sore and late. His parents were already hurrying out the door by the time he made it to the kitchen.

"Hey, how was the fireball match last night?" Rhett asked as Stone grabbed a muffin and a can of kangle juice.

Stone swallowed a bite of his muffin. "It was a great match. The Juggernauts won pretty easily. I think they're definitely going to the championship."

"I've heard Jalem has a few good teams this year," Rhett said as he walked to the door.

Brae came to Stone and put a hand on his shoulder, looking deeply into his eyes. "I'm glad you had good time with your friends," she said with a smile. "I just get a little overly concerned about you. I'm sorry."

Stone shook his head. "It's okay, mom. I get it…I really do." He leaned forward, giving her a quick hug. Out of the corner of his eye, he saw his dad offering a thumbs up. Stone pulled back. "I have something I'd like to talk to both of you about."

"Can it wait until tonight?" Rhett asked as he looked at his com band. "All of us are running late this morning."

"Yeah…sure," Stone said, realizing that he should at least let his parents know he had given his public com ID to a new friend.

Brae placed a hand on Stone's cheek. "You're a good lad, Stone Williams," she said, turning to join Rhett as he exited the door.

At the academy, Stone tried to focus on his lessons, but his mind kept wandering back to the street match with Ledger and his teammates.

Why did Ledger really ask for my com ID? Stone wondered as he sat down to eat his lunch. As careful as his parents had taught him to be regarding their secrecy, a bit of paranoia instinctively crept into his thoughts. Two of his friends joined him, which soon distracted Stone from his wary thoughts.

During his next class, Stone's com band alerted him to an incoming message.

Ledger: *Have you recovered?*

Stone stared at his com band. A message from Ledger was unexpected, especially this soon. With suspicions revived, he hesitated, but he also considered the possibility that Ledger could actually be a straight up guy who was looking for an outside friend. He knew the safest thing for him to do would be to ignore the message and move on with his day, but curiosity ate at him. He tapped his fingers on his desk as the instructor at the front of the class was lecturing on new developments in nanotech.

Mostly…still sore though, Stone typed.

Before Stone could talk himself out of it, he pressed the send icon. He waited, his fingers drumming the desk. Irrational thoughts flashed across his mind…perhaps Ledger was some secret KDF operative trying to discover him, his parents, and his Creed. Stone imagined an entire squad of KDF storming the academy just to find and haul him in. After a few seconds, Stone recovered his rational mind. He smirked at his foolish and paranoid thoughts.

Ledger: *No doubt. I took a hit like that two weeks ago, and it took three days to work out the jeebies.*

Stone took a deep breath. That sure seemed normal. As Stone thought about Ledger, he had to admit that he actually liked the guy. He played a tough, fair fireball match without a single taunt.

Stone decided he'd better let the conversation die and get on with his day. However, the brief message exchange with Ledger certainly eased his mind regarding any threat, as minimal as it might be. A part of him envied normal teens that didn't have to worry about the ever-present threat of being discovered as a Jeshuan.

Early that evening, Stone entertained a longer message exchange with Ledger, which convinced him that everything with Ledger was on the up and up. The guy seemed genuine, even opening up about his frustration with some of his teammates. He waited for any probing questions, but there wasn't even a hint at such a thing. Without realizing it, the evening passed, and any potential threat seemed to disappear completely.

Over the next couple of weeks, Stone's communication with Ledger became a daily occurrence, and the two became friends in a way Stone never expected. One evening as Stone was studying at home for an exam in his scitech class, his com band notified him of an incoming holo message. Stone stared at the request...Ledger. Finally, he clicked "ALLOW."

A holographic video of Ledger illuminated six inches above his com band.

"Hey, Stone," Ledger said offering a smile.

"Ledger," Stone grinned back. "What's up?"

"Thought maybe we could talk face-to-face for a change."

"Yeah...sure," Stone replied. "How was your match against the Blazers?" he asked, trying to break the ice.

"Brutal!" Ledger replied. "They seemed way more intent on hitting us with fireballs than on scoring." Ledger pulled up the sleeve on his right arm to reveal a large nasty bruise covering his shoulder with red burn marks around the edges.

"Yikes...that'll take some time," Stone said wincing.

"Yeah, I'm not sure why I even play the stupid game," Ledger replied.

Stone was stunned by the confession. Ledger was one of the top contenders to be selected for the Global Fireball Champion Team. He figured that it had been his goal all along.

"Really?" Stone asked. "I thought you loved the game."

Ledger got serious. "Parts of it, sure. I mostly play because my father insists on it. He says it will enhance my training."

Stone hesitated, wondering what he meant by that. It sounded a lot like something his own dad would say.

"I mean, there's certainly no future in fireball after graduation, and besides that, the other players are just so..." Ledger continued but couldn't seem to find the right word.

"Fake?" Stone offered.

Ledger looked right at Stone and slowly nodded. "That's it. And not just my teammates...everyone. Sometimes I think I have more in common with my training bot than I do the kids at the academy. I'm looking forward to doing something that really matters."

"I get it," Stone agreed. "One more year and the galaxy is ours."

Ledger's smile returned. "Nobody here gets me. I wish we weren't so far apart. I'd like to hang out."

"Jalem and Brohn aren't exactly next door," Stone said.

"For sure...take care, Stone," Ledger said. A second later the holo image disappeared.

There was a tap on Stone's bedroom door, and the door slid away.

"You okay?" Brae asked, peeking into his room. "I thought you had a friend over."

"Nah...just a holo on my com band," Stone replied.

"I didn't think Briggs liked holos," Brae said.

"A new guy. I met him playing fireball a while ago," Stone replied.

Brae fully entered his room. "I'm glad for you," Brae said with a smile. "Is he a Jeshuan?"

"Not sure yet," Stone answered. "He's genuine. If he's not, he's one in the making," Stone said with a grin.

His mother nodded, looking as though her thoughts were distant. "Aren't they all?" she said. "Just be careful, Stone. There's a lot at stake."

"I will, mom."

"Good night, son," Brae said as she came to kiss his cheek.

As she left his room, Stone replayed his exchange with Ledger in his mind, searching for any danger, but he couldn't find any. The truth was that Ledger was a great guy. Despite this fact, Stone cautioned himself about revealing too much to his new friend. Jeshuans were considered fringe and heretical by much of the masses. He would need to keep his secret life secret.

Over the next few weeks, the friendship between Stone and Ledger deepened. Stone was surprised by how honest Ledger seemed to be about everything. It was a quality Stone didn't realize he was missing in other friendships until he experienced it with Ledger.

One afternoon, Stone received a message from Ledger.

In Brohn. How about grabbing some food?

Stone smiled. It would be great to see Ledger in person again. Just as he was about to reply, caution kicked in, causing him to hesitate. He shook it off, having convinced himself that everything with Ledger was completely normal.

Sure...Kit's Diner on Sierra Drive is my favorite. 12:30?

A few seconds later, Ledger replied. *Perfect. See you then!*

Rhett and Brae had taught Stone well. Even when everything in life seemed normal, he was trained to observe and be careful. He had heard many stories of KDF operatives appearing out of nowhere to arrest and imprison a group of Jeshuans or a family.

Stone arrived at the diner 30 minutes early but parked his speeder inconspicuously across the street so he could scout the area for any unusual characters, like undercover KDF operatives. He waited until he saw Ledger enter the diner. Still clear. Stone was relieved, eager to prove that his friendship with Ledger was exactly what it appeared to be.

Stone entered the diner and walked to the table where Ledger was sitting. As soon as Ledger saw him, his face lit up. He stood to greet Stone.

"Hey, man, it's good to see you again," Ledger said, offering a hand and a one-armed hug.

They sat down, and Stone looked Ledger in the eye, searching for the genuine heart he had come to believe his friend possessed.

"I didn't think you had another fireball match here so soon," Stone said.

"We don't. My father is here on business, and I asked to come along," Ledger replied.

Stone was curious but decided to take the conversation another direction. In just a few minutes, Stone was at ease and enjoying his time with Ledger. It felt as if they had been friends for years and were just catching up. A couple of minutes later, a young waitress appeared at their table. Stone looked up to see the face of the girl that usually waited on him.

"Hey, Stone," she said with sly smile. "New friend?" she asked as she eyed Ledger.

"Hi, Ayla," Stone replied. "This is Ledger."

Through hints here and there, Stone had deduced that Ledger came from a well-off family. The apparent social divide between this simple waitress and his new friend was significant. Stone watched to see how Ledger would respond—it would tell him a lot about the true character of the guy.

"Hi, Ayla. It's a pleasure to meet you," Ledger said with a smile. "How long have you worked here?"

Ayla hesitated. She was a pretty girl, wary of flirtatious customers. After three seconds of scrutiny, she smiled. "Nearly a year now. Stone was my first customer," she said flashing her eyes his way. "What can I get you boys?"

Stone and Ledger gave Ayla their order. When she left, Ledger was grinning.

"What's up?" Stone asked.

Ledger looked Stone in the eye. "She's into you."

Stone scoffed at the notion. He shook his head. "Yeah…I don't think so."

"I'll bet that every time you come here it's not a bot waitress that serves you but it's her," Ledger said. Stone realized he was right. "Look, Stone, if there's one thing I get, it's knowing when a girl is interested. She's interested…and she's cute too."

Stone looked at Ledger. "What about you…have you got a girl?" he asked hoping to deflect the conversation.

"Just like a fireball jink," Ledger said with a laugh. "Nice move."

Stone laughed.

For the next hour, Stone and Ledger ate delicious fried suroot curls and seasoned brisket wraps while enjoying their time together talking about friends, futures, and hobbies. When Stone asked Ledger about his plans after the academy, Ledger became quite serious. He looked at Stone as if trying to decide if he dared share his thoughts.

"Truth is, I'm very devoted to trying to honor Sovereign Ell Yon with my life. That's something I don't share with my friends in Jalem."

Stone felt the hair on his neck stand straight. *Was this a hint from Ledger?* he wondered.

Stone nodded. "I get it, Ledger. Same here. Not too many guys our age are devoted to him like that."

Ledger's eyes opened wide, looking completely relieved at hearing Stone's affirming words. It seemed to have a profound effect on him.

"Now I know what it is," Ledger said.

"What's that?" Stone asked.

"Somehow I knew you were committed to Ell Yon just as much as I was."

Stone swallowed hard. If he only knew...dare he tell him about the life-saving truth of Jeshu? Could it be possible that Ledger was a—"

"What do your parents do?" Ledger asked as their time was winding down.

When Stone hesitated. Ledger held up his hand.

"Don't tell me. Our friendship must remain unbound by any social presuppositions." He glanced at his com band. "I have to go—time to meet up with my father," Ledger said. He tapped his com band and stood up.

Stone joined him.

"Talk to you later, Stone. Stay cool."

"You too. Good luck in your fireball match against the Storms this week," Stone said as they grasped hands.

Once Ledger exited the diner, Stone sat back down to arrange payment for the meal on his com band. Ayla appeared at his side.

"No need. Your friend already paid," she said as she started gathering dishes.

When Stone glanced up at her, she flashed him a quick smile.

"I was really your first customer?" Stone asked.

"Mm-hmm," she said, continuing to work.

"How come I don't see you at the academy?" he asked. "Have you already graduated?"

Stone noticed that Ayla's smile diminished. "Not exactly."

"That's a bit mysterious," he quipped back with a smile, but she became even more serious.

Ayla stopped to look straight at him. She scanned the room and sat down opposite Stone. It was a move that really surprised him. Ayla leaned forward.

"Considering who your parents are, it wouldn't hurt for you to be a little more mysterious too." Ayla's stern eyes captured Stone's attention. "You're not as anonymous as you think, so...you should be careful."

Ayla seemed to search his eyes for understanding. A few seconds later she started to stand up.

"Wait!" Stone said, reaching for her arm.

As soon as he touched her, he realized how offensive that might seem. He quickly pulled back his hand. "Sorry…I don't understand. What are you getting at? What do you know?"

Ayla eyed Stone closely. "I know a lot more than you realize."

Stone had never looked at Ayla like he was now. Her rare green eyes suddenly held him captive in a way he never expected.

"Like what?" he asked.

Ayla glanced toward the kitchen and stood up as the manager of the diner appeared.

"Not here. I'm off at six," she said then grabbed her load of dishes and left.

Ledger hurried to catch his father at the Brohn Sanctum, but he couldn't help thinking about his time with Stone. The guy was refreshingly genuine. It was a bold move to speak about Sovereign Ell Yon with such passion, but now knowing that Stone had the same heart explained why he enjoyed his friendship with him so much. He had never met anyone quite like Stone. Ledger remembered reading in the ancient writings about two men who shared kindred hearts for Sovereign Ell Yon and wondered if he might have found such a friend in Stone.

Ledger rounded the final turn on his speeder as he approached the Brohn Sanctum. He frowned as he saw a Morian commando patrol by the gate of the outer courtyard. *Will Ell Yon ever deliver the Rayleans from the oppression of this wretched empire?* he wondered.

Ledger stopped and exited his speeder. He walked past the patrol as if they weren't there. That seemed to be the preference of both Morians and Rayleans alike. Upon entering the expansive marble foyer of the Brohn Sanctum—or any sanctum, for that matter—he experienced an inexplicable pull on his mind and heart. This sensation had been with him since childhood, making him feel both unique and out of place, particularly after interacting with other children and youths. He was convinced that no one his age shared such feelings until he met Stone. After only a few minutes of guarding him in a street fireball match several weeks ago, Ledger perceived that Stone might be the only other individual on the planet who could understand him.

Ledger made his way into the oration chamber where his father was just taking the platform to address the Keepers and the Builders of Brohn. Ledger made eye contact with his father, Fasa Kylos, and nodded. The words of his father certainly stirred his soul much like the readings of the oracles of old. Ledger had grown up learning the history of his people, so he couldn't help the deep feelings of loyalty such a legacy evoked within him. Admittedly, there were far too many instances of the Raylean people falling away from the ways of Sovereign Ell Yon, but once the order of the Keepers and Builders had been established, they had stayed the course, even being diligent to eliminate those who would attempt to subvert the plans of Ell Yon through promoting Deitum Prime and heresy.

"My fellow Keepers and Builders, our mission to purify the sanctums and the people of Rayl continues. Though the heresy of the Jeshuans occasionally rears its blasphemous head in some of our major cities, the Keeper Defense Forces continue to execute their duties to protect our legacy and our future as followers of the Immortal Sovereign Ell Yon."

Kylos's last statement brought rousing cheers from the audience. Ledger joined in the applause. As his father continued his speech, Ledger's mind wandered to earlier days when his father began training him.

"We need a leader who has the diplomatic skills of a Keeper and also the tactical skills of a military general. You will be that man, Ledger," his father had told him. "You are the secret weapon that will rid our planet once and for all of the heretics that hold us back from our great future."

The commission his father had given Ledger ignited a passion that brought the stories of the ancient oracles to life. Ledger imagined the mighty Navis of old wielding the Protector and defeating entire empires. *Could I be one of those Navi?* he dared ask of himself. *When will the Sovereign restore the Protectors to the Keepers to lead their people? When will he free us from the bondage of the Morian Empire?*

Oftentimes, Ledger's mind would drift into questions that had no immediate answers, but that didn't diminish his belief in or passion for serving Ell Yon. He knew that patience was something the Immortal required, so he would wait—but in the waiting, he would prepare just as his father had taught him.

When Fasa Kylos finished his speech, the chamber gave a rousing standing ovation. Such things made Ledger proud to be his son. The respect of other devout Keepers and Builders who served Ell Yon was something few had earned.

"Excellent speech, Father," Ledger said as he greeted him at the base of the platform.

Fasa Kylos smiled, placing an arm around Ledger's shoulder as they walked toward the exit. "Thank you, Ledger. I'm glad you made it. Did you enjoy your time with your friend?"

"I did. I enjoy his company," Ledger said, reflecting on their conversation. "We share a similar devotion to Sovereign Ell Yon."

Kylos looked over at Ledger with surprise on his face. "Really? I'd like to meet him sometime."

Just before they exited the oration chamber, Kylos stopped and turned them both about to see the magnificent beauty of the sanctum's inner room.

"One day, the men and women of the sanctums will gather to hear *you* speak," Kylos said with his chin lifted. "Ell Yon has a special calling on your life, Ledger—one that will initiate the purifying leadership needed to restore our orders to their rightful place of dignity among the people of Rayl."

Ledger knew that his father was referring to the Jeshuan heretics that had spread across the planet. When he considered their treacherous efforts to undermine the ways of Ell Yon, a fierce anger began to boil within him. Ledger, in particular, had direct and immediate access to the truth about them through his father.

"Are the Keeper Defense Forces making headway against the enemies of Ell Yon?" Ledger asked.

"They are," his father said, turning about to leave the chamber. "But not as quickly as I had hoped. The heretics are elusive, and the planet is vast. That's why your training is so important. You will take our purifying cause to the four corners of Rayl."

"How can they be so deceived?" Ledger asked, disgust darkening his countenance. "There are rumors at the academy that the KDF has had to kill some of them. Is that true?" Ledger asked looking over at his father.

"Some of them are so consumed by their false beliefs that they attack our courageous KDF operatives. We must do what is necessary to defend ourselves and preserve the ways of Ell Yon."

Ledger felt the burning in his heart for protecting the legacy of Sovereign Ell Yon among his people. "I want to be part of that, even if it's dangerous."

His father nodded. "Soon, my son."

Kylos was thrilled with how enthusiastically Ledger was embracing the mission of the Keeper Order to abolish the Jeshuan sect. Kylos had masterfully orchestrated Ledger's training in both the tactical combat arena and as a future Preeminent Keeper in the Order.

He will be a master of weapons and a master of prophecies…just like the days of old, Kylos thought as his plan ripened. *It's just a matter of time before the Jeshuans are no more.*

Such thoughts were pleasant for Kylos to contemplate. What he wasn't looking forward to, however, was the meeting with Subchancellor Pylok later this afternoon when he returned to Jalem. There was never any guarantee that an encounter with the Morian governor of Rayl would end well. This time he would call on Krisha Monae to accompany him, regardless of her recent frequent display of reservation.

Kylos met Monae at the Jalem Sanctum before boarding a Morian transport sent specifically to pick them up. Monae shook her head as they took their seats.

"This can't be good," Monae said, glaring at Kylos. "Anytime Pylok arranges our transportation, I have to wonder if it's a one-way trip."

"Nonsense, Krisha," Kylos said with a crooked grin. "Subchancellor Pylok has been very cordial with me as of late," he said to reassure her, but deep down, his stomach was in a knot.

"Morian rulers are never cordial with Rayleans unless it suits their own devices," Monae countered, turning to look out the portal as they launched on a vector toward Pylok's palace.

The entrance into Pylok's Hall of Judgment was much the same as before—grand, cold, and ominous. The master Keeper and master Builder approached Pylok's seat with as much confidence as they dared.

Kylos bowed his head slightly. "Subchancellor Pylok, it is good to see you again. It's always a pleasure to serve you. Since it isn't yet time for our yearly accounting, you must have something in particular you want to discuss?"

Kylos noticed that Monae seemed uncomfortable with how familiar his tone was toward the Morian Subchancellor.

"Well, Kylos, your discernment does you justice," Pylok replied. "I have a favor to ask of you."

"Of course, Subchancellor. Anything to strengthen our mutually beneficial arrangement."

A slight smirk crossed Pylok's face, and Kylos noticed that Monae fidgeted at this last exchange. Pylok gazed at Kylos and Monae for a moment before speaking.

"It seems that we have both been plagued by two groups of people that are contrary to our established authority," Pylok said as he stood from his elevated seat. He slowly walked down the four wide steps to stand at the same level as Kylos and Monae.

This is different, Kylos thought, being careful not to show alarm.

Pylok approached both of them and stopped three feet short.

"I am referring to the Partisans and the Jeshuans, of course," Pylok continued. "These persistent and irritating factions are refusing to give up. After seventeen years of their annoying presence, I've finally arrived at a conclusion." Pylok lifted a finger and smiled. "Your KDF operatives are surely skilled and knowledgeable regarding the underground affairs of both of these nefarious Raylean factions. Since I've afforded you significant leeway in the execution of the Peace Preservation Edict, it's time you give me something in return."

Kylos swallowed hard. Pylok lowered his finger but continued to glare at Kylos with steely eyes.

"I want your KDF squads to hunt down and kill any Partisans with the same tenacity you have exercised in your hunt for Jeshuans. Such action will also be mutually beneficial since you have stated that their actions are reprehensible to you and the law-abiding Rayleans of this planet."

Kylos scrambled for words that would appease Pylok without committing to such an abominable thing. Although Kylos did not support the Partisans, many Rayleans secretly applauded their efforts to rebel against the oppressive rule of the Morians. Their declaration to free all of Rayl was a quiet hope in the hearts of every Raylean.

Kylos began to sweat as he considered his limited options. He glanced toward Monae, hoping she would offer some tactful response. After all, that is why he had insisted she accompany him. Monae stayed silent, offering nothing.

"I see, Subchancellor. The Partisans are indeed reprehensible in the acts of rebellion against the Morian Empire. I'm just not sure how we could accomplish nearly as much as your skilled commandos could," Kylos offered, hoping Pylok would leave room for his denial through flattery. But Pylok would have none of it.

"You underestimate the effectiveness of your highly trained operatives," Pylok replied with false flattery of his own. He leaned in toward Kylos. "Whispers in the dark can be very revealing."

Pylok held Kylos's gaze for a moment. He turned around and walked back up the steps to his elevated seat and sat down.

"My replacement, Subchancellor Marculus, will be arriving one year from now, and I want these Partisans eliminated before I relinquish this position and return home to Moria. I expect frequent reports from you on the number of Partisans your operatives eliminate over the next 12 months." A subtle smirk landed on Pylok's face. "And don't worry, Kylos, this will be our secret. None of your people need know of our arrangement. Within a year's time, I'm certain that a thorough purging of the

Raylean people of both these heretical factions will serve us both quite well." Pylok's eyes narrowed, and his countenance hardened. "You may go and fulfill your duty to the Morian Empire."

Kylos and Monae offered a bowing of their heads, then turned and exited Pylok's Hall of Judgment. Kylos was irritated with Monae. Her silence was insulting. As they boarded the transport, Monae leaned over to speak in hushed tones.

"That was quite cordial indeed."

Kylos scowled at her. "I've never known you to be so absent in such a situation."

Monae pursed her lips. "Agreeing to hunt down and kill our own people is something I can never condone," she whispered, her eyes full of condemnation.

"You already have, Monae. The Jeshuans are just as much Raylean as the Partisans," Kylos shot back.

Monae leaned back in her seat. "Perhaps we are wrong on both accounts."

Kylos glared at his counterpart. *Is she being swayed by the irrational and blasphemous teaching of the Jeshuans too?* he wondered.

"What do you mean by that?" he said with forced restraint.

Monae hesitated. She glanced toward Kylos. "What if we were wrong? What if we are fighting *against* Sovereign Ell Yon instead of *for* him. The mere thought of it—" Monae let her words trail off.

Kylos was stunned beyond words. The influence of this dead heretic was becoming impossible to quell.

"Our orders have become pointless, Kylos," she continued. "There are no Protectors to build and none to Keep. For thousands of years the Protectors guided our people." She looked Kylos square in the eye. "We have no Protectors! Where is Ell Yon?"

Kylos's fury was mounting. "Are you seriously questioning the legacy of our orders because of the claims of one false Navi? I thought you were stronger than that!" Kylos exclaimed, finding it nearly impossible to keep his voice quiet. His accusation didn't seem to affect the Master Builder in the least.

Not another word passed between them for the rest of the ride back to the sanctum. Once they exited and walked to the inner chamber of the sanctum, Kylos confronted Monae once more.

"Monae," Kylos said turning to directly face her. "Your growing reservations about our common goal of eradicating the Jeshuans is extremely concerning."

Monae's eyes narrowed as she turned to face Kylos. "And your willingness to become a Morian Talon blade to slay our own people is just as concerning!"

Kylos felt the fracture between them solidify. Her recent behavior and attitude were wholly unacceptable.

"I demand you resign your station as the lead Master Builder of the Builder Order," Kylos declared.

Monae glared back at Kylos. "I will have no part in the killing of our people anymore—Partisans or Jeshuans. They are all Rayleans and to do the bidding of the Morian Empire in killing our own is despicable."

Monae turned and began walking away. After she had taken a few steps, she turned back. "There are no other Builders that will agree to such a thing. The Keeper Order will do this atrocious thing on their own or the Builder Order will be no more!" Monae declared.

As furious as Kylos was with Krisha Monae, hearing her speak such words destroyed a part of him. This false Navi named Jeshu had single-handedly dismantled and destroyed one of the most honored institutions in Raylean history. He took several deep breaths as he considered this frightful dilemma, and as he did, a plot began to form—one that would complement his ultimate weapon against the Jeshuans nicely.

He ascended the steps of the oration chamber, feeling the call to stay true to his mission for Sovereign Ell Yon no matter what odds he faced.

"The Jeshuans rarely have weapons and never fight back," he said quietly to himself as he slowly walked to one end of the platform. "My people, and Ledger in particular, need to understand how dangerous the Jeshuans are even if they aren't violent. But weaker minds are too often placated by pacifists, so if we were to raid a group of Partisans but call them Jeshuans, the rest of Rayl would be fully persuaded for our cause." Kylos began to smile as he sorted out the details of his plan.

I will need someone I can trust...someone who has demonstrated complete loyalty, Kylos thought. He turned around and paced to the other end of the platform. *Chief Deklan, my Jalem lead KDF operative is the man,* Kylos concluded. *We will need to be thorough, manage publicity, and keep everything extremely confidential.*

Kylos lifted his com band and tapped an icon. Chief Deklan's face appeared, hovering just above Kylos's left arm in holographic perfection.

"Yes, Preeminent Keeper," Deklan said.
"Chief—we need to talk."

CHAPTER

14

The Zeal of a Keeper

Stone paced along the walkway outside of Kit's Diner, waiting for Ayla. At ten after six, he began to wonder if she had jilted him. He sat down at the side of the diner on a nearby planter that was home to two sprawling trees with white blossoms and a host of various flowers growing near the base. It was a pleasant place he hadn't really noticed before. After a two-minute wait, Ayla sat down next to him. She didn't seem in a hurry to talk. She looked over at him.

"Hi."

For some reason, Stone wasn't in a hurry for the conversation either. He was rather content just to have her nearby. Without her waitress uniform, Ayla looked different. He tried to remember if he'd ever seen her in regular clothes but no memory came to mind.

"Hi," he returned. "Thanks for meeting me."

Ayla offered a gentle smile and nodded. After a ten-second awkward pause, Stone figured he should broach the subject.

"So, what did you mean when—"

"I'm hungry," Ayla interrupted. "Can we get something to eat?" She looked at Stone, tilting her head slightly.

Stone took a moment to look at her…really look at her. Her bright eyes and dimpled smile were pleasant. He had never been one to be enamored with a girl, not even the pretty ones. There was too much to learn and work toward. But in this moment, some of that rigid commitment seemed to soften.

"Hungry? After working in a diner all day?" he asked.

"What…you don't think waitresses need to eat?"

Stone laughed. "Of course I do. I just thought you would have already eaten Kit's Diner food."

Ayla grimaced. "After serving it all day, I need something else."

"Hmm." Stone thought. "There's a southeastern style cafeteria three blocks over."

"I love southeastern," Ayla said, rising to her feet.

Stone left his speeder at Kit's Diner so they could walk together. The route to the cafeteria was off the main thoroughfare, which afforded them reasonable privacy to talk. When he was sure no one was within listening distance, he glanced over at Ayla.

"I didn't know you were one of us," he said.

"Our Creed haven is very small. My folks have to be very careful because of where they work," Ayla explained. "I'm not sure your parents even know about us."

That last comment told Stone that Ayla understood exactly who he was and where he came from.

"I get the impression you know me from more than just the diner," Stone said, looking at her out of the corner of his eye. He was confused because he had never seen Ayla anywhere except at the diner.

Ayla pursed her lips, glancing briefly his way. Her silence answered for her.

"How so?" he asked.

Ayla shrugged her shoulders. "You're the reason I took the job at the diner."

Stone's eyes widened. *A stalker?* he wondered.

Ayla seemed to realize his conclusion, and she put her arm out in front of him to stop them from walking. "Not for the reason you're thinking!" she quietly exclaimed. "Honest!"

Stone squinted his eyes. "For what reason then?"

Ayla took a deep breath, turned, and slowly resumed walking. Stone stepped to catch up. She seemed to struggle with an explanation. She scanned about them to make sure they were still out of earshot of any passersby.

"My family are devout Jeshuans," she said in a quiet voice. "My dad and mom are super-secret Navis. They have to be because she's a medtech master at the Brohn Medtech Facility and my father serves on the executive staff at the same place."

Stone was more than surprised, having thought Ayla came from a blue-collar family.

"My siblings and I are tutored at home by a close Jeshuan friend so we can stay off the Keeper grid as much as possible," Ayla explained.

The more Stone learned about Ayla, the more intrigued he became. There was a lot more to this girl than he had first thought.

"That still doesn't explain why you took the job at Kit's Diner because of me. Are you spying on me?" he asked.

Ayla stopped walking again. She leaned up against a fence that bordered a small park. Stone turned to face her. She looked up at him, wistful and concerned.

"With all the secret living we have to do, I've turned into a bit of a sleuth. I figure information that I know and others don't know gives me an advantage at keeping myself and my family safe while still serving the cause of Jeshu."

Stone crossed his arms, gazing into the green eyes of this intriguing girl...still waiting for information that would make sense of her story.

"I believe every single event that happens to a dedicated follower of Jeshu happens for a reason...a reason that perhaps only Sovereign Ell Yon knows."

"Ayla, you have to help me here. What is this all about?" Stone pressed.

She pursed her lips, struggling as if she were carrying some enormous burden.

"If Kylos and the Keepers had their way, you would never have been born."

Stone was rather stunned by the statement. "What is that supposed to mean?"

"It took me three years to figure this out...bits and pieces of overheard conversations...secret records and such." Ayla looked at Stone, searching his face. "Seventeen years ago, my mother was an assistant medtech to the Brohn lead medtech master when your dad brought your mother in with a fatal abdominal wound. My mother was called to assist the medtech master part way through a procedure and was ordered by the medtech master to perform a surgery to make your mother infertile."

Stone waited. He had heard his parents refer to him as a special gift, but he assumed it was just something all parents told their children.

"Assuming that is true, obviously your mother didn't do the surgery, but why didn't the medtech master do it?" Stone asked. "That doesn't make sense."

"I don't have all of it pieced together yet," Ayla replied, "but I heard my mother say that he was called away to perform another procedure. He didn't know my mother was a secret Jeshuan. When he left, my mother decided not to go through with the surgery despite the risk she was exposing herself to. She put your mom back together and then helped your parents get out of the medtech facility before the KDF could find them. I heard my mom tell my dad that if Kylos had known that Rhett and Brae Stryker were at the medtech facility, he would have killed them both."

Stone took a moment to think about what Ayla had shared.

"My parents and I owe your mom a great debt of gratitude. I'm sure they would like to thank her personally," Stone offered.

Ayla shook her head. "My parents wouldn't risk the exposure. They have been extremely careful and found a hundred ways to help fellow Jeshuans because of it."

"Can I at least visit your Creed haven with you sometime?" Stone asked.

Ayla tilted her head. "I don't think that would be such a good idea."

"Listen, I get the super-secret stuff, but all the havens still need to support each other. How can we do that if we don't even know you exist?" Stone argued.

Ayla appeared to think that over. She came close to him and grabbed his com band arm. She typed in the address of her Creed haven on a "notes" screen.

Stone looked down on her auburn hair as she typed. Having her this close caused his stomach to flutter. She finished and backed away, resuming her lean against the fence.

"There. Memorize it and delete it...okay?"

Stone read the address, repeating it a couple of times in his mind then deleted it.

"Done...when do you meet?"

"Our next meeting is tomorrow night," she said with a grin.

Stone nodded. He stepped toward her and turned, leaning against the same fence. Now shoulder to shoulder, he looked straight ahead.

"So, just to be clear...you *are* spying on me."

Ayla squirmed. "Well, I figure Sovereign Ell Yon must have a pretty important plan for your life if he went through all of that trouble to arrange your birth."

Stone looked at her out of the corner of his eye.

"Honestly…I look for where Ell Yon is working, and I go there," Ayla said dismissively. She flipped her hair and turned to look down the thoroughfare. "Besides, isn't your grandfather the great Elias Thornton…modern-day Navi that single-handedly took on Prefect Terrok and the Keeper and Builder Orders all at the same time? Can you blame me?"

Stone smiled. He liked Ayla.

"Well, I guess you'd better stick close," he quipped, sticking out his arm for her to take. "You never know when some grand Immortal plan might kick off."

Ayla turned back to look at him and his offer. She smirked, then smiled, taking his arm. "If you insist."

Stone resumed their walk to the cafeteria. With her hand resting gently on his arm, that simple touch seemed to have a profound effect on him. They were walking closer together because of it, which he liked.

"The guy you were with, are you sure about him?" Ayla asked, glancing over at Stone.

"Mostly. I've only known him for a couple of weeks. He seems like a decent guy," Stone replied. "He's from Jalem."

Ayla seemed concerned. "I don't have my Protector yet, but my first impressions are pretty good."

"And?" Stone pressed.

"And for what it's worth, I agree. He's a decent guy, but I think there's always reason to be concerned. It could be an intersection."

"Intersection?" Stone asked.

"An intersection is when two lines of an investigation converge. It always means something very significant because the coincidence of something like that is a million to one. For those who are true to Sovereign Ell

Yon, I guarantee that in some profound way, he is at work. I'm just waiting to see what your intersection will be."

Stone laughed out loud. "You are an intriguing girl," he said, searching Ayla's eyes. How could a simple waitress at Kit's Diner be so intrusive...profound... intelligent. He was looking forward to getting to know her more.

Back at the sanctum in Jalem, Ledger intended on doubling his efforts to become fully trained in the ways of the Keepers and their defense force operatives. Ever since he was a child, the sanctum and its library of wondrous historical records, the oration chamber, and the well-kept ornate courtyard with thousands of flowers and trees was where he felt most at home. Studying the writings and records of the ancient oracles was part of his daily regimen, and he loved it, which made him extremely unique among other children.

"If you continue to learn of Sovereign Ell Yon and study his words given to us by the great oracles, you will be the youngest Keeper Master in the history of Rayl," his father had said, encouraging the enthusiasm of the child.

At twelve years old, Ledger was assigned by his father, Fasa Kylos, to be trained by some of the most elite Raylean miltech personnel on the planet. His natural athleticism enabled him to excel in this new physical, strategic, and military training. He had learned about the great Daeson Starlore of old and how the Commander of the Malakians had similarly trained him to battle with the enemies of Ell Yon, so Ledger embraced his training whole-heartedly. When Ledger traveled from his home to the sanctum by himself, his father would insist that an assistance and training android accompany him for protection. One of the androids, R32, seemed to be his constant companion. Oddly enough, Ledger came to enjoy the companionship of the android. When the rest of the world didn't seem to offer a genuine friend for the boy, R32 seemed an acceptable substitute.

By the time Ledger was seventeen, Fasa Kylos was on the verge of creating a new Master Keeper in the person of his own son. Ledger wanted to make his father proud of him, but that was not the key impetus for his complete dedication. Ledger was driven by his love for the mighty and Immortal Sovereign Ell Yon, believing with his whole heart that he would be called to some great mission for the cause of his people.

"Perhaps you will lead our people to freedom beyond the shackles of the Morian Empire," his father had speculated. "Or perhaps you will prepare our world for the prophesied true deliverer," he added. "But your first mission must be to purge our people of the heretical beliefs that have beguiled them because of these violent Jeshuans."

Ten years earlier, Kylos had initiated the construction of a KDF operative training and detention complex on the outskirts of Jalem. It was equipped with an armory of weapons utilized by the KDF operatives, including the Bi-dagger Talon, often the preferred weapon of choice when stealth was required. Ledger had proven exceptionally proficient with the Bi-dagger Talon. One facility on the complex grounds was equipped with a high-tech holographic simulator to run various training scenarios. Additionally, six training and assistance androids were positioned in their charging stations at the armory. Every KDF mission had at least one android accomplice for various purposes. Although the bots were limited in their role with weapons because of the anti-AI restrictions placed on them, these mechanical assistants proved incredibly valuable when transporting and guarding suspected Jeshuan criminals.

Ledger's elite training, orchestrated by his father, had propelled him into a world beyond anything his peers could even imagine. It was the reason that so much of his non-sanctum life seemed pointless, including his dominance in the fireball competition arenas. That competition and much of his social life and acquaintances seemed quite trivial by comparison.

Today Chief Sergeant Deklan was conducting training on the use of the tactical class-one rapid-fire plasma rifle, another key weapon in the suppression of Jeshuan heretics. Ledger employed his plasma rifle with precision and deadly force against the holographic insurgents in the current training scenario with two assistance bots for support. Even Chief Deklan seemed impressed, a thing difficult to accomplish. At the end of the exercise, the holographic world of the city of Jalem with its synthetic buildings and inhabitants disappeared, and the two assistance bots stood motionless just behind Ledger. As the visuals cleared, Ledger heard the quiet clapping of an observer. Ledger turned around to see his father applauding his performance.

"Well done, Ledger," his father commended.

Ledger lowered his rifle. "Thank you, Father."

Kylos looked toward his sergeant—the man gave a subtle nod.

"Chief Deklan tells me your training is going extremely well," his father said.

It was rare for his father to offer a compliment, so Ledger wasn't sure what to say. Although Ledger had many different instructors, Chief Deklan oversaw most of his training. As the leader of the primary KDF squad in Jalem, the Chief had a front row seat to the effectiveness of the efforts against the Jeshuans.

"I think it's time you start using your skills to make a real difference for Sovereign Ell Yon," his father continued.

Ledger came to stand before his father and Chief Deklan. "Seriously?" he asked.

"What do you think, Chief…is he ready?" his father asked.

"I believe he's ready, Master Kylos," the chief replied. "But he's young and there will be danger. The Jeshuans can be ruthless."

Ledger's father looked at him, appearing to consider the warning his chief KDF operative had just given him.

"I'm ready, and I can handle anything the Jeshuans throw at me," Ledger replied with an air of confidence.

Kylos hesitated…scrutinizing his son. "Yes…I believe you can. Why don't you clean up and go home while I discuss the details of your first mission with Chief Deklan."

Ledger nodded. "R32…with me," Ledger commanded one of the assistance bots.

Ledger and the android walked toward the holo facility exit. He couldn't believe this was happening. He had waited for years for this very opportunity.

Once outside, Ledger made his way toward his two-seat speeder.

"Your training is going well, Master Ledger," R32 said.

"Thanks, R32. I can't believe I get to go on a real KDF mission." Ledger thought about the holo representations of the Jeshuan fighters. "You've been on a lot of missions?" he asked the bot.

"Yes, 158," R32 said without emotion.

"Is the simulation I just trained on realistic?" Ledger asked. "I mean…are the Jeshuans as ruthless fighters as the holo makes them out to be?"

The android hesitated. "The simulation is augmented to enhance your training."

Ledger wasn't sure what the bot meant by that, but sometimes R32 was a bit cryptic. It was his "human-like" responses at times that caused Ledger to prefer R32 over the other bots. Ledger jumped into the pilot seat, and R32 took the passenger's.

"Master Ledger?"

"Yes, R32," Ledger replied.

"It has been my observation that there are now Jeshuans in all echelons of Raylean society, and the KDF has been fighting them for the past eighteen years," R32 stated.

"Yes?"

The android paused again. Those hesitations by R32 were tells for Ledger to know that something unusual was going to be offered by the android.

"It would be interesting to know how many weapons the KDF has retrieved from their raids on the Jeshuans. The stockpile must be large indeed."

Ledger looked over at R32 as he sat motionless, staring straight ahead. The bot hadn't actually asked a question, and yet it felt like one. Ledger refocused on the thoroughfare ahead, his mind reflecting on R32's statement. Something about it jarred him. What was the bot implying? In the fortress of Ledger's mind and in his singular mission to be the ultimate vessel through which Sovereign Ell Yon could work in restoring the Raylean people to their favored status, one small fracture appeared.

Not another word was spoken until they arrived at Ledger's home.

"Will you be my assistance android on the mission tomorrow?" Ledger asked.

"It would be my honor, Master Ledger," R32 replied.

Ledger left the bot at his docking station in the speeder garage and went to his room.

R32's voice kept repeating in his head. *The stockpile must be large indeed.*

Kylos watched as Ledger exited the facility with the assistance bot. The Preeminent Keeper of all Rayl considered his next decisions carefully. To say that he was frustrated by the elusive and growing Jeshuan heretic movement was a gross understatement. He had dedicated the last eighteen years of his life to their complete annihilation and considered his effort only marginally successful, even though in reality it was a complete failure. The Jeshuan movement had somehow grown and spread across the planet in spite of his aggressive efforts. But Kylos remained undaunted by the substance of his apparent failure, for he was about to unleash the ultimate weapon on those degenerate but resilient Jeshuans. His patience was very close to paying off. He turned to Chief Deklan.

"The lad isn't ready to experience a full raid," Kylos began. "The idealistic mind of the boy must be solidified and reinforced in order to complete his training."

Chief Deklan nodded. "I understand."

"Bring in a team of operatives from Joppik to pose as Jeshuans. Let's set up an assault and counterattack scenario. Make sure every plasma rifle is secretly modified to non-lethal settings. I don't want him hurt. Do you understand?"

"Absolutely."

"He needs to see just how lethal the Jeshuans can be before he encounters them in a real scenario."

"I'll set it up," Deklan said.

Kylos could rely on Deklan. The man had executed his directives as the leader of the primary KDF squad in Jalem without question and without compromising Kylos's tenuous relationship with the Morian Subchancellor and his commandos.

"Very well, Chief...carry on."

That night Ledger could hardly sleep as he thought about his first mission with a KDF squad. He felt like he was trained and ready, regardless of how dangerous the mission might be. The anticipation was palpable, and Ledger's mind raced with thoughts of the upcoming mission. This was his chance to prove himself, to show that his training was not in vain. He had always admired the KDF operatives, their precision and bravery, and now he was on the cusp of joining their ranks in a real scenario.

At dawn Ledger, R32, and the KDF squad assembled in the briefing room. Chief Deklan laid out the plan, each detail meticulously crafted. Little did Ledger know that the operatives from Joppik, disguised as Jeshuans, were already in position, ready to engage.

"Our intelligence locates this faction of Jeshuans in a rural compound, so we should be clear of any Morian intervention, at least for thirty minutes," the Chief explained. "We make our drop two miles east of the compound and cover the rest of the way on foot."

Ledger listened intently, his heart pounding with a mix of excitement and anxiety. The room buzzed with the quiet confidence of seasoned soldiers, and he found himself both humbled and exhilarated by their presence. Chief Deklan's voice cut through the tension. "Remember, these Jeshuan heretics could be armed and dangerous. Stay focused, stay sharp, and follow orders."

Ledger nodded, gripping his plasma rifle tightly. As they moved out, the sun's first light cast long shadows across their training complex. They made their way to an assault vehicle and boarded. Once they set down and disembarked, the squad moved with practiced efficiency, their movements synchronized and precise. It took them another forty-five minutes to make it to the Jeshuan compound.

As they approached the Jeshuan holdout, Ledger's visor lit up with tactical data. He took a deep breath, steeling himself for the encounter. Every step brought him closer to the moment he had been preparing for, the moment that would solidify his place among the KDF operatives.

"I have hits on seven armed Jeshuans in that building," one of the operatives said as he scanned the compound with an advanced through-field device.

"Copy. You three cover the south entrance," Chief Deklan ordered. "You two and Ledger, with me on the west entrance."

When both teams were in place, the entrances were simultaneously breached and the fires of Gehenna unleashed. The air around them erupted in multiple bursts of rapid plasma fire. Ledger was stunned by the force and speediness of the Jeshuan reaction.

They must have known we were coming, he thought as he took cover behind the corner of a wall and returned fire.

The firefight was ferocious, but the Chief's plan to bracket them from both entrances paid off. One by one, the vicious Jeshuans fell until there were only two. Finally, they laid down their weapons and surrendered. KDF operatives rushed them and quickly placed composite fetters around their wrists. Ledger looked into the eyes of one of them and knew that his mission to purge Rayl of these heretics was justified. The man's face was filled with contempt.

"We are Jeshuans, and we will destroy the archaic ways of the Keepers and the Builders! We are called by Ell Yon to rid the planet of you and your arrogant rule!" the man shouted as he was taken outside.

Ledger scanned the other five dead Jeshuan heretics, their weapons strewn about beside them.

"They are well armed," Ledger said, looking to his assistance bot, R32.

"Indeed," the bot responded emotionlessly.

Chief Deklan quickly ushered Ledger out of the facility where the skirmish had taken place. "You've seen enough for today. Well done, Ledger," the Chief said with a proud look.

Two assault vehicles set down nearby.

"You accompany Alpha Team with the prisoners back to our complex while I take Bravo team and clean up before any Morian commandos arrive."

"Copy, Chief," Ledger said.

On Ledger's return flight to the complex, firm resolve settled in his heart, and he knew—he could not stop until Rayl was rid of the vicious and heretical Jeshuans.

Over the next few weeks, Ledger was allowed to join Chief Deklan and his squad on several more Jeshuan raids. In raids where the Jeshuans were unarmed and didn't fight back, they were arrested and incarcerated at the KDF detention facility in the complex on the outskirts of Jalem. But occasionally, the Jeshuans were well armed and fought with fierce resolve. In such instances, Ledger learned from the Chief to give no quarter nor allow any to escape.

"These are the most dangerous Jeshuans of all and cannot be permitted to continue their treacherous methods," Chief Deklan explained. "You must always be prepared for the worst-case scenario, Ledger."

"I understand, Chief," Ledger replied.

CHAPTER

15

A Secret Revealed

Over the next several months, Stone and Ayla grew closer. The more time he spent with her, the more his heart inclined toward her. This romantic relationship had taken him by surprise. His parents approved, especially since they had learned that Ayla was a devout follower of Jeshu.

Additionally, the friendship between Stone and Ledger also continued to deepen. Ledger found numerous opportunities to travel to Brohn and visit with Stone. On one such occasion, Ledger even briefly met Stone's mother. The interaction between them was extremely cordial, and Stone was pleased with Brae's approval of his friend.

Although both Stone and Ledger shared their passion to serve Sovereign Ell Yon, Stone carefully avoided discussions that might land on Jeshu. He had learned enough about Ledger to deduce that his father worked at the Jalem Sanctum and perhaps was even a Keeper. Stone's growing apprehension in that regard was becoming significant, especially since Ayla had voiced her reservations multiple times.

"I'm going to find out how he's connected to the Keepers," Ayla warned. "It's too risky, Stone!"

"I hear you, Ayla, but I can't just turn my back on him. What if Ell Yon is calling him to join us regardless of his affiliations?" Stone argued. "Besides...intersections, remember?"

Ayla smirked as she leaned into him. He wrapped his arms around her. She could always disarm him so quickly.

"He's a true friend...a guy I can really relate to," Stone said. "I think we must have been brothers in another life," he quipped.

Stone truly did hope that one day Ledger might be open to a conversation about the Son of Ell Yon, but every time he considered it, the risk seemed too great. That was all about to change.

One evening after a game of street fireball, Stone and Ledger decided to eat some food from a restaurant with Jorn influences. Jorn was the third planet in the Kayn System and closest habitable planet to Rayl.

"How are things with Ayla?" Ledger asked with a broad smile once they sat down at their table.

Stone smiled back, nodding. "It's good. I really like her."

"I told you," Ledger said. "When you two get bonded, I get credit."

"I won't deny it...you opened my eyes for sure," Stone agreed.

"You know, Stone," Ledger said as he scooped up a helping of the Jorn delicacy known as Kurin Kalamy. "You should come and visit me. Have you ever been to Jalem?"

"No, actually," Stone replied, trying to figure out how to navigate around his invite.

"Seriously...you should come. In fact, come spend a week with me. My father would love to meet you. I could show you the historical archives in the sanctum," Ledger said, getting more excited about the idea as he proposed it. "There is nothing like it on all of Rayl."

"I don't think that's going to—"

"Come on, Stone. Why not?" Ledger cut him off. "I could even get you onto the KDF training complex."

His face empty of expression, Stone stared at Ledger. This was the first time Ledger had revealed his enthusiasm for the KDF. There was no skirting it this time.

"The range for weapon firing is—"

"Ledger," Stone interrupted forcefully. "I'm not coming. I won't ever be able to come."

Ledger's brow furrowed as he set his food aside. He waited, looking intently at Stone for some explanation. Stone stared across the table at his friend, unsure what to say.

"Are you really training to become a KDF operative?" Stone finally asked.

Ledger's eyes narrowed. "I'm not training to become one...I am one," Ledger said flatly.

Stone frowned. "So you hunt and kill fellow Rayleans."

Ledger eyed Stone for a long time. "No, not usually. We're tasked with finding and detaining those individuals attempting to subvert the established ways of the Keeper and Builder Orders. Jeshuan heretics are trying to destroy the legacy of faith the Raylean people have had in Sovereign Ell Yon for eons," Ledger explained, his voice tightening with tension. "I would think you'd understand this."

Stone shook his head. "No, Ledger, I don't. KDF operatives are hunting and killing many innocent people because the Keeper Order doesn't want to lose its power over the people."

Ledger continued to eye Stone closely. "Are you sympathetic to those heretics?" he asked.

Stone stayed silent as he glared back at his friend. A horrifying thought filled his mind. "Who's your father?" Stone asked.

"My father is Preeminent Keeper Fasa Kylos, protector of the legacy of all who follow Sovereign Ell Yon." Ledger shook his head while sitting back in his chair. He crossed his arms.

Chills flitted up and down Stone's spine as he only now realized he had befriended the son of the worst and darkest enemy of all Jeshuans on the planet. He felt foolish for lying to himself these past few months, knowing deep down that something wasn't right. Ayla's words of warning briefly intercepted his thoughts. But despite all this, there was a kindred spirit about Ledger that wouldn't let go, so he had stayed.

"All along I thought you were a loyal believer in Sovereign Ell Yon and his ways. Was I that wrong about you?" Ledger asked.

Stone could hear the voice of his parents in his mind, warning him to stand up and walk away, but he just couldn't. Perhaps there was an inkling of hope for Ledger.

"Ledger, you don't get it," Stone said, leaning forward. "I *am* loyal to Sovereign Ell Yon. Jeshu wasn't a heretic. Do you have any idea what he did for the people...the incredible power he had to heal and help them? He was on a mission from Sovereign Ell Yon himself!"

Ledger's eyes widened. He leaned forward so that he was glaring into Stone's eyes. "You're not just a sympathizer...you *are* one!"

Stone reached across the table to touch Ledger's arm. "Listen to me, Ledger. Jeshu—"

"You disillusioned fool," Ledger scowled while pulling his arm away. "You are helping to destroy the heritage of faith among our people. You will be judged by the Immortal for your foolish ideas."

Silence and distance fell between Stone and Ledger, heralding the end of something good. After a few seconds of silent retreat from each other, Stone looked at Ledger with sorrow in his eyes.

"Jeshu came to save you and all the people of Rayl. Search your heart, Ledger, and search the oracles of old. The Merchant has come, and we killed him."

Ledger's eyes became fierce as he leaned forward. His jaw clenched as he prepared a response. But at the last moment, Ledger stopped. He looked at Stone with a similar sorrow filling his eyes, seeming to know that this divide would separate him from the best friend he had ever known. His countenance softened.

"You're the best friend I've ever had." Ledger's gaze fell briefly to the table then back up to Stone. "Almost like a brother. But your heretical belief in a false Navi and his blasphemous claims against the Immortal Ell Yon is unforgivable."

Ledger leaned back in his chair again. "I will do my duty as a KDF operative." Ledger stood, casting one final look at Stone. "You've been warned."

Stone watched Ledger exit the restaurant and then spent the next 30 minutes staring at his uneaten food. After much contemplation, he came to a conclusion. *There was no other possible outcome*, Stone realized. *This was inevitable.*

Later that day, Stone sat down with his parents and with Ayla in his home to reveal what he had discovered about Ledger.

"Stone!" Rhett said jumping up. "What have you done? Fasa Kylos's son?" he exclaimed.

"I'm sorry. We silently agreed from the onset that our backgrounds were off the table." Stone lowered his head. "I see how foolish that was now."

Brae and Ayla looked terrified.

"This relationship will have ramifications throughout all of the Brohn Creed havens," Brae said quietly. "How much does he know about us?"

"Almost nothing," Stone replied. "As evidenced by the fact that he only learned today I was a follower of Jeshu. He doesn't even know where we live."

Stone looked up at his dad. Seeing such disappointment in his eyes really stung. Rhett seemed to catch his gaze and came to him.

"Stone, we have to take drastic measures to protect you and the havens. Kylos could use this as an entry point into our entire Jeshuan network." Rhett looked to Brae for confirmation, but she seemed lost in her thoughts.

"Brae?" Rhett egged.

"What are the odds?" she said softly. "Our son and the son of Fasa Kylos becoming friends."

Ayla took a deep breath. "Major intersection."

Stone cringed.

"Yes, Rhett, everything must change," Brae agreed. "As pleasant as the young man seemed, we must consider the worst-case scenario."

"Kylos is ruthless," Rhett continued. "I've already heard that there is an up-and-coming KDF operative that is going to take over for Kylos. Now we know who that is."

Stone was sick at heart for causing such urgent work for all Jeshuans in the Brohn region, so he dedicated himself to helping at every turn. The ripples throughout the network were significant but quietly implemented. And although it was extremely humbling for Stone to experience, he didn't regret his friendship with Ledger. Something about their friendship was unique, and he refused to believe that Ledger would turn into the evil monster most of the Jeshuans believed him to be.

A few weeks later, both Stone and Ayla fully committed their lives to Jeshu and received their Protectors. It was a time of great celebration for both families. Together, they planned out a future that would honor and serve Sovereign Ell Yon, no matter where he called them to go.

As the weeks turned into months, Stone graduated from the Brohn Academy and Ayla from her tutored studies. Their love for each other continued to grow as they spent more and more time together. Their budding romance provided a joyful reprieve from the frequent and difficult challenges of living as oppressed and persecuted Jeshuans.

The Creed havens increased in number and continued to spread across the planet despite the severe persecution the KDF operatives were exacting on any and all Jeshuans. Most were imprisoned at the KDF complex outside of Jalem, but other facilities were built to house the increasing number of captives. The planet-wide situation was coming to a head. Much to Stone's dismay, Ledger's name became synonymous with the leading edge of Kylos's efforts to subdue and eradicate the Jeshuans. Even Ledger's academy fireball name was resurrected to describe him—Lethal Ledger. Stone never spoke to his old friend again and wondered if Ledger ever thought of him and their friendship. Though Ledger was now the dreaded enemy of every Jeshuan, Stone still believed there was good in his former friend.

One day he'll see the truth. Ell Yon, please rescue Ledger Kylos, he pleaded during his time of communing.

When Stone began accompanying his parents into the Ruah, a whole new world of purpose filled his life. He now understood why they had been so diligent about training him with such skills. At first, he was as green as any other newbie, but soon Stone established himself as a formidable warrior on behalf of the Malakians they served beside. He was particularly adept at listening to the whispers of his Protector in the heat of battle, often advantaging his squad by discerning enemy activities without much hard evidence. By the time Stone turned 20 years old, he was a warrior of the Ruah in his own right.

The Morian Empire continued to tighten its grip on the planet of Rayl, adding to the rising tension. And as they did, a rebellious response from the Partisans faced further reciprocation. To Stone, it seemed as if his planet was heading toward a political and military cliff. Everything seemed so volatile and chaotic. Even though the ways of Jeshu were completely about establishing kindness and peace among the people, the peaceful ways of the Jeshuans seemed to incite the fiercest response from non-Jeshuans. Only when Stone looked at this conflict through the lens of the Ruah did it make sense. Dracus C'fir was tireless in his effort to thwart the peace and truth of Jeshu, Son of Sovereign Ell Yon. Stone and Ayla leaned further in to the Merchant's peace as the days before them became uncertain and potentially hostile.

CHAPTER

15

Unforgivable

Ledger and his team arrived in Brohn early in the morning. They had pinpointed at least one of the havens that had secretly been established here. Ledger, Chief Deklan, and their six operatives took much of the day to organize and plan the raid. According to their intel, this was a high threat, fully armed Jeshuan faction...the deadliest sort. The raid was planned for 9:00 p.m., when the armed Jeshuans were scheduled to meet. Ledger's father would arrive early in the afternoon and conduct meetings at the Brohn Sanctum as a cover, should any Morian patrols be inadvertently involved.

Ledger had been on numerous raids in many other cities, but something about this one had him on edge. The last time he was in Brohn he'd met up with his old friend, Stone, over a year and a half ago. An ache remained in his heart for that lost friendship. *Surely Stone wouldn't be stupid enough to align with one of these radicalized factions of the Jeshuans,* he thought. Ledger dismissed the notion, reassuring himself that Stone was too much of an honorable man to do such a thing. Before long, Ledger was consumed with the final preparations.

Armed not only with sleek weapons of defense but also with the Morian Peace Preservation Edict and letters of authority from his father, Ledger and Chief Deklan led the six operatives down the back street to the entrance of the suspected Jeshuan holdout. Five minutes before the scheduled breach, Deklan received an encrypted message from Fasa Kylos.

"What's up, Chief?" Ledger radioed.

The Chief hesitated. "We're being redirected. Evidently this faction has moved. Follow me."

Ten minutes later, they arrived at the new coordinates. The team readied themselves by powering up their weapons and taking positions on each side of the doorway.

"Master Ledger, you must hold until my operatives make a first breach," Chief Deklan insisted. "This is a threat level one."

"I can't do that, Chief. I don't lead from behind," Ledger replied, powering up his plasma rifle and activating his visor symbology.

Chief Deklan scowled. "I have direct orders from your father. Give us 60 seconds to determine the level of threat. My job is on the line."

Ledger frowned. "I'll give you 20 seconds, Chief—that's it."

"Fair enough. R32, you follow Master Ledger in for cleanup," the Chief said.

Ledger leaned against the wall just to the left of the entrance with R32 behind him as the Chief gave the signal to breach the facility. Two electro-discharge mechanisms were placed on each side of the door. Five seconds later, a burst of energy disabled any locking mechanism, and the doorway slid apart from the center. Chief Deklan led all six operatives into the facility.

"Drop your weapons!" Ledger heard Deklan shout, but his warning was immediately met with multiple bursts of class-one plasma fire. The inside of the facility erupted in wild plasma salvos, and Ledger couldn't keep still. He stepped around the corner as four more rounds lit up the air in front of him. He added his firepower to the target along the far wall. Two shadowy figures fell in the far corner. Within seconds, the firefight was over.

"Enemy suppressed," Ledger heard one of the operatives radio as he made his way into the aftermath of the melee, stunned that his operatives could subdue an armed band of level one Jeshuans so quickly. R32 followed close behind.

A smoky haze hung in the air as the remnant fog of plasma residue settled. Ledger saw dozens of bodies lying throughout a large room. The carnage was horrific. One thing became immediately apparent to Ledger as the air cleared.

"Where are the weapons?" Ledger radioed to Chief Deklan as he came close to one of the prone Jeshuan heretics, his own rifle at the ready in case any of them were only wounded. Ledger inspected two more bodies—no weapons. Ledger turned to face Chief Deklan. "Where are the weapons?" he shouted.

"Chief, we need to clear out. Morian commandos will be on their way," one of the operatives said.

Chief Deklan scanned the room, his gaze coming to rest on Ledger. "Sometimes mistakes happen," Deklan responded. "We need to clear out now. R32, escort Master Ledger out."

As the Chief and his six operatives moved to the exit, Ledger found himself standing in the middle of a massacre.

"We should vacate the premises, Master Ledger," R32 said, standing next to him.

But Ledger found it impossible to move from this room of horrors. At least 20 unarmed people lay dead in a mangle of limbs, blood, and scorched bodies.

"They were unarmed," Ledger said, the muzzle of his rifle slowly falling. His stomach began to churn as he considered the carnage of innocent people—carnage he had helped create. Jeshuans or not...this was not justified.

He wasn't prepared for the raw emotions that began to well up inside him.

The distant siren of a Morian commando patrol was just discernable. R32 waited patiently beside Ledger.

Ledger heard a pained moan from across the room, the direction in which he had added his own shots. He instinctively brought his rifle to bear in that direction but realized the foolishness of his action. He dropped his rifle to its sling position, maneuvering over ten corpses to get there.

"Ledger," a raspy voice called out as he neared.

Ledger's heart quickened at the sound of it, his blood running cold as he came to realize that such a crime had been executed on someone he knew. A hand lifted up from a body propped up and slumped over in the corner of the room. Ledger went toward the raised hand, kneeling next to the wounded body with R32 following close behind. Ledger's soul languished with what he saw.

"Stone!" he cried out, his eyes filling with tears.

Ledger dropped his rifle to the floor and threw his helmet to the side as he reached for his friend.

"Stone!" he cried again, searching for some hope that his friend's wounds were survivable.

"Ledger...you are...," Stone coughed blood as he struggled to say his final words. "You are more than...a brother to me, and I forgive you."

"Don't talk, Stone," Ledger said, unsure how to help the closest friend he'd ever had. "I'll get you help!"

Stone shook his head. "Listen to me." Ledger had never seen such compassion in the countenance of another like he saw in this moment from his dying friend...a friend Ledger had abandoned. Stone lifted his right hand for Ledger to take in his, and Ledger took it. The physical contact with Ledger seemed to momentarily rally Stone.

"Sovereign Ell Yon is calling you...listen to him!"

Stone began to slip further down the wall, and Ledger grabbed his right forearm to support him. Ledger felt the firm form of Stone's vambrace, and in that single moment of touch, Ledger's world changed.

"Ledger...why do you persecute me?" a thunderous voice called out. Ledger's visual world exploded in a vibrant display of thousands of images and overwhelming sounds. The sensation was crushing, and he tried to turn away, but it was impossible because the display surrounded him on all sides. The images were flashes of memories, each with a connection to something supremely significant and powerful. Ledger cowered as he considered the might behind the leading of the display. Slowly the montage of sights and sounds converged to a single point of brilliant light that hurt his eyes.

"Who are you?" Ledger dared ask.

Out of the light, a noble form walked toward him. Ledger felt like he was nearing the presence and power of a million suns. He trembled, kneeling to the ground as this regal form approached. Ledger shielded his eyes from the glory of the being, only able to look upon his feet which were shod with shoes made of priceless elements.

"I am the Immortal whom you have killed. I am the Merchant who purchased the souls of humanity with my blood."

Ledger forced himself to look upward at the face of the one who tormented his wicked soul. "I am Jeshu, Commander of the Malakians...Son of Sovereign Ell Yon!" the voice thundered.

As quickly as the vision came, it collapsed to darkness. Ledger's gaze fell on the still form of his friend, but his friend was not there. Stone's body began to fall away, and Ledger held him. He pulled Stone onto himself, wrapping his arms around him.

"Stone," Ledger wept. "Stone...I'm so sorry."

Tears flowed freely as the magnitude of his crimes against Stone and all Jeshuans began to crush him. His sobs deepened as he held the dead form of the man who had tried to save him...had tried to tell him the truth.

Of every human being that has ever lived, I am the most wretched, Ledger cried out in his mind.

R32 knelt next to Ledger and Stone. With a voice far more tender than Ledger deserved, the bot spoke.

"Master Ledger, Stone Stryker has passed. You must leave here before it is too late."

Ledger slowly lifted his head to look at R32, unable to move from this paralysis of despair. With tears streaming down his face and his arms wrapped around the burden of his soul, he uttered, "I have nowhere to go but to follow him into death."

R32 reached for his arm. "I know a place, and Jeshu is calling you there."

Ledger looked on the bot in wonder, his profound statement briefly lifting Ledger out of the utter depths of his own despair. *How can a bot speak such things?* he wondered.

R32 gently pulled Stone from Ledger's embrace and carefully laid him on the floor. He lifted Ledger to his feet.

"Come with me, Master Ledger," R32 said, leading him out a back entrance just as a Morian patrol arrived at the front entrance.

The bot led him through a corridor with adjacent chambers on his right and left. As they were approaching an outside exit, the door opened to reveal a gathering of people with grave concern on their faces. Ledger's KDF uniform instantly identified who he was. They froze in place, as did Ledger and R32. For a brief few seconds, a bizarre exchange of fearful, dreadful, and angry looks flashed back and forth then Ledger recognized one of them as she stepped forward. Confusion, fear, and rage filled her countenance as she came to Ledger.

"What have you done?" Ayla asked.

All of Ledger's guilt crushed him further into an even darker place with no way out.

"I'm so sorry," he whispered to the one Stone had loved.

"What have you done!?" she screamed as she began to beat on his chest with her fists.

An older man from behind her came to pull her away as R32 pulled Ledger through and past the Jeshuans. As they retreated from each other, Ledger looked over his shoulder to see the anguished face of Ayla screaming at him. That visage would be indelibly etched in his mind for eternity. It was the image of justified fury for the sin he had committed against his friend and so many more. His grief swelled to an inconsolable level.

"What have I done?" he cried out, wanting the mountains of Basidia to fall on him so he could end the torment of his folly, but R32 pulled and carried him forward to a place he knew not.

Outside, Ledger found it nearly impossible to move his legs, but R32 continued to prod and pull him away from the nightmare of horrors. No matter how far he went, the horror followed after him…haunting him every second of his existence. At one point Ledger leaned up against a dark wall in the alley where R32 had taken him. He covered his face in shame, sinking to the ground in bitter tears. Wild emotions of guilt ravaged him, manifesting in physical pain like he'd never felt before. He couldn't escape that single moment when he had touched Stone's vambrace…and not just a vambrace…a Protector! The searing presence of Ell Yon was there, lingering in his mind—Ell Yon who said he was Jeshu! The words repeated in his mind, crushing him with each remembrance. How could it be? Was everything he had believed a lie?

The images and emotions of the moments leading up to the words of Ell Yon were impossible to process, yet there was a sense that even now Ledger was not aware of the full truth of everything.

Ledger rocked back and forth on his knees, head bent low, moaning in anguish, crying out for the death of his friend...a death by his hand.

"Master Ledger, we must keep moving," R32 encouraged, pulling him upward.

Ledger pushed the bot away. "Leave me!" he shouted, looking up at the android. "What's wrong with you, android? Leave me alone!"

But the bot did not leave. Instead, it knelt on one knee in front of Ledger...waiting. Ledger continued to wallow in self-indignation and utter despair...guilty of murder and of opposing the Immortal Sovereign Ell Yon for years. *Why should life continue?* he wondered as the prison of his condemnation surrounded him.

Jeshu...Stone...KDF...sanctums...Keepers...Ledger's thoughts shifted to...his father! Did Fasa Kylos know the truth? Would his father be as crushed with grief if he knew the truth that Ledger now knew?

Ledger lifted his head to see R32 still waiting. "Take me to my father," he ordered.

Brae and Rhett were together when Ayla called them on her com band. "The haven was raided tonight," Ayla said with quivering lips. "Stone is—"

"Stone is what?" Brae urged.

Ayla broke down in uncontrollable weeping as the holo became a mess of unintelligible pixels. Brae's heart nearly stopped.

"Oh, Rhett...please no!"

Within seconds, she and Rhett were speeding to Ayla's Creed haven. When they arrived, the haven was filled with wailing friends and families. Brae and Rhett found Ayla in the corner holding Stone's body in her arms, his face wet with her tears. She looked up at them, unable to speak. Brae collapsed onto the ground beside her, cradling her only son. Ayla wrapped her arms around Brae as together they cried out in anguish. Rhett knelt beside them, and Brae could see anger burning in his eyes like an unquenchable fire. He reached to touch Stone's arm.

Ayla looked at the grieving parents. "I saw him…it was Ledger Kylos," she muttered between sobs. "How could he have done this to his own friend? He's a butcher!" she screamed.

Brae felt like her soul was being torn in two. Kylos had once more pierced her heart with abject sorrow. Would it ever stop…would he ever stop?

Ell Yon, she cried out in her mind. *When will you end the evil of Kylos?*

She bent low to kiss Stone's beautiful face, unaware of anything else around her. For ten long minutes, she clung to Stone, unable to remove herself from his presence. When she lifted her head, Rhett was gone.

"Ayla…where is Rhett?" Brae exclaimed.

"I…I don't know."

Brae's heart sank even further, knowing exactly what Rhett would want to do. But she also knew that such revenge would destroy him…both of them. She stood, wiping her tears away while continuing to search for her mate. But Rhett was nowhere to be found.

Ayla continued to hold Stone as she looked up at Brae.

"He's going to kill him," Brae said. "I have to stop him. I can't lose both of them in a single day."

Ayla bit her lip and nodded. "Go."

Brae sprinted out of what was left of the haven, desperate to stop Rhett from killing the murderer of their son.

Jeshu…please help me. Please save Rhett! she pleaded.

"I said, take me to my father," Ledger commanded R32 again.

R32 still hesitated, as if contemplating how to disobey his order. A new emotion surfaced as Ledger faced the obstinance of a robot. He stood, and R32 stood with him. "Go malfunction around someone else!" Ledger shouted, walking past the bot. He began looking for a grav-rail terminal. R32 stayed close beside him. When Ledger entered a main thoroughfare, R32 approached a two-seat speeder. He placed his hand near the front quarter of the vehicle, and a few seconds later the wing doors began to open. Ledger looked at the bot, stunned once again by its malfunctioning actions.

"What are you doing, R32?" Ledger asked.

"We need to borrow this speeder. Time is of the essence."

Ledger looked up and down the thoroughfare, wondering if being arrested by a Morian patrol was going to be his next plight. However, stealing a speeder seemed a small thing at the moment. R32 had no difficulty starting the speeder, which troubled Ledger even more. As he navigated toward the Brohn Sanctum, Ledger began replaying every conversation he'd had with his father regarding his destiny to purge Rayl from all Jeshuans. Was his father as deceived as he was? Ledger became consumed with questions about his entire life... 21 years of preparation all undone in a single moment. How would his father respond to it all? Did he have the answers?

"Why is this happening to me?" Ledger mumbled out loud as the buildings on either side blurred by him.

"Truth is painful, and there is more pain to come," R32 said without turning his head to look at Ledger.

Ledger glanced over at the bot, completely at a loss regarding the android. Something about him frightened Ledger. He would abandon R32 once they arrived at the sanctum...once he had his answers.

As Ledger approached the sanctum, all his emotions began to build once again—the shame...the pain...the anger. Ignoring all safety measures of approach and speed, Ledger shut down the speeder's engine, exiting the cockpit before it had come to a full stop, much too close to the sanctum's outer court gate. Being late at night, the outer court of the sanctum was empty. There would be only a couple of sanctum guards inside the main entrance to the sanctum structure. Ledger entered the large outer courtyard, ten thousand white Wild Crimson Roses greeting him in silent condemnation.

"Father!" Ledger screamed, walking to the center of the broad courtyard.

All around him, the beautiful structure of the sanctum seemed to herald his crime against humanity. He dared not enter the house of Ell Yon.

"Father!" Ledger screamed louder. Tears began to stream down his face once more as the weight of his wicked acts pressed hard upon his soul. He turned about, his arms outstretched. Silently he called down the judgment of Ell Yon upon himself.

A figure appeared near the courtyard entrance from behind one of the hundred columns, but it wasn't his father. The man approached out of the shadows. As he neared, a fully energized glowing Talon blade appeared in the man's right hand. Though he had never met the man, Ledger knew who he was. This was Stone's avenger...the father of his best friend. The fury in the man's face was everything Ledger would expect. R32 stepped in front of Ledger, but Ledger pushed him aside.

"Go away...this man is justified," Ledger declared.

Rhett Stryker raised his Talon to strike. Ledger opened his palms to the man, waiting...silent. The buzz of the Talon stasis field filled the night air, a prelude to execution.

"No!" came a piercing cry from a woman at the courtyard gate.

Ledger turned just enough to see her sprinting their way. The man before him pulled back to release his death blow, but something stayed his arm.

"Rhett...no!" the woman screamed again.

At the same time, Ledger's father appeared at the sanctum's main entrance along with Chief Deklan and his team of six armed KDF operatives.

Rhett came at Ledger, his left hand grabbing him by the collar, the Talon in his raised right hand still poised to strike. Rhett's face was now just inches from Ledger's—pain and fury evident in each anguished crease.

"I'm so sorry," Ledger whispered. It was a paltry plea of repentance to parents that deserved to have the blood of their son atoned for.

The woman arrived, trying desperately to separate Ledger from Rhett.

"No, Rhett. You can't kill him!" Brae cried out. She pushed the two men away from each other, turning her back to Ledger. She touched Rhett's cheek soothingly, begging him to recant. Ledger fell to his knees, all resistance to his just punishment abandoning him.

Rhett's fierce countenance of fury transformed into a portal of abject pain. Ledger saw tears swelling in the man's eyes. "Why not?" Rhett screamed. "Our son is dead...he killed our son!"

"Get off your knees, my son!" Kylos commanded as he approached with his armed escort.

Within seconds Brae and Rhett were surrounded, six plasma rifles trained on their chests. Rhett slowly lowered his Talon, his countenance a mix of sorrow and lingering rage.

"Why did you stop me, Brae...why?"

Brae turned to face Ledger. She took a step toward him. Then she did something that stunned every person in the courtyard, especially Ledger. She tenderly reached for him, placing her right hand against his cheek.

"Because Ledger is our son too."

Her words hung in the air, locking each actor of this bizarre scene in place. Ledger looked up into the compassionate eyes of this woman he had met only once. Her shocking declaration shattered the last vestiges of his false life. Ledger slowly stood, gazing into the soul of this woman. He looked past her to Rhett and then to his father. Fasa Kylos did not correct her.

"What does she mean?" Ledger asked.

Kylos frowned. He left the safety of Chief Deklan and his operatives and came near to Ledger. "My son, you were born to purge Rayl of the heresy of the Jeshuans. Come with me and fulfill your destiny."

Ledger's mind twisted with jarring realization—could everything in his life be a lie...even his father? "How could you do this to me?" he asked, scanning Kylos's face. "What does this all mean?"

His father seemed unwilling to answer. The truth now evident to Ledger wasn't just painful...it was horrifying.

"You used me to..." Ledger began, turning toward Brae and Rhett. "To get to them."

Full realization of the heinous actions exposed the horrid character of the man he had called father.

"You caused me to kill my...my brother! Why?" Ledger pleaded, turning back to Kylos. "I loved you...I wanted to be you!" he screamed. "Why?"

"It's not too late, my son," Kylos offered. "We still have much work to do."

Ledger began shaking his head. "Don't you understand? I came here to tell you that Jeshu spoke to me...the Son of Ell Yon spoke to me! We are wrong about this...about all of this!"

Kylos's countenance slowly transformed from sympathy to fierce rage as the realization of Ledger's confession took hold. "You ignorant boy, I would have given you everything! The power and prestige of my position was yours for the taking. I took care of you as my own, and you repay me with insolent blasphemy!"

Ledger had never seen such disdain on the face of the man he had called father. The utter betrayal he felt was visceral. The work of Dracus was evident.

"No matter," Kylos declared, lifting his chin while stepping back from Ledger. He turned to glare at Rhett and Brae, an evil leer on his face. "My revenge is complete. When you showed up at the medtech facility, you were dying, and you were pregnant. I spared your life and stole your child, transforming him into the enemy of my enemy. Your deaths will be the final judgment of your malicious crimes against Sovereign Ell Yon."

"Chief Deklan...execute all three of them!" Kylos said, separating himself from Ledger, Rhett, and Brae.

The Chief and his six KDF operatives refocused their weapons on the chests of each of the three. As the Chief's finger pressed against his rifle's trigger, R32 stepped forward with both hands before him. A brilliant blast of energy exploded outward at the armed men, throwing them all backward ten feet. A moment later, the KDF operatives all lay unconscious on the ground in a mash of uniforms and weapons as a brilliant white light shone down from above. A transport descended, nearly landing on their heads. Kylos ran for protection into the sanctum while Ledger, Brae, and Rhett took cover near the courtyard gate. More guards and operatives would soon arrive.

The small transport landed, and the cockpit canopy opened. A seasoned pilot waved them to enter.

"It's Major Kamp," Rhett said. "We must go!"

Brae reached for Ledger, but he couldn't move. He shook his head.

"Come, my son," Brae pleaded.

"I can't," Ledger said, backing away. There was too much to process...too much to atone for. "I can't," he repeated, backing further away from them. He couldn't stop the urge to flee—flee from everything. How could the killer of Jeshuans face them? *Run!* It was the only thing he knew to do.

"Lady Brae," the android said, coming to stand between the two of them. "I have been with him from birth."

Brae looked at Rivet, peace in her eyes. "Go, Rivet... protect him."

Ledger turned and ran toward the courtyard gate, his android following close behind. Ledger recovered the stolen speeder, barely waiting for R32 to join him. He dashed away from the Brohn Sanctum as fast as the speeder would take him, running from everything. He left the city limits, traveling in a random direction into the middle of nowhere. There were no more emotions to try. After flailing about in confusion and pain, he arrived at a numb emotional state. The overload was shutting him down. In the middle of the night, a hundred miles from Jalem near the towering rocky spires of the Garden of the Immortals, Ledger stopped the speeder. He exited and walked to the edge of a rock shelf that overlooked the massive gorge. Like a shadow that would not disappear, R32 quietly came to stand beside him.

After thirty minutes of trying to decide if there was any reason he should continue living, Ledger inched closer to the edge of the cliff. He felt used, deceived, and trapped, unable to go forward or retreat. To not exist seemed an easy way out. As Ledger's mind waffled on the brink of self-destruction, the image of a powerful Immortal pierced his thoughts just as a frightful winged creature swooped up the edge of the cliff to appear in its full horrific glory just three feet in front of Ledger. It roared an ear-piercing shriek while flapping massive wings to momentarily hover in front of him. Fur and feathers meshed together with four powerful legs ending in two-inch talons around each paw. Part wolf, part cat, part eagle, the creature's glowing orange eyes glared at Ledger while barring its menacing razor-sharp teeth.

Ledger stumbled backward at the sight of it, falling to the feet of R32. Ledger wondered if the creature would devour him and end his miserable life. His heart was pounding as he considered his actions, but instead R32 stepped forward, lifting his hand to the creature. By some bizarre connection, the creature seemed mesmerized by the bot's actions. It closed its mouth, pushed the crown of its head against the android's hand, then tucked its wings, kicked off the edge of the rocky ledge, and disappeared down the vertical wall of the cliff. R32 turned around and reached for Ledger, offering him a hand up.

"That was a Valraven," the bot said calmly. "They are very rare. Legends claim they are infrequently used by the Immortals to deliver messages to humans. I should think that his message to you was quite clear."

Ledger took Rivet's hand. The bot lifted him without effort. Ledger eyed R32 closely, his whole perception of this strange android shifting with each passing minute. It took him a couple of minutes to recover from the frightful sight of the creature.

"What are you?" Ledger finally asked, weary of all his other ugly thoughts.

"Originally, I was a maintenance android at the robotics facility in the capital city on Mesos. My designation was RI-6482. Your grandmother, Raviel Starlore, redesignated me as Rivet."

Ledger looked at the bot. He slowly shook his head. Starlore? Grandmother? The reference for the whole of his existence had shifted so far that he had no footing to set his thoughts upon. He would have to figure that all out later.

"But what are you?" Ledger asked, leaning against a large rock outcropping.

Rivet came to stand next to Ledger. He slowly turned his head toward him.

"You have been my liege ever since I was disconnected from Brae Stryker. For you, I am your protector. I am truth."

The android unnerved him. For years he had considered R32 just his training bot, but now even the android was a false character in his life.

"You are truth?" Ledger scoffed. "That's rich coming from an AI android that has been a secret operative inside the Keeper Order for the last 21 years."

"I relayed KDF targets to Major Kamp in order to minimize loss of life while maintaining my primary directive," Rivet stated without emotion.

"And what is your primary directive?" Ledger asked.

Rivet looked into Ledger's eyes. "To protect you."

"Who gave you that directive?" Ledger asked.

The bot hesitated, which always made Ledger uncomfortable. "Unclear."

Ledger frowned. "Then how am I supposed to trust you? For all I know, you could still be part of my fath—Fasa Kylos's—plan or worse yet, Lord Dracus. Obviously, you are fully AI, capable of violating any or all the anti-AI code rules. Not to mention that you also communicate with strange animals."

Rivet's head turned straight to look out over the gorge. He remained silent.

"I'm just a pawn in somebody's nefarious plan, and I don't even know whose. How can I believe anything anyone ever tells me again, including you?"

Ledger looked over at the perfectly still android. The bot slowly turned his head back to look at Ledger.

"You met him. You know now what truth looks like."

The hair on Ledger's arms stood straight. *How did this android know such things?* he wondered. But he was right. That brief ten-second exposure to Sovereign Ell Yon through Stone's Protector had pierced through all the darkness of his soul like he could never have imagined.

All of a sudden, Ledger felt like his body weighed a thousand pounds.

"I'm tired, Rivet."

"Yes, my liege."

Ledger sat down, then leaned over to lay down on the hard rock bed and fell into a fitful sleep.

Four hours later, Ledger awoke to a cold and dreary dawn, the anguish of his wretched deeds just as oppressive as the night before. Dark clouds above filled the air with a misty haze that obscured the gorge. He was cold, wet, and miserable. He recovered to the speeder, hoping there was enough fuel to take him to a port someplace.

"What is your plan, Master Ledger?" Rivet asked.

"Everything I thought to be true is a lie, and I've killed my best friend. My plan is to run as far away from Rayl as possible. Perhaps on the other side of the galaxy there's a place for wretches like me."

"As you wish," Rivet said.

Brae had no words to describe the pain that was pulling her into an emotional abyss. But besides the pain and sorrow, there was extreme anger. The evil plot of Kylos wasn't just about eliminating Jeshuans…it was about having his revenge and reveling in the torment Brae and Rhett were experiencing. Kylos had stolen her embryo to deliver to a birthing center and spared their lives all for the dark satisfaction of revenge. *How dark the darkness is!* Brae thought.

Despite her own raw emotional turmoil, Brae knew that Rhett was equally broken and enraged. She clung to him, holding tightly to the one who had been her lifeline to hope many times over.

"Don't you leave me, Rhett," she pleaded through her tears.

"I would never leave you, Brae," Rhett said, cradling her in his arms.

Brae shook her head. "That's not what I mean. Promise me this will not destroy you...your ability to love...your faith in Ell Yon."

Brae pulled back to look him eye to eye. "You have to promise me, Rhett. I can't lose you too."

Rhett swallowed hard, his words slow to come. "I don't even know how to process all of this." He leaned into her, resting his forehead against hers. "Thank you for stopping me. How did you know?"

"When he looked at me, Daeson's eyes were looking back. I knew then that Kylos had taken our child from us when I was injured 20 years ago."

Brae wrapped her arms around Rhett's neck. "But Sovereign Ell Yon will give him back. And his work for Jeshu will be great."

It was in that moment that Brae remembered the words that Jeshu had whispered into her ear 21 years earlier.

"Your joy will sustain you, and your sorrow will be the catalyst to save millions." Brae realized that the sorrow of Sovereign Ell Yon's people was precious to him—sorrow not wasted.

ABOUT THE AUTHOR

Chuck Black graduated from North Dakota State University with a degree in Electrical and Electronic Engineering. After traveling the world as a tactical combat communications engineer for the United States Air Force, he was accepted into pilot training and served the nation as an F-16 fighter pilot. He is the author of twenty-three novels, including the popular *Kingdom Series*, *The Knights of Arrethtrae* series, the *Wars of the Realm* series, *The Starlore Legacy* series, and *Call to Arms: The Guts and Glory of Courageous Fatherhood*. *Kingdom's Dawn* was on CBA's top ten best sellers list twice in 2008 for all Christian Youth Literature.

Chuck is also an entrepreneur with sixteen patents and is currently the president and general manager for FlowCore Systems, a chemical injection automation company in the oil and gas industry located in Williston, North Dakota.

Chuck is a believer in Jesus Christ as Lord and Savior and in the Holy-Spirit-inspired, infallible Word of God. He is devoted to his wife, Andrea, their six children and spouses, and numerous grandchildren. It is his desire to inspire people of all ages to follow the Lord with zeal and to equip parents, pastors, and youth leaders to accomplish the same through his allegorical and Scripture-based novels, seminars, podcast, and published articles.

More Books by Chuck Black

The Starlore Legacy
Science Fiction Biblical Allegory

The Kingdom Series
A Medieval Adventure Allegory of the Entire Bible

The Knights Series
Legendary Tales of Heroic Valor

Wars of the Realm
Modern Day Spiritual Warfare

Dramatized Audiobooks
Available for Every Title

www.ChuckBlack.com

CHUCK BLACK
THE STARLORE LEGACY
NOVA
EPISODE ONE

THE STARLORE LEGACY
NOVA

A mighty empire. A lowly slave. A galaxy to save.
Will a hero rise?

Daeson Lockridge was born of royal blood, and all of his plans are falling into place now that his performance flying the legendary Starcraft at the academy places him as the second ranking cadet in his class. Only his cousin, Prince Linden Lockridge ranks higher. But a chance encounter with a lowly Starcraft mechanic shatters his perfect plan. The mysterious Raviel intersects his life and everything he thought he knew about himself, his family, his planet, and his galaxy seems a lie. Exposed as a fraud and with no one to trust he must flee the mighty Jyptonian fleet and search for the truth... a truth that will change his life and the future of the galaxy forever, for the Immortals are watching.

Published by
Perfect Praise Publishing
Williston, ND

PERFECT PRAISE
PUBLISHING

ALL RIGHTS RESERVED

CHUCK BLACK

THE STARLORE LEGACY

FLIGHT

EPISODE **TWO**

FLIGHT

Ancient prophecies promise a future of hope, but who dares face the wrath of a powerful tyrant?

Daeson seeks the counsel of the oracle that propelled him into a life of ruin and terrifying adventure. But the ruthless Chancellor Lockridge offers no quarter to his life-long friend turned traitor. Lockridge's thirst for revenge spills the blood of thousands of innocent Rayleans, and Daeson bears the burden of global calamity. Rejected by all except the spirited Raviel, Daeson struggles to carry on. When the whispers of the Immortal Ell Yon beckon Daeson to a remote moon of the planet Mesos, he must find the courage to face his deepest fears. Can Daeson trust the words of an ancient Immortal and inspire the slaves of Jypton to rise up? Not only does the future of his people hang in the balance, but the entire galaxy as well!

Published by

Perfect Praise Publishing

Williston, ND

CHUCK BLACK
THE STARLORE LEGACY
LORE
EPISODE THREE

THE STARLORE LEGACY
LORE
The Raylean people teeter on the edge of annihilation.
Can Daeson lead the quest for their promised homeworld?
Daeson finds himself a prisoner in a tribal world where the law of survival rules. Gone is the hope of the promised homeworld given by the mighty Immortal, Ell Yon. Daeson must fight to restore a future to the Raylean people, but to succeed he must overcome the marauders of cruel worlds, the tragedy of quantum peril, and the arch-enemy of the Sovereign Ell Yon, Lord Dracus. The odds are mounting against him. The relentless loyalty of his friend, Tig, sustains him as he rediscovers the power of the Protector. Can he lead the Rayleans to freedom once more?
Published by
Perfect Praise Publishing
Williston, ND
PERFECT PRAISE
PUBLISHING
ALL RIGHTS RESERVED

www.ingramcontent.com/pod-product-compliance
Lightning Source LLC
Chambersburg PA
CBHW031031310726
48969CB00007B/1944